W9-CEJ-912

"COME ALONE. . . ."

By the time Sheriff Monte Carson, Louis Longmont, and the rest of the people from Big Rock arrived at the Sugarloaf, Smoke and Sally's cabin had burned to the ground.

Monte got off his horse and walked over to where Emmit Walsh and Jim Sanders were standing over the bodies of Will Bagby and Sam Curry, lying next to the bunkhouse. Their hats were in their hands and expressions of sorrow were on their faces.

Doc Spalding ran over and knelt down next to the bodies and examined them for a moment, taking note of the gunshot wounds. He glanced up at Emmit and then over at the smoldering ruins of the cabin. "Any sign of Sally, boys?" he asked, dreading the answer.

Emmit shook his head. "No, sir. We even checked the bunkhouse just to make sure she wasn't in there."

Monte followed his gaze toward the pile of smoking logs and wood where the cabin used to stand. "I guess we're gonna have to comb through the rubble to see if Sally's in there somewhere."

Louis walked up, stood next to Monte, and stared down at the bodies. He noticed a piece of paper stuck on the front of Sam's shirt. He pointed his finger. "You might want to take a look at that, Monte," he said.

Monte bent down and took the paper, holding it up so he could read it. "Smoke Jensen," he read out loud, "we got your wife. Come to Pueblo one week from today and go to one of the saloons. Come alone if you ever want to see her alive again. If you bring the law, you'll find pieces of her scattered all over the mountains."

Monte glanced at Louis. "Son of a bitch!" he said, his voice tight with anger. "They've taken Sally."

"Is there a signature on the paper?" Louis asked.

Monte nodded. "Yeah, it's signed W. Pike."

<u>BOOK YOUR PLACE ON OUR WEBSITE AND MAKE THE READING CONNECTION!</u>

We've created a customized website just for our very special readers, where you can get the inside scoop on everything that's going on with Zebra, Pinnacle and Kensington books.

When you come online, you'll have the exciting opportunity to:

- View covers of upcoming books
- Read sample chapters
- Learn about our future publishing schedule (listed by publication month *and author*)
- Find out when your favorite authors will be visiting a city near you
- Search for and order backlist books from our online catalog
- Check out author bios and background information
- Send e-mail to your favorite authors
- Meet the Kensington staff online
- Join us in weekly chats with authors, readers and other guests
- Get writing guidelines
- AND MUCH MORE!

**Visit our website at
http://www.kensingtonbooks.com**

TREK OF THE MOUNTAIN MAN

WILLIAM W. JOHNSTONE

PINNACLE BOOKS
Kensington Publishing Corp.
http://www.kensingtonbooks.com

PINNACLE BOOKS are published by

Kensington Publishing Corp.
850 Third Avenue
New York, NY 10022

Copyright © 2002 by William W. Johnstone

All rights reserved. No part of this book may be reproduced in any form or by any means without the prior written consent of the Publisher, excepting brief quotes used in reviews.

If you purchased this book without a cover, you should be aware that this book is stolen property. It was reported as "unsold and destroyed" to the Publisher and neither the Author nor the Publisher has received any payment for this "stripped book."

All Kensington Titles, Imprints, and Distributed Lines are available at special quantity discounts for bulk purchases for sales promotion, premiums, fund-raising, and educational or institutional use. Special book excerpts or customized printings can also be created to fit specific needs. For details, write or phone the office of the Kensington special sales manager: Kensington Publishing Corp., 850 Third Avenue, New York, NY 10022, attn: Special Sales Department, Phone: 1-800-221-2647.

Pinnacle and the P logo Reg. U.S. Pat. & TM Off.

First Pinnacle Books Printing: December, 2002
10 9 8 7 6 5 4

Printed in the United States of America

ONE

William Pike, known to one and all as Bill, stood up in his stirrups and stretched his neck and back, groaning with pleasure as the knots and kinks in his muscles relaxed. It had been a long ride from Corpus Christi, Texas, to the Rocky Mountains of Colorado.

He sat back against the cantle of his saddle and turned to look at the nine men riding with him. They were a disreputable and dangerous-looking lot. Most had beards, some grown to cover knife or bullet scars, others just worn because of the lack of hot water while riding the owlhoot trail.

Pike and his men thought of themselves as Regulators—a fancy term for bounty hunters that shot first and asked questions later. They were fresh from the infamous Nueces Strip, a corridor of land stretching from Corpus Christi down to the Mexican border. They'd made a good living there, killing or capturing the Mexican *bandidos* who came up from Mexico looking for easy pickings among the many settlers coming to the area from the East. That had all come to a grinding halt when the Texas Rangers sent in a man named McNally and a corps of other Rangers every bit as tough and ruthless as Pike and his Regulators. Suddenly, the pickings were as slim as the twelve-inch stiletto Pike carried in his boot. The *bandidos* began to shy away from the area, and the other robbers and rapists and footpads were of such a small danger they carried very low prices on their heads.

Looking for a new territory to ply their trade, Pike and his men had ridden to Utah, home of many outlaws trying to hide from John Law. There he'd come upon what he thought to be a golden opportunity—a wanted poster offering a king's ransom for one man, a man who lived in Colorado.

Pike turned his glance from his men to stare down the ridge on which he'd stopped his mount.

"Hey, Bill," Rufus Gordon called from the rear of the line of men.

"Yeah, Rufe, whatta ya want?" Pike answered without looking back.

"You said once we got to Colorado, you'd tell us why you brung us here. How about it?"

Pike nodded. He guessed it was about time to let the men in on it. He reached inside his coat and pulled out a yellowed, wrinkled paper. He unfolded it and held it up for the men to see. "This here wanted poster is gonna make us rich, boys," he said, his grin exposing blackened, crooked teeth under his handlebar mustache.

"What's it say, Bill?" Gordon asked. "I can't read it from back here."

Hank Snow, a stone killer who was himself wanted for murder and rape in three states, laughed out loud. "Hell, Rufe, you couldn't read it if'n it were in your hands."

He was referring to the fact that Rufus Gordon carried a sawed-off ten-gauge shotgun in a holster on his hip instead of a pistol because he was so nearsighted he couldn't see anyone more than a few feet away from him.

"That's a lie an' you know it, Hank," Gordon replied. "I can read as good as you any day."

"That's not sayin' much," Blackie Johnson sneered. "Hank never learned to read neither."

Pike cleared his throat to get his men's attention. "Well, here's what this poster says, boys." He read aloud:

WANTED
DEAD OR ALIVE
THE OUTLAW AND MURDERER
KIRBY "SMOKE" JENSEN
$10,000.00 REWARD
Contact the Sheriff at Bury, Idaho Territory

"Ten thousand greenbacks, boys," Pike continued. "That's nothing to sneeze at."

"Hell," Gordon said, counting on his fingers, "that's . . . uh . . . exactly how much is that for each of us, Bill?"

"That is one thousand dollars apiece, gentlemen," Bill answered.

Hank Snow shifted the chaw of tobacco from one cheek to the other, leaned over, and spat a stream of brown juice at a horned toad sitting on a rock watching the men. "That's if none of us gets killed 'fore we collect it," Snow said around the tobacco. "More if a couple of us catch a lead pill."

"Hank, the poster's fer one man, not a whole gang," Gordon argued. "How's one man gonna stand up to us, the meanest, baddest gents west of the Pecos?"

Snow looked at Gordon and spat again, his eyes as black as the beard on his cheeks. "Yore forgittin' somethin', Rufe," he said in a low voice. "Ten grand on one man's head must mean he ain't no pilgrim hisself." He turned his gaze to Pike. "What'd this *hombre* do to make hisself so valuable, Bill?"

"Yeah," Gordon added, "what did the sheriff up there tell ya?"

"I didn't exactly talk to the sheriff, boys," Pike said. "I didn't want nobody else to know we was after this Jensen feller. I got my information, along with this wanted poster, from a miner I met in a saloon up in Utah."

"Well," Snow said, "we're waitin'."

"This miner said he was in Bury, Idaho Territory, a few years back when some gents named Stratton, Potter, an' Richards rode into town with a gang of outlaws. He said there were 'bout twenty or so of 'em all told. A little later, this Jensen, along with a bunch of old mountain men, surrounded the town and told all of the miners and townsfolk to get outta town. They'd come for the gang."

"What'd the gang do to get Jensen an' the mountain men all riled up?" Blackie asked.

Pike grinned. "Nothin' much. Just killed Jensen's wife an' baby boy, an' stole all the gold he'd spent a year minin'."

"So Jensen an' his gang rode into town an' shot up the other feller's gang?" Snow asked.

Pike shook his head. "Nope. The old miner said all of the folks in town gathered on the ridges overlooking Bury and sat an' watched as Jensen rode into town alone to face down the gang."

"You mean one man went up against over twenty outlaws by hisself?" Gordon asked.

Pike nodded. "Yep. The miner says it was like a war down there, an' when it was over, Smoke Jensen was the last man standing."*

"Jesus," Gordon said. "I can see why he's worth ten thousand dollars."

Return of the Mountain Man.

Pike scowled. "I didn't say it was gonna be easy, boys. But a thousand dollars apiece is more'n we made in a year down on the Nueces Strip."

"You're forgettin' one thing, Bill," Snow said. "How the hell are we gonna find one man in these mountains?"

Pike grinned and pointed over his shoulder down the ridge. "Easy. That there's Smoke Jensen's ranch, the Sugarloaf. I hear he's given up his guns and turned into a peaceable gentleman rancher. I figger we'll ride in and surround the place. Kill any son of a bitch that makes a move toward a gun. This poster says he's wanted dead or alive, so it's just as easy, maybe easier, to kill the bastard."

Blackie Johnson cleared his throat. "Uh, Bill. That there wanted poster don't say nothin' 'bout no ranch hands being wanted dead or alive."

Hank Snow laughed and slapped his thigh. "Hell, Blackie," he called as he punched brass into his six-gun. "You weren't so particular who you killed down Corpus way last year."

"That was different," Blackie growled back at Snow. "Them was Mexicans up from Mexico, an' you know a Mexican's just a little better'n an Injun."

"Don't worry about it, Blackie," Bill Pike said. "We won't kill nobody unless they draw down on us first."

His men began loading their shotguns and rifles while they looked down on the Sugarloaf, thinking this was going to be the easiest money they'd ever earned.

"He'll most likely have a woman with him, so we'll take her too an' have some fun with her tonight," Pike said.

When Blackie started to speak, Pike held up his hand. "Now, go easy Blackie. We won't kill her, just work her a little bit to have us some fun."

Blackie scowled but held his tongue, not wanting to be labeled a sissy by these tough men. He remembered how Whitey Jenkins had been brutally beaten down near Harlingen when he'd objected to Hank raping a young girl in her teens who they'd come upon on the road back to Corpus Christi.

Hank had cut the girl up pretty bad, and then he'd beaten Jenkins within an inch of his life. None of the men had stood up for Jenkins, with most saying he'd deserved what he got for being such a sissy about what Hank had done. Blackie didn't intend to make the same mistake.

Once the men were ready, Pike held up his hand and yelled, "Let's ride, boys!"

The ten men, loaded for bear, spurred their mounts down the ridge toward Smoke Jensen's ranch. As they rode, holding out six-shooters, rifles, and shotguns, Pike grinned as he thought about how they were going to kill Jensen and all his hands and take his woman for their pleasure. . . .

TWO

"You cold-mouthed son of a flea-bag good-for-nothin' . . . !" Pearlie yelled, struggling to hold on as his horse bucked and tried to swallow his head in the chill morning air.

Cal looked up from the morning fire, staring through steam rising off his coffee, and laughed. "Hey, Pearlie. When are you gonna learn to walk that hoss of yours around a little bit 'fore you try and mount him?" he hollered.

Pearlie held on to the saddle horn with one hand and the reins with another as his horse crow-hopped and danced around the cowboys' camp.

Smoke Jensen smiled as he screwed a cigarette into his face and bent over a match. He tipped smoke out of his nostrils, and watched as Pearlie finally regained some control over his mount and walked it toward the fire.

"Maybe he just needs a little coffee," Smoke offered while he took the blackened coffeepot off the coals and poured a cupful for Pearlie.

Pearlie jumped down out of the saddle, gave his horse a baleful look, and flicked the reins over a limb of one of the numerous cottonwood trees that lined the stream where they'd camped the night before.

He was still muttering to himself when he gratefully

accepted the cup of steaming brew from Smoke and took a deep draught.

Cal winked at Smoke and approached them. "Say, Pearlie," he said, trying to suppress a grin. "I know a man who's right handy with horses over at Big Rock. He could probably train that mount of your'n so he wouldn't do that every morning when you get on him."

Pearlie glared at Cal over the rim of his cup, his eyes flat and his expression black. "Cal, you know there ain't nobody in Big Rock knows any more 'bout horseflesh than I do," Pearlie said in an even voice.

Cal cut his eyes over at Cold, the name Pearlie had given his horse when it became evident he was extremely cold-mouthed in the morning and would buck for five to ten minutes the first time Pearlie got on him every day.

"Oh, yeah," Cal replied, now openly grinning. "I can see how well-trained Cold is."

Pearlie set his cup down and began to make himself a cigarette out of his fixin's.

"Just because that broken-down old nag of yours doesn't have enough spirit to buck, don't mean he's any better trained than Cold," he said.

Cal looked at Smoke and rolled his eyes. Smoke was used to this byplay between Cal and Pearlie, and would've been worried if it ever stopped. He knew the two would each put their lives on the line for each other without a second thought.

Smoke took a final drag of his cigarette and threw the butt in the fire. "If you two children are through jawing at each other," he said, "we've still got some beeves to move."

"Yes, sir," Cal said, dumping his coffee on the hot coals of the fire and beginning to put the dishes from their breakfast away. "I'll be ready in a few minutes."

He looked over his shoulder and grinned. "After all, I don't have to spend a lot of time gettin' my mount ready to ride."

They were moving a small herd of fifty or so heifers south from the Sugarloaf to a distant neighbor's spread. The neighbor, a man by the name of Wiley, had made the mistake of buying some cattle from a seller who'd gotten them in south Texas the year before. Wiley's herd had been almost completely wiped out by Mexican tick fever carried by the Texas cattle.

When Sally, Smoke's wife, heard about the Wileys' plight from the man's wife one day in the general store in Big Rock, she'd immediately offered to stake them to a new starter herd.

"But Mrs. Jensen," the woman had said with tears in her eyes, "we don't have no money to buy a new herd with right now. In fact, Sam's been talking about heading back East to try and get a stake to start over."

"Don't you worry about paying us for the herd, Mrs. Wiley," Sally had said. "There'll be plenty of time to talk about that after you've built the herd up enough to sell some to market."

"But you don't hardly know us at all," Mrs. Wiley said.

"You're our neighbors," Sally answered. "That's all I need to know."

So now, in the final days of autumn before the winter snows would come to the Colorado high country, Smoke and the boys were making good on Sally's promise and driving the young beeves to the Wiley ranch.

As they got mounted up, Pearlie held up a coin. "Call it, Cal," he said.

"We ain't flippin' no coin for the drag position today, Pearlie. I rode it all day yesterday an' my throat is plumb raw from all the dust I ate."

The drag position on a trail drive, riding at the rear of the herd to round up stragglers, is the worst possible place to be. A moving herd of cattle throws up a lot of dust in the air, most of which is breathed in by the drag rider.

"Hey, Cal," Pearlie argued. "As the youngest man on the team, you're supposed to ride drag every day. I think I'm bein' right nice to give you a chance to win the point position by flippin' for it."

"But I always lose!" Cal complained.

"It ain't my fault you the unluckiest man in Colorado," Pearlie countered.

"Oh, all right," Cal said. "I call tails."

Pearlie held out his left hand and flipped a coin. He caught it and turned it over onto the back of his right hand. "Heads," he said shortly, and spurred his horse toward the front of the herd.

As Pearly rode past, Smoke said, "Don't you ever feel guilty, cheating Cal like that?"

"Why?" Pearlie asked, his face a mask of innocence as he slowed his horse to a stop in front of Smoke. "What do you mean?"

Smoke shook his head. "I know all about those two coins you had made by the blacksmith in town. One with two heads and one with two tails."

Pearlie looked over his shoulder to see if Cal had heard what Smoke said. The boy was already fifty yards away and fast disappearing in the dust cloud that rose behind the herd. "You gonna tell Cal, Smoke?"

"No. The boy is a grown man now, and he's got to learn to find these things out for himself. It's not up to me to teach him how not to be cheated . . . especially by his best friend."

Pearlie got a pained expression on his face. "Aw,

Smoke, I ain't exactly *cheatin'* Cal," he said, though it was clear he wasn't proud of what he'd done.

Smoke shrugged and smiled. "If it's not cheating, what exactly would you call it, Pearlie?"

Pearlie opened his mouth to reply, stopped, and just hung his head as he rode off toward the rear of the herd to change places with Cal.

Smoke was proud of him. Both of the young men were far more to him than just hired hands. In fact, both he and Sally felt as if the two were members of their family, and treated them accordingly.

As one of the beeves bolted from the herd and ran past Smoke, he pulled his rope off his saddle horn, let out a four-foot section, and whirled it in a circle as he spurred his horse, Joker, after the errant animal. Time to quit daydreaming and get to work, he thought, exulting in being back on the trail after a summer of working around the ranch.

Smoke had come to the high country of Colorado almost twenty years before with his father from Missouri to make a new life for them. Here they'd met up with an old mountain man named Preacher, who took both the pilgrims, as he called them, under his wing and taught them the facts of life on the frontier.

After Smoke's father was killed, Smoke rode with Preacher for many years, learning all the experienced mountain man could teach him about the mountains he so loved. It wasn't long before Smoke himself became one of the region's most famous mountain men, becoming a legend in his own time among that strange breed of men who had no use for civilization and its trappings.

After outlaws killed his wife and son, Smoke and Preacher tracked them down to Idaho and Smoke killed every one of the sons of bitches in face-to-face combat. This put him on the owlhoot trail for a time and he was a wanted man, until some federal marshals found out the truth and got him a pardon from the governor.

It was shortly after that when Smoke met up with a schoolteacher named Sally Reynolds and married her. They moved to the area where they lived now and founded their ranch, the Sugarloaf. Smoke had stayed on the right side of the law ever since.

Once the herd was bedded down for the night, Smoke and the boys made camp near a stream so they'd have water for cooking, though it was much too cold for bathing.

As they sat around the fire, eating beans and fatback bacon cooked in a skillet, Smoke reached in a paper sack and took out a handful of biscuits Sally had prepared for them before they left the Sugarloaf.

He pitched a couple to Cal and to Pearlie and kept some for himself.

Pearlie used the biscuit to sop up some of the juice from the bacon and popped it in his mouth. He closed his eyes and moaned at the excellent taste. "Boy, Smoke, these sinkers Miss Sally made are sure tasty," he said.

Smoke nodded, too busy eating to reply.

Cal glanced over at Pearlie. "How would you know how good they taste, Pearlie? You're such a chowhound you don't even chew 'em 'fore you swallow 'em."

Pearlie grinned back at Cal, bacon juice running down his chin. "You don't have to chew these, Cal boy, they plumb melt in your mouth."

He took a deep drink of his boiled coffee, glanced down at his empty plate, and then looked over at Smoke, a wistful look in his eyes.

"You don't happen to have any of them bear sign Miss Sally made, do you?"

Sally Jensen was famous for miles around for the quality of the sweet doughnuts she baked that were called bear sign by mountain people. Pearlie was one of her most ardent admirers and had been known to eat an entire batch of bear sign on his own and then clamor for more.

Smoke looked in the paper sack. He reached in and pulled out two bear sign and held them up. "I see there's two left," he said, keeping his face serious.

He pitched one to Cal and kept one for himself. "Sorry, Pearlie, but if I remember correctly, you had a mite more than your share at our nooning today."

Pearlie's face looked panicked. "Smoke, you know you can't do that to me. You and Cal wouldn't eat those bear sign in front of me without sharin', would you?"

Cal winked at Smoke. "I know, Pearlie," he said slyly. "Why don't we flip a coin for the last one?"

Pearlie smiled quickly, and then his face fell and he hung his head. "I knowed I shouldn't have told you 'bout those two-sided coins, Cal."

Smoke laughed and threw his bear sign to Pearlie. "Here you go, Pearlie. You can have mine."

"But don't you want it?" Pearlie asked, though he made no effort to return the pastry.

Smoke shook his head. "No." He patted his stomach. "Sally's been after me to lose some weight so she won't have to spend all winter letting out my britches."

Pearlie laughed. Smoke was anything but overweight. Standing a little over six feet tall, with shoulders as wide as an ax handle, a stomach that looked like a washboard, and arms as big around as Pearlie's neck and as hard as granite, he certainly didn't need to lose weight. Pearlie knew it was simply Smoke's way of letting him have the bear sign without any argument.

Pearlie sighed. "I just can't do it, Smoke," he said, tearing the bear sign in half and throwing part of it back to Smoke. "But I will let you share it with me," he added, popping his half in his mouth before he could change his mind.

Smoke took the bear sign and dunked it in his coffee cup. "I agree with you, Pearlie," he said after devouring the doughnut. "Sally is the best cook in the territory."

"In the territory, hell," Pearlie added as he bent to light a cigarette off a burning stick from the fire. "She's the best cook in the world!"

THREE

Bill Pike held up his hand to slow his riders as they crossed several large pastures while moving toward the log cabin in the distance.

When the riders had slowed their mounts to a walk, Rufus Gordon pulled up next to Pike. "What's goin' on, Bill?" he asked.

Pike gave him a look. "I'm thinkin', Rufe," he answered. "Somthin' you don't know nothin' about."

Gordon pushed his hat back on his head and scratched his forehead with the barrel of a .44 pistol he was carrying. "What's there to think about, Bill? I thought we was gonna head on into Jensen's ranch and blow hell out of him."

Pike reined his horse in. "That's just it, Rufe. Does it look like anybody's workin' this here ranch?"

Gordon and the other men looked around. There were numerous cattle and some horses milling around in the fenced-in pastures between them and the cabin on the horizon, but no cowboys or other workers were present.

Gordon pursed his lips. "Now that you mention it, Bill, it do look a mite slow fer a workin' ranch."

"And what does that tell you, Rufe?"

"Uh, I dunno, Boss. You're the brains of this outfit."

Pike nodded. "Yeah, and don't you forget it. Now,

what I think is that either Jensen is in that cabin, or he is somewhere else on the ranch outta sight."

"So, what's that mean?" Gordon asked, his brows knit in puzzlement.

"It means we don't want to go riding in all hell-bent for leather and warn him we're coming if he's in the cabin. Nope. We're gonna ride in nice and slow, like we've just come to pay a nice visit."

"But what if'n he comes outta that cabin blastin' away with his six-killers?" Gordon asked.

"Then, we'll cut him down like autumn wheat," Pike replied. He stood up in his stirrups to get a better look at the area around the cabin. He saw it was surrounded on three sides by heavy forest, though none of the trees were within a hundred yards of the house.

He nodded, talking low to himself. "Yeah, that Jensen is a careful feller all right. He's cut the trees back away from the cabin to give himself a clear field of fire in all directions so nobody can't sneak up on him when he's there."

Pike saw another building fifty or so yards from the cabin that had the look of a bunkhouse to it.

"And he's smart enough to keep the bunkhouse close so his men will be nearby in case he needs 'em," he mumbled to himself. "This ain't gonna be no easy hombre to corral," he said out loud to the men in his group. "He's careful and he's smart."

"What do you want us to do, Bill?" Gordon asked.

"Rufe, you take two men with you and ride on around to the left there and come up to the cabin from over there," he said, pointing to the trees off to the cabin's left side.

"Blackie, you take two men and circle off to the right and do the same thing. The rest of you come with me and we'll head straight on in toward the cabin. That way, if Jensen's in there and he sees us comin', he won't have no place to go to."

Sally Jensen was in the kitchen, frying some chicken for the ranch hands to eat for lunch when they got back from Big Rock. She'd sent them in to get some fencing supplies to have on hand for the upcoming winter season. The heavy snows of the high country always played havoc with their fences, and much of the winter season was spent repairing the ravages of the storms that came through the high valleys.

Though she and Smoke didn't have many employees, the few they had were well paid and treated as friends rather than employees. There were six men besides Cal and Pearlie that were full-time workers, and a dozen more who'd come in and help out part-time when it was calving season or if some beeves needed to be moved to market.

Four of the men were in Big Rock, and the other two were working on the walls of the bunkhouse, filling up holes so the winter winds wouldn't whistle through while they were sleeping.

Sam Curry stood up from the board he was sawing and stretched his back. "I'm going outside for a smoke, Will," he said. "You want me to see if Miss Sally has any coffee hot 'fore I come back?"

Will Bagby took some square-headed nails out of his mouth and nodded. "Yep, that'd be right nice, Sam," he answered. "That north wind is already startin' to get a mite chilly."

Curry laughed. "Hell, this is like summer compared to a month from now when you'll be freezin' your *cojones* off."

He fished the canvas sack containing his tobacco

out of his shirt pocket, and was just taking one of his papers out of its packet when he stepped out of the bunkhouse to find four men on horses coming up the trail from the north pasture.

Curry, who knew just about everyone in the county, didn't recognize the men, and furthermore, he didn't like the look of them either. The had the look of trouble written on their faces, and the way they wore their guns tied down low on their hips let Curry know they weren't ordinary cowhands looking for work.

He'd left his own pistol on a peg in the bunkhouse, and it was too late to go for it now, so he just gave a low whistle as a signal to Will that there was possible trouble brewing.

"Howdy, gents," Sam said, nodding his head at the four men while he continued to build himself a cigarette. "What can I do for you?"

Bill Pike's eyes drifted down, and he saw the man standing in front of him wasn't wearing a side arm. "Howdy, mister," he said, smiling and trying not to look dangerous. "We're looking for a Mr. Smoke Jensen, and we was told this was his ranch. Is he around?"

Curry stalled for time. "Uh, what do you want to see Smoke about?"

Pike tried to keep his voice neutral and unthreatening. "Why, I don't think that's any of your business, sir," he said, smiling widely.

Suddenly, Will Bagby stepped from the bunkhouse door with a twelve-gauge shotgun cradled in his arms. "Well," he said, keeping his eyes on the men with Pike, "we work for Mr. Jensen. So if you don't want to state your business, you'll just have to ride on back to town," Bagby finished.

Pike's smile faded and he began to frown. "That's

not very friendly, mister, pulling an express gun on us like that."

Pike's eyes raised and he stared behind Curry and Bagby, and then he nodded once.

A shot rang out and a hole as big as a fist appeared in Bagby's chest as the bullet Rufus Gordon fired into his back came out. Bagby flopped forward, blood pouring from his mouth and nostrils.

Curry yelled, "You bastards!" and bent to try to grab Will's shotgun.

Pike calmly drew his pistol and shot him in the face, blowing him backward up against the bunkhouse wall.

The door to the log cabin slammed open and a beautiful, dark-haired, hazel-eyed woman appeared on the porch. She was holding a sawed-off ten-gauge shotgun in her right hand and a short-barreled, silver pistol in her left hand.

"Hold on there!" she yelled, her eyes wide with horror as she saw her friends lying dead on the ground. "Drop those guns or I'll blow you to hell!" she said.

Rufus Gordon laughed and began to move his pistol toward her. She fired without aiming, and the pistol along with two of Gordon's fingers flew through the air.

"Ow . . . God damn!" Gordon yelled, bending over and cradling his right hand up against his belly to stop the bleeding. "She blowed my goddamn fingers off!" he moaned, tears of pain in his eyes.

As Pike's gun hand began to move, Sally eared back the twin hammers on the ten-gauge and smiled grimly at him. "Just twitch, mister, and give me a reason to scatter your guts all over my front yard," she said menacingly.

Pike, who'd rarely ever feared a man, and never a woman, felt his guts turn to ice and knew he was as close to dying as he'd ever been in his life. He let go of his pistol and let it swing down to hang by the trigger guard on his trigger finger.

Sally shook her head. "That won't do, mister. My husband invented the border shift. Just drop the pistol on the ground."

Pike smiled, though he had to force his lips to move. "Would your husband be Smoke Jensen, ma'am?" he asked.

Sally didn't answer, but turned her attention to the other men riding with Pike. "Now, all of you. Unbutton those gunbelts and let them drop."

Pike noticed some movement behind the woman out of the corner of his eye, but he kept his gaze fixed on her face so she wouldn't be warned.

Spreading his arms wide to get her attention, Pike said, "We don't want no trouble, ma'am. We just wanted to talk to Smoke about some business," he said, trying to keep his voice level.

Sally's eyes flicked to the two dead men lying next to the bunkhouse.

Before she had a chance to respond, Blackie Johnson stepped up to her from around the corner of the cabin and stuck his pistol in her back. "Drop that scattergun, little lady," he growled.

Sally's finger tightened on the triggers of the shotgun, and for a moment, Pike thought she was going to fire anyway. He felt his bowels rumble at the thought of what ten gauge buckshot would do to him, before her face fell and she lowered the two guns to the porch and raised her hands.

Pike grinned with relief and stepped down off his horse. "Check out the cabin, Blackie," he said as he bent and picked up his pistol and held it pointed at the woman.

Blackie entered the door and returned a moment

later. "All clear, Boss," he said, holstering his pistol. "There ain't nobody else around."

Pike walked up to the woman and backhanded her with his left hand, snapping her head back and drawing blood from her full, red lips.

"Now, unless you want to end up like your men over there, tell us where your husband is, Mrs. Jensen," he snarled.

Sally sucked the blood off her lips, grinned, and spat directly into Pike's face. "You'll find out soon enough, you coward," she said evenly, showing not the slightest trace of fear. She looked again at the dead men and smiled grimly. "In fact, his face will be the last thing you ever see when he finds out what you've done and comes to kill you."

"You talk big for someone who's lookin' down the barrel of a six-gun, lady," Pike said, admiring her courage in spite of his frustration at not being able to cower her.

"I've looked down the barrel of guns before, mister," she replied, "and I'm still here, which is more than you'll be able to say after Smoke gets through with you."

Pike took a deep breath as he looked around the ranch. "Well, I guess he's not here, so our best bet is to take his woman and hightail it off his home territory, boys," Pike said to his men.

"Where're we going, Boss?" Blackie asked.

Pike's eyes went to the mountains in the distance. "Let's head on up into the high country. We'll leave Jensen a note telling him if he wants to see his woman alive again, he'll come up there to talk to us."

He looked back at Sally. "Tie her up good and tight and put her on a horse while I write Mr. Smoke Jensen a note," he said.

While his men tied Sally's arms behind her and saddled up one of the horses in the nearby corral, Pike wrote a note to Smoke, and then he pinned it to Sam Curry's shirt.

Blackie, who was watching him, asked, "Why don't you leave it in the cabin, Boss?"

Pike grinned maliciously. "'Cause I've got other plans for the house," he said.

Once the men had Sally up on the horse and had bandaged Rufus Gordon's right hand, Pike went into the cabin. He stripped the sheets off the bed and piled them in the middle of the kitchen floor, poured kerosene on them from the lanterns, and then put a match to the pile of cloth.

By the time he was on his horse and they'd ridden out into the pasture toward the distant mountains, bright orange flames were licking the roof of the cabin sending clouds of dark smoke into the overcast sky.

Sally glanced back over her shoulder, tears of loss and frustration in her eyes.

FOUR

Peg Jackson, owner of the general store in Big Rock along with her husband, Ed, checked the list in her hand for a final time while Emmit Walsh looked on.

"Well, Emmit," Peg said, "I think we've gotten just about all of the things Sally sent you into town for, with the exception of the gingham cloth she wanted. Just tell her I'm expecting that in on the next shipment from Colorado Springs and it ought to be here next week."

"Yes, ma'am," Emmit said as he filled his arms with some of the packages of foodstuffs and canned goods Sally Jensen had asked him to get from the store.

"You want Ed to help you load those things?" Peg asked.

Emmit shook his head. "No, ma'am, thank you. I can handle it."

He carried the bags out to the buckboard parked in front of the store where the other men from the Sugarloaf were waiting for him.

The back of the buckboard was stuffed with bales of wire, stacks of fence posts, buckets of nails, four salt-lick blocks, and other sundry ranching necessities they'd picked up from the feed store down the street.

"That about got it?" Josey McComb, another of the hired hands, asked.

"Yep," Emmit replied.

Monte Carson, sheriff of Big Rock, ambled by, taking a stroll down the boardwalk. He was, as usual, smoking his pipe and sending clouds of evil-smelling smoke into the chilly autumn air.

He stepped over to the buckboard and stopped to lean his arms on the sides of the wagon. "Looks like Smoke's gonna have you boys busy doing some fencing 'fore the winter snows come," he observed cheerfully.

When Emmit and Josey nodded, Carson added, "Well, don't let Smoke work you too hard."

Emmit laughed. "Oh, Smoke's not there right now, Sheriff. He and Cal and Pearlie are taking some beeves over to the Wiley spread to help them out after all their cattle died of tick fever. It's Miss Sally that's being the slave driver. I've never seen a woman work so hard to make a place look good."

Carson grinned. "Yeah, Sally Jensen is a perfectionist all right, but they've got a right nice place to show for it."

"You can say that again," Josey said. "She's even got us putting little wooden tags with numbers on 'em on the beeves' ears so we'll know when each one of 'em drops their calves. She keeps it all in a little book up at the cabin."

"That's what you get for working for an ex-schoolmarm," Carson said, shaking his head. "Teachers like to keep things neat and orderly."

"I don't mind," Emmit said. "The Jensens are about the nicest folks I've ever worked for, and the food is the best in the area."

Carson nodded. "Especially those bear sign Sally's so famous for, huh?"

"Stop it, Sheriff," Josey said. "You're makin' my mouth water just thinkin' 'bout 'em."

Carson tapped out his pipe on the side of the buckboard, put it in his shirt pocket, and moved back to the boardwalk. "Well, see ya later, boys," he called, waving over his shoulder.

"See ya, Sheriff," they answered, and Emmit jumped up on the hurricane deck of the wagon and slapped the horses with the reins to get them started back toward the Sugarloaf.

Josey and the other two cowboys followed on their horses, singing old campfire tunes as Josey played on his mouth-harp.

As they passed the city limits sign, Emmit pulled out his pocket watch. "Looks like we'll be back home just in time for lunch."

"I sure hope Miss Sally has that fried chicken ready when we get there," Josey said.

When the buckboard crested a small rise about ten miles from the Sugarloaf, Emmit jerked back on the reins. "Oh, shit!" he called.

"What is it?" Josey asked, letting his horse come up even with Emmit.

"Looky there," Emmit said, pointing up ahead.

Josey followed his gesture and saw a large cloud of black smoke rising and spreading across the sky.

"Damn!" he exclaimed. "That looks like it's comin' from the cabin area."

"Josey," Emmit said, "you hightail it on back to town and get the sheriff and anyone else you can find an' bring 'em out to the Sugarloaf. Tell 'em it looks like Miss Sally's in trouble."

"Jim," he said to one of the cowboys as he jumped down off the buckboard, "give me your mount an' you bring the buckboard on along. I'm gonna ride as fast as I can to see if'n there's anything I can do until we get some help."

He swung up onto Jim's saddle and whipped the horse with the reins as he dug his spurs into its flanks. "Giddy up, hoss!" he yelled as he and the other cowboy bent over their mounts' necks and raced toward the ranch.

Monte Carson was in his office, sitting leaned back in his chair with his feet up on his desk, enjoying his fifth cup of coffee of the morning, when Josey burst through his door.

When the door burst open and slammed back against the wall, the noise startled Carson so much he jumped and spilled coffee all down his shirt.

"God damn!" he yelped, and hurriedly brushed at the scalding liquid as it burned his chest.

"Sheriff, you got to come quick!" Josey McComb yelled. "There's a big fire out at the Sugarloaf."

Carson stopped fussing with his shirt and stared at Josey. "What?" he asked.

"On the way out to the ranch we saw a big cloud of smoke coming from the area of the cabin," Josey said, still breathing hard from his ride into town.

"Is Sally all right?" Carson asked as he grabbed his hat off a rack next to the door.

"Don't know, Sheriff. Emmit told me to get back here an' get some help to come out to the ranch."

Carson ran out of the door and stopped on the boardwalk. "You go on over to the general store and get Ed and Peg! I'll get Doc Spalding and anyone else I can find!"

As Monte Carson ran down the street toward Dr. Colton Spalding's office, his heart was filled with dread to think that something might have happened to Sally Jensen. Smoke and Sally were his closest friends in Big Rock, and were responsible for him being sheriff.

Before he came to Big Rock, Carson had been a well-known gunfighter, though he had never ridden the owlhoot trail.

A local rancher, with plans to take over the county, had hired Carson to be the sheriff of Fontana, a town just down the road from Smoke's Sugarloaf spread. Carson went along with the man's plans for a while, till he couldn't stomach the rapings and killings any longer. He put his foot down and let it be known that Fontana was going to be run in a law-abiding manner from then on.

The rancher, Tilden Franklin, sent a bunch of riders in to teach the upstart sheriff a lesson. The men killed Carson's two deputies and seriously wounded Carson, taking over the town. In retaliation, Smoke founded the town of Big Rock, and he and his band of aging gunfighters cleaned house in Fontana.

When the fracas was over, Smoke offered the job of sheriff of Big Rock to Monte Carson. Monte married a grass widow and settled into the job like he was born to it. Neither Smoke nor the citizens of Big Rock ever had cause to regret his taking the job.

Monte Carson knew he owed the Jensens a debt he could never repay, and he'd be damned if he was going to let anything happen to Sally while Smoke was away.

Louis Longmont, owner of Longmont's Saloon, was sitting at his usual table, sipping on a china cup filled with his favorite chicory-flavored coffee. Even though it was still mid-morning, he was playing poker with three trail hands who'd come to town the previous night. The game had been going on for over twelve hours, and showed no signs of stopping anytime soon. He was in the process of what he called teaching amateurs the laws of chance.

Louis was a lean, hawk-faced man, with strong, slender hands and long fingers, nails carefully manicured, hands clean. He had jet-black hair and a black pencil-thin mustache. He was, as usual, dressed in a black suit, with white shirt and dark ascot—something he'd picked up on a trip to England some years back. He wore low-heeled boots, and a pistol hung in tied-down leather on his right side. It was not for show, for Louis was snake-quick with a short gun and was a feared, deadly gunhand when pushed.

Louis was not an evil man. He had never hired his gun out for money. And while he could make a deck of cards do almost anything, he did not cheat at poker. He did not have to cheat. He was possessed of a phenomenal memory and could tell you the odds of filling any type of poker hand, and was one of the first to use the new method of card counting.

He was just past forty years of age. He had come to the West as a very small boy, with his parents, arriving from Louisiana. His parents had died in a shantytown fire, leaving the boy to cope as best he could.

He had coped quite well, plying his innate intelligence and willingness to take a chance into a fortune. He owned a large ranch up in Wyoming Territory, several businesses in San Francisco, and a hefty chunk of a railroad.

Though it was a mystery to many why Longmont stayed with the hard life he had chosen, his best friend Smoke Jensen thought he understood. Once, Louis had said to him, "Smoke, I would miss my life every bit as much as you would miss the dry-mouthed moment before the draw, the challenge of facing and besting those miscreants who would kill you or others, and the so-called loneliness of the owlhoot trail."

Sometimes Louis joked that he would like to draw against Smoke someday, just to see who was faster. Smoke allowed as how it would be close, but that he would win. "You see, Louis, you're just too civilized," he had told him on many occasions. "Your mind is distracted by visions of operas, fine foods and wines, and the odds of your winning the match. Also, your fatal flaw is that you can almost always see the good in the lowest creatures God ever made, and you refuse to believe that anyone is pure evil and without hope of redemption."

When Louis laughed at this description of himself, Smoke would continue. "Me, on the other hand, when some snake-scum draws down on me and wants to dance, the only thing I have on my mind is teaching him that when you dance, someone has to pay the band. My mind is clear and focused on only one problem, how to put that stump-sucker across his horse toes-down."

Louis had tried his best not to take all of the cowhands' money during the long night, though it would have been relatively easy for him. He knew the men had worked over three months on the trail to amass the money they were now risking in the poker game, and he had no desire to take all of it from them. However, he didn't mind taking enough to pay for his time and to teach the men that poker wasn't really a game of chance so much as a game of skill.

The man across the table from him raised Louis's bet. Louis was considering whether to let the man have the pot so he'd be able to stay in the game a while longer, or whether he should just go on and clean him out so he could go home and get some sleep, when Monte Carson and Doc Spalding rushed through the batwings as if their pants were on fire.

Louis turned his head and raised his eyebrows in question. It wasn't like Monte to get so riled up this early in the morning.

"Louis," Carson said, rushing over to the table. "There's a fire out at the Sugarloaf. Emmit says it looks like it might be the house, and Sally's there alone."

Without a second thought, Louis flipped his cards onto the table. "I'm out of the game, gentlemen."

As he stood up, the man across the table scowled. "You can't leave now," he growled. "You got to give me a chance to win my money back."

"It took you twelve hours to lose it, pilgrim," Louis said as he scooped the money in front of him into his pocket. "How long do you think it'd take you to win it back?"

"That ain't the point," the man said, jumping to his feet with his hand next to the butt of his pistol.

Before he could blink, Louis had drawn his Colt and cocked it and had the barrel inches from the man's nose. "You might want to reconsider your words, mister," Louis said in a low voice. "I'm in a bit of a hurry, so either pull that hog-leg and go to work, or shut up and sit down."

The man gulped and sat down, his face pale and sweating.

Louis smiled and holstered his weapon. "Andre," he called to his French chef. "Fix these men anything they want to eat and put it on my bill," he said, and then he whirled around and raced out of the saloon behind Carson and the doctor.

When he got on his horse, Louis noticed it looked like half the town was in the street heading out toward the Sugarloaf. The Jensens were well liked in Big Rock and the citizens were on their way to help.

FIVE

By the time Sheriff Monte Carson and Louis Longmont and the rest of the people from Big Rock arrived at the Sugarloaf, Smoke and Sally's cabin had burned to the ground.

Monte got off his horse and walked over to where Emmit Walsh and Jim Sanders were standing over the bodies of Will Bagby and Sam Curry, lying next to the bunkhouse. Their hats were in their hands and expressions of sorrow were on their faces.

Doc Spalding ran over, and knelt down next to the bodies and examined them for a moment, taking note of the gunshot wounds. He glanced up at Emmit and then over at the smoldering ruins of the cabin. "Any sign of Sally, boys?" he asked, dreading the answer.

Emmit shook his head. "No, sir. We even checked the bunkhouse just to make sure she wasn't in there."

Monte followed his gaze toward the pile of smoking logs and wood where the cabin used to stand. "I guess we're gonna have to comb through the rubble to see if Sally's in there somewhere."

Louis walked up, stood next to Monte, and stared down at the bodies. He noticed a piece of paper stuck on the front of Sam's shirt. He pointed his finger. "You might want to take a look at that, Monte." he said.

Monte bent down and took the paper, holding it up so he could read it. "Smoke Jensen," he read out loud, "we got your wife. Come to Pueblo one week from today and go to one of the saloons. Come alone if you ever want to see her alive again. If you bring the law, you'll find pieces of her scattered all over the mountains."

Monte glanced at Louis. "Son of a bitch!" he said, his voice tight with anger. "They've taken Sally."

"Is there a signature on the paper?" Louis asked.

Monte nodded. "Yeah, it's signed W. Pike."

"W. Pike? Have you ever heard Smoke mention that name, Monte?" Louis asked, his expression puzzled.

Monte shook his head. "Not that I remember."

Doc Spalding stood up. "Sam Curry wasn't armed, Monte," he said, "but it looks like Will had a shotgun." He inclined his head toward the scattergun lying next to Will's body.

"Sam never wore a gun, Sheriff," Emmit said. "He kept one in his saddlebags in case of snakes or wolves or such, but he didn't believe in wearing one."

"It looks like Will was shot in the back, Monte, and Sam was shot in the face," Doc Spalding said.

Monte shook his head. "Bastards gunned them down without giving them a chance."

Louis looked at Emmit. "When was Smoke due to arrive at the Wileys' ranch?" he asked. Everyone in town was aware of the Jensens' charitable gift to the Wileys, and a couple of other ranchers had donated some cattle for Smoke to add to the ones he was taking there.

"He should be gettin' there today sometime," Emmit answered.

Louis looked at Monte. "We'd better head on over there and let Smoke know what's happened," he said.

"Maybe he'll know who this Pike is and why he'd want to do this."

"I'll take care of the bodies and see that they get a proper burial," Doc Spalding said.

Ed Jackson stepped forward. "Tell Smoke the people of Big Rock will take care of cleaning up the cabin. We'll save whatever we can."

Monte and Louis swung up into their saddles. "Peg, would you let my wife know where I'm goin'?" Monte said. He and his wife lived a short way out of town on a small spread, and she wouldn't have heard what was going on yet.

"Sure, Monte. Ed and I'll go by there on our way back to town."

"Just a minute, Sheriff," Emmit said, and he ran over to the corral behind the bunkhouse. He returned a few minutes later with two horses with dally ropes on their halters. "Take these broncs with you. That way you can change hosses when yours get tired."

Monte and Louis each took a dally rope in their hands, and jerked their horses' heads around and put the spurs to them, heading off toward the Wiley ranch. It would normally be a two- or three-day ride, but if they pushed it and used the extra horses, they could make it in a day and a half.

Smoke and Cal and Pearlie pushed the beeves they were herding over a crest above a valley, and looked down at the Wiley ranch in the distance. It wasn't a particularly large spread, just big enough for Mr. and Mrs. Wiley and one hired hand to run by themselves.

Cal moved up from the drag position on the herd next to Smoke. "Jiminy, what's that smell?" he asked, wrinkling his nose up at the smell of charred and burning flesh.

Smoke pointed off to the side of one of the Wileys' pastures. A large pile of what looked like cattle was being burned. "Mr. Wiley is burning the carcasses of his cattle that died from tick fever," he said. "That's about the only way to stop the fever from infecting other cattle he puts on the ranch."

"That's good," Cal said, taking off his hat and slapping dust off his clothes. "I'd sure hate to drive these beeves all this way and have them take sick too."

Smoke looked up as a light dusting of snow began to fall from dark clouds overhead. "The cold weather and snow will help too," he said. "It should kill off any ticks that still have the disease before they can make the new cattle sick."

Pearlie rode over to join Smoke and Cal. "You two gonna sit here jawin' all day, or are we gonna get these beeves down to the Wileys?"

Smoke laughed. "What's your hurry, Pearlie?" he asked.

"It's time for lunch, Smoke, an' I'm so hungry my stomach thinks my throat's been cut."

As they moved the cattle down the ridge toward the valley, Mr. Wiley and his hired hand saw them coming, and got on their horses and rode out to help them bring the herd in.

Bill Wiley shut the gate on his north pasture behind the last of the beeves, dusted his hands off on his britches, and turned to Smoke and the boys. "Come on up to the house, men. Martha oughta have lunch ready by now."

Smoke drew a startled look from Pearlie when he said, "We don't want to impose, Mr. Wiley."

"Don't be silly, and please call me Bill. When I saw you boys up on the ridge, I told Martha to cook us up a couple of turkeys I trapped this fall."

"Turkeys?" Pearlie said, almost drooling at the thought of a turkey dinner.

"Yep, with all the fixin's," Wiley said.

SIX

Snow began to fall from dark, ominous-looking clouds and the temperature started to fall. Sally, riding near the front of the band of outlaws, shivered and felt her hands begin to grow numb.

Bill Pike looked at her, noticing for the first time she was only wearing a relatively thin housedress. Her heavier clothes and coats had been in the cabin they'd burned, and none of the men had thought to get something more suitable for Sally to travel in before the house was torched.

Pike reached behind his saddle and pulled a yellow poncho out of his saddlebags. Even though it was thin, it was made of oilcloth and would keep the worst of the wind and snow off the woman. He kneed his horse over next to Sally's and prepared to drape it over her head and shoulders.

Sally glanced at him, her eyes flat and emotionless. "Since you're being so thoughtful, would you mind loosening my hands?" she asked.

Pike glanced at her hands, and saw that they were pale and almost blue from lack of circulation. Though he wasn't sure just yet what he was going to end up doing with this woman of Smoke Jenson's, he wasn't totally heartless.

He slipped a long-bladed knife from a scabbard in his boot and sliced through the ropes binding

Sally's hands behind her back. Holding the knife point in front of Sally's face as she rubbed her hands trying to get feeling back in them, he growled, "I'm gonna leave your hands untied, Mrs. Jensen. But I'm warnin' you, if you try to run or cause any other trouble, we'll catch you, an' then I'll use this knife on your face so even Smoke won't ever want to look at you again."

Sally looked at the knife. "Point taken," she said in an even tone, showing no fear.

"What?" Pike asked, not understanding the term.

"I understand what you're saying," Sally said, carefully not promising not to try and escape.

"That's good," Pike said, "'Cause my problem is with Smoke, not you, an' I'd hate to have to hurt you."

Sally's eyes narrowed. "What problem do you have with my husband, Mr. Pike?" she asked.

Pike gave her a nasty grin as he put the knife back in its scabbard. "That's none of your business, Mrs. Jensen."

"I think it *is* my business, Mr. Pike. After all, when a woman's husband has to kill a man, it's only right she should know why he had to do it."

Pike threw back his head and laughed. "I think you got it backward, little lady. Smoke ain't gonna kill me, I'm gonna kill him."

Sally smiled sweetly and shook her head, her eyes sad. "Do you have any idea how many men before you have said that, Mr. Pike, and how many men are dead because they underestimated Smoke Jensen?"

Pike's expression darkened, and he clamped his jaws shut tight and spurred his horse on up ahead of Sally so he wouldn't have to talk to her anymore.

He rode up next to Rufus Gordon, who was riding bent over with his ruined hand pressed tight against his belly. Gordon glanced at him and then back over his shoulder at Sally. "I'm hurtin' awful bad, Bill," he groaned.

Pike nodded. "I know, Rufe. We'll get you some laudanum when we get to Canyon City. We got to pass through there on the way to Pueblo."

Gordon cut his eyes back to Sally. "And when the time comes, I want to be the one to kill her, Bill. I owe her for what she done to my hand."

Bill grinned. "Maybe you ought to thank her instead, Rufe. From where I sit, it looks like she coulda put that bullet in your brain just as easily as in your hand."

"That don't matter, Bill. She damn near shot my hand off an' I'm gonna make her pay!"

Pike's eyes got hard and his expression soured. "You'll do exactly what I tell you to do and nothing else, Rufe!" he snarled back. "I'm still head man of this outfit, and I'll tell you what you can do and what you can't do. Got me?"

Gordon's eyes fell. "Yeah. I ain't tryin' to cross you, Bill."

"That's good, Rufe, 'cause what that lady did to you ain't nothin' to what I'll do to you if you ever try to go against me."

After they finished the turkey dinner, Mr. Wiley and Smoke and the boys went out on Wiley's porch for coffee and smokes. While Wiley filled an old corncob pipe with black tobacco, Smoke and Cal and Pearlie all built themselves cigarettes.

Wiley stood at the porch rail and watched as the snow became thicker. "I think it'd be best if you men spent the night here, Smoke," he said. "There ain't no use in you trying to get started tonight with this storm brewing."

Smoke took a drag on his cigarette and chased it with some of Mrs. Wiley's excellent coffee as he stared out into the early evening snowfall. "We wouldn't want to put you and Martha out, Bill," he said.

Wiley waved his pipe in the air. "Don't be silly, Smoke," he said. "It won't be any trouble at all, and you and the boys can start out fresh in the morning after a good breakfast."

At the mention of food, Pearlie's ears perked up. "That sounds good to me, Smoke," he said, licking his lips.

"Any time somebody mentions food it sounds good to you, Pearlie," Cal said, laughing.

Smoke and Wiley joined in the laughter, and Smoke said, "We'll accept your hospitality, Bill, but only if Martha will let Pearlie and Cal do the dishes after we eat."

"That's a deal," Wiley said.

The storm broke during the night, and the day dawned with clear skies and the temperature just above freezing. After a hearty breakfast of scrambled hens' eggs, deer sausage, and biscuits almost as good as Sally made, Smoke and Bill Wiley went out on the porch to finish their coffee while Cal and Pearlie helped Martha Wiley clean up the kitchen dishes.

As they sat there, smoking and drinking coffee, Smoke's sharp eyes saw two figures appear on the ridge above the Wileys' valley.

"Looks like you have company coming," Smoke said.

Wiley got to his feet and walked over to the edge of the porch. "Must be something important," he said.

"The poor bastards must've ridden all night through that storm to get here."

Smoke stepped into the house and got his binoculars out of his saddlebags. When he put them to his eyes, he was startled to recognize the riders as Monte Carson and Louis Longmont.

"Damn!" he muttered to himself, his heart racing. The presence of his two best friends way out here could only mean serious trouble back home. His mouth grew dry and his stomach churned at the thought that maybe something had happened to Sally.

Bill Wiley stuck his head back in the door to the house. "We got company coming, Martha. Better put on some more coffee and fix up some more breakfast."

Smoke jumped off the porch and ran through ankle-deep snow to meet Monte and Louis in the front yard.

"What's wrong?" he asked, not waiting for them to get off their horses.

Monte and Louis looked at each other, neither wanting to be the one to break the news to their friend.

Finally, Louis spoke. "Someone attacked the Sugarloaf, Smoke. They killed Sam Curry and Will Bagby, burnt your house down, and took Sally with them."

Smoke stopped dead in his tracks. "Are you sure they took her?"

Monte and Louis climbed stiffly down off their horses. Snow and ice were packed on their hats and shoulders. "Yeah," Monte said, reaching in his pocket. "They left this note."

As he handed the note to Smoke, Bill Wiley came out of the house and took their horses' reins. "You men get on in the house 'fore you freeze to death out here. I'll have my hand take care of your horses."

Minutes later, while Monte and Louis warmed up by eating breakfast and drinking several cups of coffee, they explained what had happened at the Sugarloaf to a rapt audience.

When they finished, Smoke read the note for the fifth time, trying to remember if he'd ever crossed paths with anyone named W. Pike.

"You have any idea why this Pike fellow would do such a thing, Smoke?" Monte asked. He knew Smoke had made a lot of enemies in his many years on the frontier.

Smoke started to shake his head, and then he remembered a day long ago when he and Preacher rode into Rico. . . .

Smoke and Preacher dismounted in front of the combination trading post and saloon. As was his custom, Smoke slipped the thongs from the hammers of his Colts as soon as his boots hit dirt.

They bought their supplies, and had turned to leave when the hum of conversation suddenly died. Two rough-dressed and unshaven men, both wearing guns, blocked the door.

"Who owns that horse out there?" one demanded, a snarl in his voice, trouble in his manner. "The one with the SJ brand?"

Smoke laid his purchases on the counter. "I do," he said quietly.

"Which way'd you ride in from?"

Preacher had slipped to his right, his left hand covering the hammer of his Henry, concealing the click as he thumbed it back.

Smoke faced the men, his right hand hanging loose by his side. His left hand was just inches from his left-hand gun. "Who wants to know—and why?"

No one in the dusty building moved or spoke.

"Pike's my name," the bigger and uglier of the pair said. "And I say you came through my diggin's yesterday and stole my dust."

"And I say you're a liar," Smoke told him.

Pike grinned nastily, his right hand hovering near the butt of his pistol. "Why . . . you little pup. I think I'll shoot your ears off."

"Why don't you try? I'm tired of hearing you shoot your mouth off."

Pike looked puzzled for a few seconds; bewilderment crossed his features. No one had ever talked to him in this manner. Pike was big, strong, and a bully. "I think I'll just kill you for that."

Pike and his partner reached for their guns.

Four shots boomed in the low-ceilinged room, four shots so closely spaced they seemed as one thunderous roar. Dust and birds' droppings fell from the ceiling. Pike and his friend were slammed out the open doorway. One fell off the rough porch, dying in the dirt street. Pike, with two holes in his chest, died with his back against a support pole, his eyes still open, unbelieving. Neither had managed to pull a pistol more than halfway out of leather.

All eyes in the black-powder-filled and dusty, smoky room moved to the young man standing by the bar, a Colt in each hand. "Good God!" a man whispered in awe. "I never even seen him draw."

Preacher moved the muzzle of his Henry to cover the men at the tables. The bartender put his hands slowly on the bar, indicating he wanted no trouble.

"We'll be leaving now," Smoke said, holstering his Colts and picking up his purchases from the counter. He walked out the door slowly.

Smoke stepped over the sprawled, dead legs of Pike, and walked past his dead partner in the shooting.

"What are we 'posed to do with the bodies?" a man asked Preacher.

"Bury 'em."

"What's the kid's name?"

"Smoke."

A few days later, in a nearby town, a friend of Preacher's told Smoke that two men, Haywood and Thompson, who claimed to be Pike's half brother, had tracked him and Preacher and were in town waiting for Smoke.

Smoke walked down the rutted street an hour before sunset, the sun at his back—the way he had planned it. Thompson and Haywood were in a big tent at the end of the street, which served as saloon and cafe. Preacher had pointed them out earlier and asked if Smoke needed his help. Smoke said no. The refusal came as no surprise.

As he walked down the street, a man glanced up, spotted him, then hurried quickly inside.

Smoke felt no animosity toward the men in the tent saloon—no anger, no hatred. But they'd come here after him, so let the dance begin, he thought.

Smoke stopped fifty feet from the tent. "Haywood! Thompson! You want to see me?"

The two men pushed back the tent flap and stepped out, both angling to get a better look at the man they had tracked. "You the kid called Smoke?" one said.

"I am."

"Pike was my brother," the heavier of the pair said. "And Shorty was my pal."

"You should choose your friends more carefully," Smoke told him.

"They was just a-funnin' with you," Thompson said.

"You weren't there. You don't know what happened."

"You callin' me a liar?"

"If that's the way you want to take it."

Thompson's face colored with anger, his hand moving closer to the .44 in his belt. "You take that back or make your play."

"There is no need for this," Smoke said.

The second man began cursing Smoke as he stood tensely, legs spread wide, body bent at the waist. "You're a damned thief. You stolt their gold and then kilt 'em."

"I don't want to have to kill you," Smoke said.

"The kid's yellow!" Haywood yelled. Then he grabbed for his gun.

Haywood touched the butt of his gun just as two loud gunshots blasted in the dusty street. The .36-caliber balls struck Haywood in the chest, one nicking his heart. He dropped to the dirt, dying. Before he closed his eyes, and death relieved him of the shocking pain by pulling him into a long sleep, two more shots thundered. He had a dark vision of Thompson spinning in the street. Then Haywood died.

Thompson was on one knee, his left hand holding his shattered right elbow. His leg was bloody. Smoke had knocked his gun from his hand, and then he'd shot him in the leg.

"Pike was your brother," Smoke told the man. "So I can understand why you came after me. But you were wrong. I'll let you live. But stay with mining. If I ever see you again, I'll kill you."

The young man turned, putting his back to the dead and bloody pair. He walked slowly up the street, his high-heeled Spanish riding boots pocking the air with dusty puddles.*

---

* *The Last Mountain Man*

SEVEN

Monte Carson, noting the faraway look in Smoke's eyes, shook him gently by the shoulder. "Smoke, are you all right?" he asked.

Smoke's eyes cleared and he shook his head. "Uh, yeah, Monte. I was just remembering a time long ago when Preacher and I went up against some men." He glanced around the table. "One of them I killed was named Pike."

"Do you think this W. Pike who kidnapped Sally is related to the man you killed?" Louis Longmont asked.

Smoke shrugged. "I don't know, Louis." He thought for a moment. "There was another man there, named Thompson, who said he was Pike's half brother."

"Did you drill him too, Smoke?" Cal asked.

Smoke shook his head. "No. As I remember, after I shot him in the arm and the leg, most of the fight went out of him, so I let him live."

Louis shook his head. "You know better than that, Smoke," he said.

Smoke's eyes met Louis's. "I was only in my teens at the time, Louis. I hadn't learned yet not to ever leave a man alive who has reason to come after you later."

Bill Wiley, standing over at the counter next to his

wife, Martha, cleared his throat. "Gentlemen, I ain't exactly an expert in all this, but I think we're getting off the point here. It don't matter why this galoot took Smoke's wife. The question is, what are we gonna do about it?"

Smoke glanced over at Wiley, a sad expression on his face. "There is no *we*, Bill. Pike, whoever he is, made it clear in his letter that I was to come after him alone. I can't risk any harm coming to Sally by charging up to Pueblo with a posse, even if they are my best friends."

"But Smoke," Pearlie said. "You can't go after them alone. They're sure to be waitin' for you along the trail. You wouldn't stand a chance."

Smoke ignored Pearlie and asked Monte, "Did you check out the tracks around the cabin, Monte? Any idea of how many men were riding with Pike?"

Monte nodded. "Louis and I both took a look, Smoke. It wasn't real clear, but it looked like between eight and twelve different tracks in the area."

Smoke got to his feet. "Well, they probably didn't know where I was, or they would've come up here to get me, so that gives me a slight edge. I can be in Pueblo a couple of days ahead of the deadline, before they're expecting me."

"So could Monte and I, Smoke," Louis said.

Smoke shook his head. "No, it's too dangerous, Louis. Both you and Monte are too well known around Big Rock. If this Pike sent a couple of men to look the town over before attacking the Sugarloaf, they might have seen you around."

"That don't apply to Cal and me," Pearlie said. "We been with you the whole time, so they couldn't have seen us."

Louis nodded. "Pearlie's right, Smoke. Having a

couple of extra guns around just might give you the edge you need to save Sally."

"I agree, Smoke," Monte said. "If, God forbid, they do manage to get the drop on you, there'd still be Cal and Pearlie there to maybe save Sally."

Smoke thought for a moment, and then he slowly nodded. "You're right, as usual, Louis, and saving Sally is the most important thing to think about."

He stepped over to his saddlebags and pulled out a wrinkled map of Colorado. Spreading it on the table, he bent over it. "See here, if they head straight for Pueblo from the Sugarloaf, they're going to have to go through Canyon City first."

He looked at Louis. "Louis, I need to borrow some of that cash you always carry. I didn't bring much with me when I left the Sugarloaf."

Louis grinned and pulled a large, black wallet from his coat pocket. He pulled out a wad of greenbacks and handed it to Smoke. "There ought to be about five thousand dollars there, Smoke, give or take a hundred."

Smoke handed the bills to Pearlie. "I need for you to get me some supplies in Canyon City. Things I'm gonna need to take on this gang of Pike's."

He asked Martha if he could get a sheet of paper and a pencil, which she quickly pulled from a kitchen drawer and handed to him. While he made a list of the things he wanted Pearlie and Cal to buy, he asked Bill Wiley, "Bill, do you happen to have any dynamite or a long gun of any kind handy?"

Wiley nodded. "Got all the dynamite you'll need, Smoke. We use it to clear stumps out when we cut wood. As for the long gun, the only thing I have is an old Sharps buffalo rifle my daddy used when we first started this ranch."

Smoke grinned. "That'll do just fine, Bill. They don't make 'em any better than the Sharps."

He handed the list to Pearlie, who asked, "What do you want us to do after we get this stuff, Smoke?"

"Just hang around town and keep your eyes open," Smoke answered. "I don't think they'll dare take Sally into town, but if these men have been on the trail for a while, I doubt if they'll pass up the chance to visit a saloon if they get a chance. I need you two to try and find out just how many men we'll be going up against and to get some idea of how good they are." He paused, and then he added, "But I don't want you or Cal to try anything that will make them notice you."

"What are you gonna do, Smoke?" Monte asked.

"I'm going to try and cut their trail before they get to Canyon City. It shouldn't be too hard, with the recent snowfalls."

"And then what?" Louis asked.

Smoke grinned, but it was a terrible grin without a trace of humor in it. "I'm going to follow them and keep a close eye on them. If I get a chance, I'll go in and take Sally away from them. If not, I'll bide my time until they get to Pueblo and make their camp. Sooner or later, they'll let their guard down enough for me to make my move."

While Bill Wiley got the Sharps and dynamite together, Smoke put his saddlebags on his horse. When Wiley came outside, Smoke packed the dynamite on one of the extra horses Louis and Monte had used, along with the Sharps and a bag of extra ammunition for it, and some .44 cartridges for Smoke's pistols and the Winchester rifle he always carried with him.

"I don't know if this'll be of any help, Smoke," Wiley said, handing him a short-barreled ten-gauge shotgun and a couple of boxes of shells, "but if you get in close, this thing will blow a barn door down."

"Much obliged, Bill," Smoke said, adding the shotgun and shells to the packhorse.

Martha Wiley came out of the house and handed Smoke another sack. "I've put some fried turkey, fatback, beans, and a handful of biscuits in there for you Smoke. You're going to need some good food up in those mountains when the snows come."

"Thank you kindly, Martha," Smoke said as he swung up into the saddle. He tipped his hat.

"And if you need another gun, I'm at your service too," Bill said.

"I'll let you know, Bill." Smoke looked around at his friends, realizing that with the odds he was going up against, this might be the last time he saw them. "See you later," he said, and then he put the spurs to his horse and took off toward the distant mountains, pulling the packhorse behind him.

Pearlie slapped Cal on the shoulder. "We'd better git movin' too, Cal."

"Just a minute, Pearlie, and I'll fix you up a sack of food for your journey," Martha Wiley said, rushing back into the house.

Cal grinned. "Better make it two sacks, Mrs. Wiley. You've seen how he puts it away."

Louis stepped over to Pearlie. "There's a telegraph in Pueblo, Pearlie. If things look like they're going badly, wire me at Big Rock and I'll come running."

Monte nodded. "*We'll* come running."

EIGHT

At mid-afternoon of their first day on the trail, snow again began falling from low-hanging, dark clouds. The air became so cold and so dark that Bill Pike decided to make camp and build a fire before he and his men froze to death in their saddles.

They were still in the foothills of the mountains, and were not making as good a time as he'd hoped, though he knew that the foul weather would bother anyone who was trying to follow them as much as it was slowing his men.

He held up his hand, signaling the men riding behind him to stop. "Rufe, tell the men to make camp here," he said, moving his horse off the trail and under a stand of tall ponderosa pine trees nearby.

Sally, who'd been riding with her head down to keep the blowing snow out of her eyes, glanced up as the man holding the reins to her horse jerked it to a stop.

The man had a deformed right arm, with what appeared to Sally to be a frozen right elbow. His right leg hung out straight from the side of his horse, and was affixed with two wooden braces with leather straps that ran from his upper thigh down to his ankle. She'd noticed that he continually stared at her with hate-filled eyes, though she had no idea why since she hadn't heard him open his mouth the entire journey.

"Are we making camp here?" she asked the strangely silent man.

He merely grunted, and awkwardly swung his right leg over his saddle and hopped to the ground.

Bill Pike tied his horse's reins to one of the pine trees, and then he walked over to help Sally down off her horse. "Come on down, Mrs. Jensen," he said in a not-unkind voice. "We're gonna make a fire to get some of the chill out of our bones and heat up some food."

Pretending to be more helpless than she was, Sally let him take her elbow as she got down off her horse. She figured if he thought she was a helpless female, it would improve her chances of escape later.

She did not have to fake her shivering, however, since the poncho she was wearing did little to keep her warm. Since she'd been taken without a hat or gloves, her hands and ears felt numb and tingly, almost in the first stages of frostbite.

As the flames of the campfire rose, casting an orange glow over the gloom of the copse of trees they were under, she moved as close as she could, holding her hands out almost in the flames to heat some life back into them.

Shortly, Bill Pike handed her a steaming tin cup filled with dark boiled coffee. "Sorry," he said, inclining his head in a short bow. "We ain't got no sugar nor milk."

"That's okay," Sally said, gratefully downing half the cup to get some heat into her stomach. "I take it black."

"Humph!" the man with the crooked arm snorted from across the fire, where he sat nursing his coffee and staring at Sally with grim eyes.

She glanced at Pike. "What is wrong with that man

over there?" she asked. "He looks like he wants to kill me."

Pike laughed shortly. "Well, he probably does, Mrs. Jensen, an' you can't hardly blame him. It were your husband who ruined his arm and his leg for him."

"Smoke did that?" Sally asked.

"Yep."

"When did this happen?"

Pike chuckled again. "More'n twenty year ago."

Sally finished her coffee and handed the cup back to Pike. "And he's just now getting around to doing something about it?"

"Well, it seems old Zeke there spent some time in a prison over at Yuma . . . for rape and murder," Pike said, staring at Sally with flat eyes. "And he said the whole time he was doin' it to that woman, he was plannin' in his mind what he'd do to Smoke Jensen's woman if he ever got the chance."

Sally shook her head. "That poor man."

"What?" Pike asked, astounded at her reaction.

"Yes. To be eaten up with hatred for all those years must have made his life miserable." She hesitated, and then she looked Pike in the eye. "But I do know one thing. If Smoke did that to him, then he deserved it, because Smoke Jensen never shot a man except in self-defense or that he needed shooting."

Pike's expression turned sour. "I'll be sure an' let Zeke know that," he said.

"What is his last name?" Sally asked.

"Thompson. Zeke Thompson," Pike replied. "He's my half brother."

Sally nodded. "So that's why you attacked my men and burned my house down. To avenge Mr. Thompson's wounds."

"No, not really," Pike answered. "I don't give a damn about Zeke. Never did like him much anyway."

"But then why?"

"'Cause, right before Jensen shot Thompson, he shot and killed my full brother, Ethan Pike. I didn't know about it till Zeke got outta prison a year or so ago and looked me up. When I found out, I decided to make things right and to make Smoke Jensen pay for what he done."

"So, your heart's filled with hate also," Sally said, giving Pike a look of pity.

He shrugged. "No. I didn't particularly like my brother Ethan either, but there are just some things a man's gotta do, an' killin' the man who kilt his kin is one of them."

Sally smiled back at Pike. "Could I have another cup of coffee, please?" she asked.

"Sure," Pike said. "Wouldn't want you to freeze to death 'fore the boys have had a chance to help keep you warm tonight."

As he handed her the cup, Sally, her face showing no fear whatsoever, said in a casual voice, "So, that's how it's going to be, is it?"

Pike shrugged. "It's been a long time since the boys have seen a woman as pretty as you, Mrs. Jensen. It'd be a shame to disappoint them."

Sally took a drink of her coffee and nodded. "I can understand that, but. . . ."

"But what?" Pike asked, wondering why this woman wasn't cowering with fear and begging for her life.

"It's just that I thought you said you wanted revenge on Smoke Jensen."

"Yeah, we do," Pike agreed.

"Raping and killing me out here in the wilderness wouldn't be near as satisfying as waiting until you have Smoke Jensen prisoner and then doing it in front of him, don't you think?" Sally said, her voice still as calm as if she were discussing the weather.

Pike threw his head back and laughed. "You're just hoping that Jensen will get the best of us and save you before that happens."

Sally looked at him, her eyes wide and innocent. "Well, of course I am, Mr. Pike. But that doesn't change the fact that if you want the ultimate revenge on Smoke Jensen, that would be the way to do it."

Pike sipped his coffee and stroked his mustache, thinking for a few minutes. Finally, he looked back over at Sally. "I'll tell you one thing, Mrs. Jensen, you've got sand."

"Well," Sally said, "what do you think about my idea?"

"I think you're right. If Smoke truly loves you, I can't think of anything that'd make him suffer more than to see my men take you on right in front of him." He nodded to himself, as if the whole thing had been his idea. "So, I guess that's the way it's gonna be."

Sally looked around the fire at the men sitting there, drinking coffee or whiskey and staring at her with hungry eyes. "I don't know, Mr. Pike," she said easily. "It looks like your men may have other ideas."

Pike straightened and puffed out his chest. "My men do what I tell them to do, Mrs. Jensen. Don't you worry none about that."

"I hope so," Sally said under her breath, waiting to see how things would turn out.

Blackie Johnson, who was the group's designated cook since he was the only one present who could make biscuits that were at all edible, finished frying several large slabs of fatback bacon. He took a large knife and sliced the slabs up while they were still sizzling in the pan. "Meat's ready," he called, and stood back as the men rushed over with tin plates in their hands to help themselves to the bacon, some beans he had cooking in a pot on the fire, and more coffee.

Johnson took it upon himself to fix a plate of food for Sally and take it to her. "Here you go, Mrs. Jensen," he said, his eyes not quite meeting hers.

Sally sensed this man was different from the rest, not quite as coarse and rough. Even his voice was cultured, as if he'd actually gone to school some.

Sally took the plate, searching Johnson's face as she said, "Thank you."

"You're welcome," he replied.

"Would you tell me your name?" she asked as she began to eat.

"Uh, Zechariah Johnson," he replied. "But most of the men call me Blackie."

Sally cocked her head and looked at him with appraising eyes. "Forgive me for saying so, Mr. Johnson," she said, "but you don't look like you belong with these other men."

He gave a half smirk and shook his head. "Don't let me being polite fool you, Mrs. Jensen. I am no better than the rest of the gang."

"But you speak as though you've had some education," Sally replied.

He nodded. "Yes, ma'am. I finished high school, and even had a year of college back in Ohio. I wanted to be a veterinarian."

"What happened to change your mind?"

He shrugged. "I came upon this man beating a team of horses that couldn't pull a wagon he had loaded too heavy, and when he refused to quit hitting them, I hit him."

"That's understandable," Sally said.

"Yeah, but it seems I hit him too hard. When I saw he was dead, I hightailed it out of town and headed

West." He smiled, but it had more sadness in it than mirth. "I've been on the owlhoot trail ever since."

Just then, the man named Zeke Thompson stepped around the fire and shoved Blackie aside. "Don't you go tryin' to get this bitch into your blankets tonight, Johnson," he growled in a husky, whiskey-roughened voice. "She belongs to me first, an' if'n there's anything left when I'm done, you can have it."

Pike moved behind Thompson and grabbed him by the shoulder and spun him around. "Shut your pie-hole, Zeke!" he said in a loud voice, his eyes blazing. "Ain't nobody touching Mrs. Jensen until I say so."

Zeke, who was wearing a pistol on his right hip with the handle facing forward for a cross-handed draw, let his left hand move toward his belly. "That ain't what we planned, Bill, an' you know it."

Quick as a flash, Pike's pistol was in his hand and the barrel was pressed up against the underside of Thompson's chin. "Now, Zeke, you just calm down and try an' remember who's the ramrod of this gang," Pike said in a voice loud enough for all the men to hear. "Any time you think you can do a better job, you're welcome to try and take over," he added, locking eyes with Thompson.

Thompson blinked and looked down. "Aw, you know that ain't it, Bill. I just wanted to teach this uppity slut a lesson."

"You'll get your chance, Zeke, but not until I say it's time." He glanced over his shoulder as he eased the hammer down on his Colt and put it back in his holster. "And that goes for the rest of you too. Mrs. Jensen will be left alone until I give the word. Anybody who touches her will have to answer to me."

Sally, watching this byplay, thought she saw a small smile curl Blackie Johnson's lips. She made a mental note that he might turn out to be a valuable ally when it came time for her to attempt to escape.

"If you're through eating, Mrs. Jensen, it might be better if you turned in for the night," Pike said. He leaned close and whispered so no one else could hear. "I want to get you out of sight so the men can quit thinking about what they're all thinking about."

Sally nodded and got up off the ground. She followed Pike over to where he'd fixed a couple of blankets on top of a groundsheet under a pine tree. "I'm gonna put you over here next to me so nobody will mess with you," he said.

Sally eyed him. "Does that include you, Mr. Pike?" she asked.

He grinned. "Oh, it's not that I wouldn't like to, Mrs. Jensen, but I gave you my word nothing will happen until we have captured your husband, an' that's the way it's gonna be."

"Good night then, Mr. Pike," Sally said, and she crawled beneath the blankets and pulled them up under her chin.

NINE

While Cal and Pearlie headed north by northeast toward the small town of Canyon, Smoke took off on a more directly eastern direction, hoping to cut across the trail the kidnappers would have to take to travel from the Sugarloaf to get to Canyon City and then Pueblo.

Fall was rapidly changing to winter as chilly winds flowed from Canada down into the area of the Rocky Mountains, occasionally accompanied by glowering skies, overhanging clouds, and intermittent snow flurries. Smoke hoped the snow continued, for it would help him track the band of men who held his wife prisoner.

He would have to cross the Sangre de Cristo Mountains to get to Pueblo, but that would be no problem for Smoke, who knew most of the mountains in Colorado Territory as well as he knew the pastures and features of the Sugarloaf.

It took him almost twenty-four hours of continual riding to arrive at the small village of Silver Cliff, a town built up to supply the many miners in the area with food and mining utensils and such. Like most mining towns, Silver Cliff consisted mainly of saloons, gambling parlors, and a couple of general stores, along with a ramshackle hotel for the miners to stay in when they visited the town to buy supplies and blow off steam from their isolation the rest of the year.

All but asleep on his horse after his long journey, Smoke decided he wouldn't be much good to Sally when he found the kidnappers unless he was rested, so he got a room in the hotel and asked the proprietor if a hot bath was available.

The man chuckled. "Yeah, we got a bathtub, mister, but it ain't used much this time of year. Most of the miners don't bathe much between September and April."

Smoke nodded. He knew how that went. When he'd lived up in the mountains with Preacher years before, the man had told him it was plumb unhealthy to bathe more than once or twice a year.

"How long will it take you to get the water heated?" Smoke asked.

"Oh, 'bout an hour, if I crank up the stove now."

"Is there any place in town that serves good food while I wait?"

"That depends on what you mean by good," the man answered with a straight face. "If you mean can you eat it without getting' poisoned, yeah, there is. If you mean does it taste good, well, that's a different story."

Smoke laughed. He liked this man, who seemed to have a good sense of humor, which was sometimes rare in a mining town where everyone usually seemed to be eaten up with gold fever.

The man came out from behind his counter and walked to the front door. He leaned out and pointed down the muddy main street toward a small clapboard building at the edge of town, sandwiched in between what appeared to be a whorehouse and a saloon. "That there is called Ma's Place, though if the old lady who runs it was ever a mother, I'll eat my hat."

Smoke glanced at the big Regulator clock that hung on the wall behind the counter. "I'll be back in an hour for that bath," he said.

"I'll have the water hot enough to take the feathers off a chicken by then," the man promised.

Smoke walked down the roughshod lumber along the street that served as a boardwalk until he was across from the building with the sign on it that read MA'S PLACE. Seeing no help for it, he hopped across the mud puddles still rimmed with ice that covered the middle of Main Street and entered the eating establishment.

True to the hotel man's word, almost every table was taken up by miners and workers eager to have some cooking that they hadn't done themselves for a change.

A portly woman in an apron, with hair that hadn't seen a comb in some time, walked up to Smoke. "Table, mister?" she asked.

The only empty table was in the center of the room. Since his gunfighting days, Smoke had made it a practice never to sit with his back to a door or window or where someone could sit behind him. He glanced over at the corner table and saw that the four men sitting there were finished eating and were talking and smoking over final cups of coffee.

He nodded his head toward them. "If it's all the same to you, I'll wait until that table is unoccupied," he said.

Ma looked over at the table, and then she stared back at Smoke. Her eyes fell to how he wore his twin holsters low on his hips, the left-hand gun butt-first and the right hand one butt-back. "Oh, so it's like that, is it?" she asked, a knowing look on her face.

Smoke shrugged.

She grinned and stuck out her hand. "My name's Ellie May, but everyone around here just calls me Ma."

He took her hand. "I'm Smoke Jensen," he said.

Her eyes widened a bit, showing that even here in this backwater town she'd heard the name before. "I'll see what I can do, Mr. Jensen."

"Just Smoke," he said.

She smiled back over her shoulder, revealing teeth that showed it'd been as long since she'd seen a dentist as it had since she'd been to a hairdresser.

She went over to the table, leaned over, and said something to the men in a low voice. As all their heads turned to stare at Smoke, he nodded at them in friendly greeting.

They hurriedly got to their feet, picked up their coffee cups, and moved to the center table, leaving theirs vacant.

As he walked past them, Smoke tipped his hat. "Much obliged, gentlemen," he said.

One of the men put out his hand and touched Smoke's arm. "Is it true, Mr. Jensen, that you've kilt over a hundred men?" he asked.

Smoke took a deep breath and stopped to look down at the man. "I don't know, mister. I don't keep count," he answered. "Putting a number on a man's life trivializes killing. And killing is never trivial."

Smoke turned his back and walked to take a seat at the vacant table by the window, with his back to the corner. Questions like that used to make him angry, but as he got older and more famous, he got used to it. Ever since he'd been featured in several of Erastus Beadle's dime novels, it had only gotten worse.

Ma walked over. "What'll it be, Smoke?" she asked.

"It's a little late for breakfast and a mite early for lunch."

Smoke smiled. "How about we compromise? Some eggs, a couple of flapjacks, and a small steak on the side would be excellent."

"Elk steak or beef steak?" she asked. "I've got both."

"Elk, please."

She nodded. "And to drink? I've got some fresh milk just brought in an hour ago."

Smoke's mouth watered. He'd drunk so much coffee on the trail his gut was burning. "That would be great, Ma."

"It'll be right out."

While Smoke waited for his food, he built himself a cigarette. More to keep himself awake than because he felt the urge for one.

As he bent over the lucifer to light it, he noticed the men he'd talked to at the table stop on their way out of the café and talk to a couple of young boys at the far side of the room.

One was dressed in black shirt and trousers and had a black leather vest on with silver conchos around the edges as decoration. Smoke noticed he wore a brace of pearl-handled Colt Peacemakers on his hips and had them tied down low on his leg.

When the boy, who couldn't have been more than eighteen or nineteen, stared over at him, Smoke knew there was going to be trouble. Damn, he thought, I knew I shouldn't have given my right name.

Ma appeared from the kitchen with a tall glass of milk in one hand and a platter of biscuits in the other. She put them on Smoke's table. "Here you go, Smoke. You can nibble on these till that steak is done. Won't be long."

Smoke cut his eyes toward the far table. "Who is that at that table over there, Ma?" he asked.

She looked, and then she frowned when she looked back at Smoke. "That there is trouble," she said. "Trouble with a capital T. He calls himself the Silver Kid, and he's always going around trying to pick fights with someone so he can show how fast he is with those six-guns on his hips."

"And his friend?"

"Oh, he's Buck Johansson. He follows the other one around like a lapdog, trying to act as tough as his friend, but he ain't near as mean as he tries to make out."

While Smoke was listening to Ma, he heard a chair scrape back from across the room and saw the Silver Kid approaching out of the corner of his eye. "Better get on back in the kitchen, Ma. I think there's going to be trouble."

Before she could reply, the Silver Kid brushed her aside and stood in front of Smoke with his hands on his hips. "I just can't hardly believe it, boys," he said, talking loud so everyone in the room could hear him. "The great Smoke Jensen drinking milk like a little bitty baby."

Smoke leaned back, loosening the hammer thong on his right-hand Colt under the table and straightening out his right leg so he could draw faster if he needed to. "And you are?" he asked.

"I'm known as the Silver Kid," the boy answered, letting his chest puff out a little.

Smoke noticed the Kid's friend standing behind him and a little off to one side, sweat tricking down his face. He clearly wanted no part of this.

Smoke reached out and took a deep drink of the milk, using his left hand. He smiled. "That's funny," he said. "I've never heard of you."

The Kid blushed. "Well, everbody's gonna know my

name after I kill Smoke Jensen," he said, his voice cracking on the word *kill*.

Smoke smiled, slowly shaking his head. "How old are you, son?" he asked, not unkindly.

"Uh, I'm almost nineteen," the boy answered, making his voice lower this time.

Smoke nodded. "That's a good age. It'd be a shame if you don't live to see it."

The Kid grinned insolently. "Oh, I'll live to see it, Jensen. It's you that's gonna die today."

At these words, the men at the surrounding tables all got up and moved out of the line of fire.

Smoke shrugged. "Maybe," he said. "But let me show you something first. All right?"

The Kid looked puzzled. "Show me what?" he asked, his right hand hanging next to the butt of his pistol, his fingers twitching.

Smoke got to his feet and faced the boy, his hands out in front of him at waist level. "Hold your hands like this," he said.

"Why?"

"Just do it," Smoke said. "I won't hurt you."

The Kid blushed and did as Smoke asked, his hands out a foot or so apart.

Smoke clapped his hands together. "Now, do that," he said, a half smile on his face. "As fast as you can."

The Kid smirked and slapped his hands together with a loud snap.

"Now," Smoke said, his hands still out in front of him. "Do it again, faster this time."

The Kid did it, but this time, so fast no one saw his hands move, Smoke drew his right-hand Colt and had it out and cocked so that the boy's hands clapped on it.

"Jesus!" the Johansson boy breathed. "I never even saw him clear leather."

The Kid's face paled at the speed of Smoke's draw. "You want to try it one more time?" Smoke asked, holstering his Colt.

The Kid nodded and spread his hands, closer together this time.

Smoke nodded and the boy moved, but this time Smoke drew his left-hand gun and had it between the Kid's hands before they could come together.

Now it was the Kid's face that had sweat trickling down off his forehead.

"I have an idea," Smoke said as he holstered his Colt for a second time. "Why don't you boys join me and I'll buy you some breakfast?"

Buck Johansson nodded and slapped the Kid on the shoulder. "Gee, that'd be great, Mr. Jensen."

Smoke sat back down. "Call me Smoke, Buck."

The two boys took seats at Smoke's table and everyone else went back to their eating.

Ma came out of the kitchen with a large platter with Smoke's food on it and gave him a wink as she put it on the table.

"I think we're gonna need some more eggs and steak, Ma. These are growing boys and they need some good grub," Smoke said.

The Kid grinned. "Golly, Smoke, I ain't never seen nobody as fast as that before."

Smoke began to dig into his food. "Fast is overrated, Kid," he said. "Accuracy is what counts when you're facing a man that wants to kill you. Being able to put that first bullet where it'll do the most good is what keeps a man forked-end-down instead of the other way around."

The rest of the breakfast was spent with the boys asking Smoke questions about what it was like in the "old" days, something that made Smoke laugh, and at the same time made him wish he was twenty years younger and still back up in the mountains with Preacher.

Still, he did his best around mouthfuls of food to give the boys some idea of what it'd been like back when white men were as rare in the High Lonesome as hen's teeth.

He told them of Preacher, a man who'd spent his entire adult life living alone in the mountains until he took Smoke under his wing as his "adopted" son, and had them laughing until they cried at tales of Puma Buck, Beartooth, Powder Pete, and Deadhead, men who lived life to the fullest and still had time to laugh at the vagaries of life in the mountains of Colorado Territory.

At one point, the Silver Kid asked Smoke if he ever kept in touch with the old men and if many of them were still alive.

Smoke's face grew sad at the question. "I still see a few of the younger ones, boys," he said, "though most are in their seventies or eighties. Unfortunately, their way of life has just about passed away with the ones who've died. There are just too many people around now, and the Indians who still live in the mountains have been so corrupted by the white man's ways that it just isn't the same anymore."

When they finished eating, he got up and shook the boys' hands. "Let me give you some advice, boys," he said. "Killing a man, taking from him all that he has or ever will have, is not something to wish for. Once you've done that, you'll never be the same. You can live with it if it's forced on you and you don't have a choice in the matter. But if you go out looking for it for no good reason other than to build a reputation, it sours something deep inside and you'll regret it for the rest of your lives. You'll be as dead inside as that man you planted in Boot Hill."

TEN

When Smoke pulled a wad of cash out of his pocket and peeled a couple of bills off the top to give to Ma for their breakfast, he didn't notice a group of four men sitting at a nearby table watching.

One of the men, a hard case named Jeremiah Jones, punched the man next to him with his elbow. "Hey, Willy, would you look at the size of that man's stash?" he said, his eyes wide.

Willy Boatman, Bob Causey, and Sam Bottoms, Jones's partners in a failed mining venture, had been in the surrounding mountains for almost a year and had little to show for their efforts. They'd come to Colorado Territory expecting to find gold lying around for the taking, with very little knowledge of how and where to dig for it.

Desperate now, down to their last few dollars, and unable to find anyone who would stake them to another try, they'd been talking about trying to rob a store or a bank, but had as little knowledge about that as they did about how to go about finding honest work.

Willy nodded, his eyes hard. "How about we follow him and see if maybe he'll agree to share some of that with us?" he said, chuckling at his wit.

"Sure," Bob Causey agreed, "we shouldn't have no problems with it bein' four agin one."

* * *

Smoke walked back to the hotel, with the four men following a short distance behind.

"Is my bath ready?" he asked the proprietor when he entered the hotel lobby.

"Sure is, mister," he said. "I got that water so hot you can take a steam bath if you want to."

Smoke handed him a dollar. "Thanks for your trouble," he said. "I'll leave my things in my room while I bathe. Could you have a boy take my horses over to the livery and get them some grain and a good rub-down?"

"Sure thing, Mr. Jensen," the proprietor answered, taking a key from the rack behind the counter. "Your room is 312, up on the third floor. Same floor as the bath."

Neither man noticed the man standing just inside the door listening as the proprietor told Smoke his room number.

Smoke dropped his saddlebags and the larger bag containing his supplies and extra weapons on his bed, locked the door, and went looking for the bathtub down the hall.

Smoke found the room and tested the water in the tub with his hand. True to the proprietor's word, the water was steaming hot, and there was a pile of towels, a bar of soap, and a bath brush on a chair next to it ready for his use.

Smoke stripped out of his clothes, hanging them along with his gunbelt on a peg on the wall next to the door. Out of longtime habit, he took one of his Colts from its holster and placed it under one of the towels, then slipped into the hot water, sighing with relief as the heat began to loosen muscles stiff from a day and night of constant riding.

He leaned his head back against the tub and closed his eyes, luxuriating in the feeling of a hot bath.

Jeremiah Jones took out his pistol and quietly knocked on the door to Room 312. When there was no answer, he tried the doorknob and found it locked. "Damn," he muttered under his breath.

"I told you he was gonna take a bath," Bottoms said.

"We could kick the door in," Causey offered.

"Naw," Jones answered. "He's probably got his money with him anyway. Let's just go find him and git it."

They eased down the hall, walking on tiptoes so as not to warn Smoke of their approach. When they got to the room with a hand-painted sign on it that read BATH, Jones held his gun out in front of him and opened the door.

At the sound of the door opening, Smoke opened his eyes and sat up in the tub, letting his right hand hang over the side next to the pile of towels.

He smiled when he saw the hard-looking men enter, each with a pistol in their hands. "Sorry, gentlemen," Smoke said easily, with no fear in his eyes. "This bath is already spoken for."

"Shut your mouth, asshole," Jones growled. "We didn't come for no bath."

Smoke wrinkled his nose at the men's ripe odor. "I can see that, though it might be a good idea for you all to take one," Smoke said, his fingers inching under the towel slowly. "You all smell like you've been sleeping with skunks."

Jones's face flushed red at the insult. "Where's the money, sumbitch?" he asked, relaxing a little when he saw Smoke's gunbelt hanging on the peg next to the door. He didn't notice that one of the pistols was missing.

"Oh, you mean my money?" Smoke asked, planning in his mind the order in which he was going to kill the four men.

"No, I mean our money," Jones replied, letting his eyes roam over Smoke's clothes on the peg.

Suddenly, from the hall behind the men, a voice called out, "Drop them guns and get your hands in the air!"

As the men turned to look over their shoulders, Smoke pulled his .44 out from under the towel.

When all four of the men pointed their guns at the unseen voice, Smoke let the hammer down just as he heard a series of shots from the hall.

Smoke shot Jones in the side of the head, the bullet entering just above his ear and blowing half his head and all of his brains all over the men standing behind him.

Causey and Bottoms, still standing out in the hallway, both were hit at the same time, one in the chest and the other right between the eyes. As they danced backward under the impact of the slugs, falling with arms flung out onto their backs, Smoke fired a second time and shot Boatman in the neck.

The man whirled around, both hands at his throat trying to stem the flow of blood from his ruined windpipe. He gurgled and choked, dropped to his knees, and died swallowing his own blood within seconds.

Smoke stood up, still holding his Colt out in front of him until he found out who was in the hall.

A young man's grinning face appeared in the doorway. It was the Silver Kid. "Howdy, Smoke," he said, his eyes still glittering with the excitement of the gunfight, his silver-plated Peacemaker pistol still smoking.

Smoke shook his head and smiled. "Mighty glad to see you, Kid," he said, putting his pistol down and wrapping himself in one of the large hotel towels as he stepped out of the bathtub.

"After you left Ma's Place," the Kid said, "I noticed these galoots following you. I figured they might be up to no good, so I trailed along to see what they were up to."

Smoke nodded as he dried off. "I'm sure glad you did."

"When I saw them at the door, I thought they had the drop on you, so I drew down on 'em," the Kid said.

Smoke raised his eyebrows. "That was mighty brave of you, Kid, to take on four men by yourself."

The Kid shrugged. "I didn't have no choice, Smoke." He grinned sheepishly. "I didn't know you had that six-killer with you in the bathtub."

"Still, it was a very courageous thing for you to do, Kid. Not many men would take on four armed desperados to help out a stranger."

"Hell, Smoke, you ain't a stranger, you're my friend," the Kid said, blushing a bright red.

"You've got that right, Kid."

Just then the proprietor ran up the hallway, a shotgun in his hands. He stood there, the shotgun hanging in his hands as he stared openmouthed at the dead bodies littering the hallway and the blood pooling on the wooden floor.

Smoke looked at him. "Say, after you get someone to haul this trash away, would you heat me up some more water? This batch has gotten kind of cold."

Cal and Pearlie rode into Canyon City in the middle of a snowstorm. Snow and ice piled on their shoulders and ice rimmed Pearlie's mustache as they rode with heads down against the north wind down the main street of the small town high in the Sangre de Cristo Mountains.

Pearlie reined his horse to a stop inside the livery stable on the edge of town and they both got down out of their saddles. A young boy grabbed the reins. "Good thing you men got to town when you did," he said as he helped them get the saddles off their mounts. "Looks like it's gonna get a mite cold later tonight."

Cal glanced at Pearlie. "Yeah, good thing we got here while it's still warm," he said with a sour smile.

Pearlie handed the boy a couple of dollars. "See that the horses get a good rub and plenty of grain."

"Yes, sir!" the boy said, unaccustomed to being paid so well.

"Is there a good hotel in town where we can get some food and a place to stay?" Pearlie asked.

"Yes, sir. The Palace is about the bestest in town. It's a mite expensive, but it's got the best food an' it's even got a saloon right next door."

Cal, who was standing in the doorway looking at the town, thought from the looks of the place that just about every building in town was next to one saloon or another, since saloons seemed to be in great abundance.

"Thanks," Pearlie said to the boy, handing him another couple of coins for his trouble.

"Why don't you head on over there," the boy said. "I'll bring your bags an' such after I see to your hosses."

Twenty minutes later, Cal and Pearlie were sitting in a large dining room ordering steaks and fried potatoes. "And bring us a large pot of coffee," Pearlie added after giving their orders to the waiter. "We need something to get the chill out of our bones."

The waiter, evidently used to this kind of weather, glanced out the window. "Oh, this ain't cold, mister," he said, grinning. "It ain't too much below zero out there yet. Just wait till we get a real storm."

After the waiter went off to get their food, Cal wrapped his arms around his shoulders and shivered. "You know, Pearlie, livin' down low like we do at the Sugarloaf, I'd 'bout near forgot how cold it gets in the mountains."

Pearlie nodded. "I ain't been this cold since Smoke took us up into the High Lonesome a couple of years ago to show us how he and Preacher used to live."

"It's funny how the cold never seemed to bother Smoke none," Cal said.

"I guess his blood must've gotten thick after all those years he spent up there with Preacher an' the other mountain men," Pearlie said.

The waiter reappeared with a pot of coffee and two thick mugs. "You boys want sugar an' milk?" he asked.

Pearlie shook his head, but Cal nodded.

"The steaks'll be right out, but here's some home-made bread and some strawberry preserves for you to get started on."

Pearlie cut a big slice of bread and spread a thick helping of preserves on it. After he took a huge bite, he rolled his eyes. "Boy, that hits the spot."

"Is it as good as Miss Sally's?" Cal asked, fixing his own slice.

"Of course not, Cal. You know nobody's as good a cook as Miss Sally, but it ain't all that bad neither."

After the waiter brought their meal, the boys ate and discussed their plans to buy the supplies on the list Smoke had given them.

Cal, who could read better than Pearlie, went down

the list while Pearlie stuffed his face. "1 can see why Smoke would want most of this stuff, like the guns an' ammo an' explosives, but some of it's a mystery to me," he said.

"Like what?" Pearlie mumbled around a mouth full of steak and potatoes.

"Well," Cal said, holding the list up to the light of the lanterns around the walls, "take, for instance, these picks and shovels and empty tin cans, and this barrel of horseshoe nails and bale of barbed wire." He looked up at Pearlie across the table. "You'd think from this Smoke was plannin' on doin' some mining or stringing up some fences or somethin'."

Pearlie shrugged and held up the empty coffeepot for the waiter to refill.

"And," Cal added, "what about the fifty tent stakes on here? You know Smoke never sleeps in no tents. He always makes a lean-to shelter out of pine branches an' such."

As Pearlie refilled their coffee mugs, he looked at Cal. "Now, Cal boy, you know whatever's on that list Smoke made, he's got a use in mind for it, so let's just get it and worry about what he wants it for later."

They both built cigarettes and leaned back, stomachs full, and enjoyed their after-dinner smokes and coffee.

When they finished, Pearlie called the waiter back over. "You wouldn't happen to have any pie for dessert, would you?" he asked.

The waiter raised his eyebrows and stared at Pearlie's thin frame and the number of empty plates and platters on the table. "Sure, we got apple and peach pie both, but I'm darned if I know where you're gonna put it, mister. You done ate enough for four men as it is."

Pearlie grinned. "You just bring it an' I'll figure out where to put it," he said.

"Uh, which kinda pie do you want?" the astonished waiter asked.

"How about a slice of each?" Pearlie asked.

Cal motioned the waiter down and whispered, "You can't tell it, mister, but my friend there has a hollow leg. He won't stop eating until it's plumb full up to his waist."

ELEVEN

Smoke was up and on the trail before dawn, feeling refreshed and rested after a good twelve-hour sleep in the hotel in Silver Cliff. He headed south out of the town toward the pass between the Crestone Peak and Deer Peak mountains. He knew that the outlaws who'd kidnapped Sally would have to travel through the pass to get to either Canyon City or Pueblo, since the mountains were too high for inexperienced men to cross this time of the year.

He hoped to get there ahead of them, but he knew it was going to be close. If they were traveling fast, they might have already gone through the pass, in which case he'd be able to pick up their trail through the snow that had been falling for the past few days.

In fact, Bill Pike had been pushing his men hard. He wanted to get to Pueblo a few days ahead of Smoke Jensen so he'd be able to pick a campsite that would be easily defended and remote enough so Jensen couldn't expect any help from the local authorities.

They'd reached the pass between Crestone and Deer Peaks the night before, and had elected to camp there until morning. Both his men and their horses were exhausted from the effort to climb up to the pass, being unused to both the thin air of the mountains and the extreme cold temperatures.

When the outlaws woke up, they were grumpy and tired and breathing heavily with even the slightest exertion. A large fire was built and Bill encouraged them to eat as much as they could to fortify them against the cold.

Joe Rutledge, called Sarge because of his stint in the Army until he'd been cashiered for stealing Army horses and selling them to settlers and Indians, moved closer to the fire and held his hands out close to the flames, trying to get them warm.

"Jesus, Bill," he complained, "I'm 'bout near freezing my balls off up in these mountains."

A couple of the other men nodded sympathetically. All of them had coats and clothes more suited to the tropical climate of south Texas and Mexico, where they'd worked for the past couple of years.

Bill, who was wearing two pair of trousers, three shirts, and a medium-heavy coat, agreed. "Yeah, I know what you mean, Sarge," he said. "I checked the map last night and we're gonna be going near Canyon City tomorrow. We'll send some men in to get some warmer clothes and more supplies when we get close enough."

Sally kept her head down to hide her smile at the outlaws' discomfort. Even though she was wearing only one set of clothes and had only a poncho to keep her warm, she was more used to the cold and wasn't particularly bothered by the temperatures.

"Well," Blackie Johnson growled, "just what do you think we should do until then?"

Pike shrugged, tired of the men's bellyaching. "I'd suggest you put on every bit of clothes you have in your saddlebags. That's about all we can do until we get some warmer clothes."

Hank Snow sat on the ground near the fire and put

his boots almost into the coals. "I can't hardly feel my feet, Bill. You suppose I'm gettin' frostbite?" he asked.

Pike moved over to stand over him. "Slip them boots off and let me take a look," he said.

Sally glanced up from across the fire. "I wouldn't do that if I were you," she said, cupping her hands around her tin coffee cup to keep them warm.

Pike looked over at her, a scowl on his face. "And why not, Mrs. Jensen?"

She got to her feet and moved over to Pike. "Because, Mr. Pike, if his feet are that cold, then when he takes his boots off, they are going to swell up. He probably won't be able to get them back on then."

"What do you suggest, ma'am?" Snow asked, watching as steam rose off his boots as they heated up from the fire.

"Get your feet as warm as you can by the fire. Just before we leave, cut a couple of strips off your groundsheet and wrap them around your boots. That should keep them dry and warm enough until we stop for lunch and build another fire."

"Who said we're gonna stop for lunch?" Pike asked Sally. "I want to make Canyon City by tomorrow."

Sally glanced over at the horses, which were standing in a group with their heads down, pawing at the snow, looking for grass to eat.

"Mr. Pike, it's not up to me to tell you your business, but unless you want to walk the rest of the way to Canyon City, you're going to need to let those horses rest some. I noticed you didn't bring any grain for them to eat, and the grass up here is under two feet of snow. Also, they're not used to the air up here. If you continue to push them as hard as you have been, they'll flounder by nightfall."

He looked at her suspiciously. "Why are you trying to help us, Mrs. Jensen? Are you just trying to slow us down so your husband can catch us 'fore we get to Pueblo?"

Sally sighed. "Mr. Pike, it will do me no good if Smoke catches up to us after we've frozen to death because you've managed to kill our horses, will it?" She moved over and held out her cup to Blackie Johnson for a refill, and then she glanced back over her shoulder. "I'll tell you for a fact, Mr. Pike, a man on foot up in these mountains is as good as dead. If those horses die, you'll be frozen solid within twenty-four hours."

"She's makin' good sense, Boss," Blackie said as he filled her cup. "My hoss ain't had nothin' to eat since yesterday."

Pike reluctantly nodded. "I see what you mean, Mrs. Jensen."

He turned to the men sitting around the fire. "Rufus, you and Sarge take your shovels and dig up some of that snow so them horses can find some grass while we eat breakfast, and then we'll do the same thing when we take our nooning."

Sally smiled to herself. Though she'd been telling the men the truth, she also knew that by now Smoke was on their trail and anything she did to slow them down made it easier for him to catch up to them.

She sat down next to the fire and nursed her coffee. When she saw Bill Pike building himself a cigarette, she got an idea. "Mr. Pike, do you suppose I could have one of those?" she asked.

He raised his eyebrows in surprise. "You smoke, Mrs. Jensen?"

She shrugged. "Just occasionally, when I'm very cold," she answered.

He handed her the cigarette he'd made and began to make himself another one.

Sally took the cigarette, reached into the edge of the fire, and got a burning twig to light it with. After a couple of puffs, she blew out the twig and used the charcoal end of it to write Canyon City on the hem of her dress when the men weren't looking. After a few minutes, she stood up and began to move toward the bushes a short distance from the campfire.

"Where're you goin', Mrs. Jensen?" Pike hollered after her.

"I need to . . . " she said hesitantly, as if embarrassed.

"Oh, all right, go ahead," Pike said.

"You need some help, ma'am?" Rufus Gordon asked, grinning salaciously.

"No, thank you," Sally answered coldly. "I can manage."

Once she was out of sight in the bushes, she bent down, tore off the part of her dress with the words *Canyon City* written on it, and stuffed it in the front of her dress where it couldn't be seen.

An hour later, after both the horses and the men had eaten their fill, Pike broke camp. As the men began to get up on their horses, Sally quickly placed the piece of dress under one of the campfire stones before she got on her horse.

As Pike led his men down through the pass toward the distant Canyon City, Sally glanced back over her shoulder at the message she'd left for Smoke, hoping it wouldn't be covered by the light snow that was beginning to fall.

Later that afternoon, when Smoke got to the pass, he found the campfire cold and most of the tracks of the men covered with snow. He knew from the horse droppings there had been at least eight or more horses, but he couldn't tell which direction they'd taken down out of the pass. If they went northwest, they were heading toward Canyon City. If they went northeast, then they were going directly to Pueblo.

As he knelt by the fire, touching the coals to try and determine how far behind them he was, he noticed a scrap of gingham cloth sticking out from under one of the stones around the coals.

He pulled it out and grinned when he recognized Sally's dress cloth. He was relieved to see that she was still alive. As he examined the cloth, he noticed it had something scrawled on it. He held it up to the light and read the words "Canyon City."

He smiled and shook his head. Sally had managed to let him know where the men were headed and she'd done it right under their noses. The poor sons of bitches didn't know who they were dealing with when they took Sally prisoner, he thought.

Judging from the coldness of the coals, he figured he was at least twelve hours behind the men. Well, he'd give his horses some of the grain he'd brought along, fix himself a small fire to heat up some coffee, and have a cold breakfast. And then he'd be on his way. If he pushed it, he could make up at least four hours on the men by nightfall.

While he ate the last of the turkey Mrs. Wiley had given him and drank his coffee, Smoke hoped Cal and Pearlie were getting the supplies he'd asked for.

With any luck, they'd be ready and waiting for him when he got to Canyon City. If that were the case, then they would probably be able to catch up with the group of outlaws before they made it to Pueblo.

Smoke's jaws clenched when he thought of what he was going to do to them if they'd harmed one hair on Sally's head.

TWELVE

Cal and Pearlie awoke after a good night's sleep in the Palace Hotel. "Man," Pearlie said, glancing across the room at the other bed, where Cal was just opening his eyes. "That sure felt good to have a real feather mattress under my butt instead of cold, hard ground."

The boys, though they had plenty of cash for two rooms, were of such a nature that they hated to waste money unnecessarily. Besides, after sleeping in bunkhouses for most of their lives, they were used to someone else snoring nearby and probably wouldn't have been able to get to sleep in a quiet room.

Cal stretched and yawned. "Yeah, an' I have a feeling we better enjoy the feeling 'cause once we leave here it's gonna mean sleeping out in the snow."

Pearlie jumped out of bed and began to put his clothes on. "Time to get goin', Cal boy. I think I can hear breakfast callin' my name."

Cal rolled over and covered his head with the blankets. "You go on, Pearlie. I want to catch another few winks."

"All right, if that's the way you want it," Pearlie said as he opened the door. "But remember, after today, all we're gonna have to eat is our own cookin'."

That threat did it. Cal groaned and rolled over out of bed. He and Pearlie were spoiled living on the Sugarloaf. Sally Jensen was one of the best cooks in the county, and Cal and Pearlie weren't used to trail food. Greasy fatback bacon and boiled beans just couldn't compare to Sally's fried chicken and mashed potatoes and corn and such.

By the time Cal got dressed and made his way to the dining room, Pearlie already had a large pot of coffee on the table along with two mugs and a jar of sugar. He knew Cal liked his coffee sweet when he could get it that way.

Just as Cal took his seat, the waiter they'd had the night before came out of the kitchen with a burly, fat man following him. "See?" the waiter said, pointing to Pearlie. "There's the man who ate all that food last night. I told you he was thin as a rail."

The fat man, who had a half-smoked cigarette dangling from the corner of his mouth, just shook his head, a look of amazement on his face.

The waiter explained, "This is our chef. After you left last night, he wouldn't believe that the person who ate two complete dinners and two desserts didn't weigh three hundred pounds."

The cook grinned and patted his more than ample stomach. "How do you do it, mister?" he asked. "If I just smell food I gain five pounds."

"Just lucky, I guess," Pearlie answered, blushing a little at the unexpected attention.

"I'll tell you one thing," Cal said. "It ain't 'cause he works it off, that's for sure."

The waiter, with the cook still watching over his shoulder, asked, "What will you have this morning?"

Pearlie stroked his chin, thought for a moment, and then he said, "I'll have half a dozen hens' eggs, a short stack of flapjacks, and some pork sausage if you have it."

Cal shrugged and said, "I'll have the same."

The waiter grinned and turned to the cook. "See, I told you so!"

While Cal and Pearlie were eating breakfast, Bill Pike and his men arrived at the outskirts of Canyon City. Pike reined in his horse and looked at the town sitting down in a small valley below them.

"We gonna git to go into town and have a few drinks and git me some laudanum for my hand?" Rufus Gordon asked.

Pike shook his head. "No, I don't think there's gonna be any drinking in town, boys. I don't want us to draw any attention to ourselves until we know for sure where Smoke Jensen is."

"But Boss," Hank Snow complained. "I ain't had a drink since we got to Colorado. And I done forgot what it's like to have a woman on my lap."

Pike glared at him. "Don't forget who's running this outfit, Hank, or it might be the last thing you ever forget."

Hank clamped his lips shut and looked down at the ground.

"Now, I'll stay out here with Mrs. Jensen. The rest of you can go into town and buy the supplies we need, and you can get yourselves a couple of bottles of whiskey if you want, but I don't want you drinking it in town. Wait until we make camp tonight. And you, Rufe, if there's a doc in town, you might wanta have him take a look at that hand. Maybe he can fix it so it don't hurt so bad."

"Anything special you want us to get in the way of supplies, Boss?" Blackie Johnson asked.

"Yeah, Blackie. Get some warm clothes and a heavy coat for Mrs. Jensen. I don't want her freezing to death 'fore we meet up with her husband."

He thought for a moment, and then he added, "And you might want to pick up some heavier coats for the rest of us too. We're gonna be going up into the mountains and it's bound to get colder the higher we get. And pick up some more ammunition, just in case Jensen brings help with him and makes a fight of it."

"You think he'll do that after you told him you'd kill his wife if he didn't come alone?" Johnson asked, glancing worriedly at Sally.

Pike pursed his lips. "I don't know." He too looked over at Sally. "What do you think, Mrs. Jensen?"

Sally smiled. "Smoke won't need any help to kill you men, and he probably won't even break a sweat doing it."

Pike threw back his head and laughed out loud. "You think he's that tough?" he asked Sally.

She nodded. "You can't imagine just how tough, but you'll find out soon enough." She looked over at the other men, sitting on their horses watching her and Pike talking. "And you men had better take some time to enjoy the town while you're there, because it is liable to be the last town you visit while you're still alive."

A couple of the men laughed, but the others just eyed her with worried looks on their faces. They weren't used to anyone not showing fear when confronted by the Pike gang, most especially women.

Pike cleared his throat. "Get on into town, boys, and get those supplies. And don't forget, I'll shoot any man who comes back here drunk."

Cal and Pearlie had finished breakfast, and were in the general store picking out the supplies Smoke had written on his list, when a group of hard-looking men walked into the room.

As the men spread out and began to gather supplies of their own, one of the men walked up to the store owner behind the counter and asked, "You got any women's clothes here?"

Cal's face got hard and his hand moved toward the butt of his pistol, until Pearlie put a hand on his arm. "Careful," he whispered.

The store owner nodded. "I got some pants and shirts that oughta fit a woman, but I don't have no fancy dresses or nothing like that."

"Pants and shirts will be all right," the man said. He held out his hand about level with his shoulder. "She's about this tall, and she's built thin, not real heavy."

The store owner walked to a rack of clothes on one wall and began to pick out trousers, flannel shirts, and some long-handle underwear.

"Oh, an' she's gonna need a heavy coat too," the man added as the store owner piled the clothes in his arms.

Pearlie motioned to Cal with his head and walked out of the store, leaving their supplies in a pile near the counter. When they got outside, he said, "That's got to be Miss Sally he's talking about."

"Yeah, I agree," Cal said.

"Now remember," Pearlie said, "Smoke said not to do nothin' to draw attention to ourselves, so don't you go off half-cocked until Smoke gets here."

"But, we can't just let 'em ride outta town without doin' somethin'," Cal pleaded.

"We are gonna do something," Pearlie answered. "I'm gonna follow 'em and see which way they're headed and make sure Miss Sally's all right."

"But what am I supposed to do?" Cal asked.

Pearlie handed him the wad of cash Smoke had

given them. "You get the rest of the supplies on the list and take it over to the hotel. Then, go to the livery and pick us out a packhorse to carry it on. Once I see where they're going, I'll come back to town and get you."

"And what if Smoke isn't here by then?" Cal asked.

"I don't know. We'll just have to figure something out when the time comes."

THIRTEEN

As soon as Cal moved back toward the general store, Pearlie took off at a dead run for the hotel. He knew if he was going to follow the kidnappers up into the mountains, he needed to get prepared.

Taking the steps two at a time, he ran up the stairs to the room he shared with Cal. He grabbed his saddlebags, stuffed some extra clothes into one, and put a sack of beans, a hunk of fatback bacon wrapped in waxed paper, and a small can of Arbuckle's coffee in the other side.

He started to leave the room, hesitated, and went back to the dresser and picked up his Winchester rifle and an extra box of cartridges. There was no telling what he'd run into up in the High Lonesome and he wanted to make sure he had everything he might need for the journey.

Closing the door, he again ran down the stairs and turned left out of the door toward the livery stable. He hoped the boy there had given his horse plenty of grain. He likely wouldn't have time to stop and let it graze while he was on the trail of the outlaws.

Blackie Johnson stepped up to the counter at the general store, and waited patiently while the owner totaled up their purchases. While he was waiting, he noticed a young man nearby also gathering up a load of supplies. Blackie smiled and nodded to the fellow. "Looks like you're gonna be doing some mining up in the mountains," he said companionably.

Cal, startled by the man's words and somewhat surprised at the congeniality of the outlaw, nodded. "Yeah, my partner and I plan to give it a try."

Blackie glanced out of the window at the gray day. "Mighty poor weather to be going up in the mountains," he said.

Cal shrugged and inclined his head at the pile of heavy coats and other clothing on the counter in front of the man. "Looks like that's where you're headed too," he said.

Blackie nodded. "Yeah, but we're just passing through, not planning on staying too long. We're from Texas and it don't get that cold down there."

Zeke Thompson sidled up next to Johnson and stared suspiciously at Cal. He glanced at Blackie with a frown on his face. "You gonna jaw all day or get our gear ready?"

Blackie stared back at Thompson, not giving an inch. He didn't like the man and made no pretense to. "I'll pay up when the clerk has the total ready. You got a problem with that, Zeke?" he asked, standing nose-to-nose with the man.

Zeke cut his eyes at Cal. "Don't get testy, Blackie, but there's no need to discuss our business with every stranger you meet."

Blackie reached over to the counter and picked up a bottle of whiskey Thompson had gotten off the shelf. "Here, Zeke," he said, sneering. "Pour yourself a drink. It looks like you need one."

"Damned if I don't," Thompson said, and took the bottle and limped off toward the door.

"Sorry about my friend," Blackie said to Cal, who

was watching Thompson tilt the bottle to the ceiling and take a large swallow. "He ain't too personable."

Cal nodded. "I can see why," he said. "That leg of his must ache something fierce in this cold weather. I busted a knee once when I was herding beeves, an' it still hurts in cold weather."

Blackie looked over at Thompson. "I suppose so, but my guess is he's just an asshole. He don't need no excuse to be snake-mean."

The owner of the store cleared his throat and handed Blackie a piece of paper with a list of their supplies and how much it cost. Blackie looked it over, and then he pulled out a wad of bills, counted out the correct amount, and handed it to the clerk.

"Much obliged," he said to the store owner. "Hey, boys," he called to the men who were still browsing in the store. "Come and get this stuff so we can head back to camp." He paused for a moment, and then he added, "Hank, you think you could go see if Rufus is through with that doctor? I want to make sure he doesn't stop off at any saloons before he heads on back here."

After they'd gathered up their supplies, Blackie tipped his hat to Cal. "Good luck to you with your mining, mister," he said.

"Thanks," Cal answered. "And I hope you get where you're goin' without freezing your balls off."

Blackie laughed. "Me too."

After the men in the store gathered up their order and left, Cal stepped to the door and watched them load their supplies and begin to walk their horses out of town.

A few minutes later, Pearlie could be seen riding past the store, following the men at a safe distance.

He glanced over at Cal standing in the doorway and winked and tipped his hat.

Cal grinned and went back into the store, where he proceeded to fill the rest of the order Smoke had given them. When he had it all stacked up on the counter, the owner of the store shook his head as he totaled the bill. "You and your partner must be planning to do a lot of blasting with all this powder."

"Yeah, it's a mite easier than using a pick and shovel," Cal answered.

The owner laughed. "That it is. But one thing, though," he added as he counted the boxes of cartridges Cal had gotten. "I don't know as you're going to need all these shells. The Indians haven't been giving the miners any trouble for some time now."

Cal nodded grimly. "It's just that my partner and I like to be prepared for whatever may happen."

"Looks to me like you're ready for the next war," the owner said as he handed Cal the bill.

Cal counted out the correct amount from the cash Pearlie had given him. "Here you go," he said. "Do you mind if I leave this stuff here for a while until I can get me a packhorse from the livery?"

"Not at all, son, I'll just pile it over here in the corner until you come back."

In less than an hour, Cal had purchased a packhorse from the livery man, loaded up their supplies, and taken the animal back to the livery, where he unpacked the boxes and bags of powder, stakes, nails, and cartridges and piled them in the stall where the livery man had his horse stored.

"I'm gonna leave these supplies here for a day or two, if you don't mind," Cal said. "My partner's out of town for a while and when he gets back we may have to leave in a hurry."

"Don't make no never mind to me, young'un," the

elderly man said. "I don't 'spect nobody will bother it none."

"Thanks," Cal said, and he went back to the hotel to wait for Smoke to come.

It was mid-afternoon and Cal was lying on the bed taking a nap when the door opened and Smoke walked in.

Cal jumped to his feet and rushed over to shake Smoke's hand. "Jiminy, I'm glad to see you, Smoke."

Smoke nodded and smiled, and Cal could see he was dead tired from his time on the trail.

"Any word on the kidnappers?" Smoke asked as he set his saddlebags on the bed.

"Yeah, there was a group of 'em here this mornin'," Cal answered. "They bought some supplies at the store an' Pearlie followed them out of town."

"They didn't have Sally with them?"

Cal shook his head. "No. They must've left a couple of men with her so nobody would see her when they came to town," Cal said.

"Which way did they go when they left town?" Smoke asked, standing by the window and staring out at the street three stories below.

"That away," Cal answered, pointing northeast.

Smoke nodded. "Then they're headed for Pueblo, like they said they were," he said.

"Smoke, you look like you could use some food and a lie-down," Cal said, worried at the tiredness in Smoke's eyes.

"Yeah, I've been pushing it pretty hard trying to catch up to them," Smoke said. "Is the food any good here?"

Cal smiled. "Pearlie thinks so."

"Pearlie would eat anything that didn't eat him

first," Smoke said. "Come on, let's get some grub and then I'll get some shut-eye. If Pearlie's not back in a few hours, we'll head out on our own down the trail toward Pueblo."

They went down to the dining room and ordered some food and a large pot of coffee. While they were waiting for the food to be cooked, Smoke told Cal about his trip following the men and the note Sally had written on a piece of her dress telling him where they were headed.

Cal grinned. "Miss Sally is too smart for them galoots," he said.

"That's for sure," Smoke said, and leaned back to let the waiter put their food on the table.

FOURTEEN

When they finished eating, Smoke called the waiter over to the table. "Hey, partner, would you have the chef fry us up four or five chickens and wrap them up for us to take with us later?" Smoke asked.

"Uh, we don't usually . . . "

Smoke handed the man a twenty-dollar bill. "Will this take care of it?" he asked, adding, "You can keep whatever's left over for yourself."

"I'll see that it gets done, sir," the waiter said, his lips curled in a wide smile. His tip would be more than he usually made in a week.

As they walked up the stairs to their room, Cal asked, "Why'd you do that?"

Smoke looked at him. "If we're going to be following these men up in the mountains, we're not going to be able to make a fire big enough to cook on without it being seen, so I wanted us to have something we could eat cold."

"Oh," Cal said, relieved that Smoke was doing the thinking for them, because he and Pearlie would never have thought of that.

Smoke went into the room and flopped down on the bed. "Wake me up in four hours whether Pearlie's here or not."

Before Cal could answer, Smoke was snoring softly and fast asleep.

* * *

Cal woke Smoke up and they were ready to leave just before nightfall. On the way out of the hotel, Smoke told the desk clerk to tell Pearlie they were on the trail heading toward Pueblo in case he returned after they left.

By the time they got the packhorse loaded up and were on their way, it was full dark and a light snow was starting to fall. "That's good," Smoke said, staring at the dark clouds in the night sky. "The clouds and snow will keep the temperatures from falling too low in the high country."

"It'll help us track the kidnappers too," Cal observed.

Smoke nodded. "That's true, if they try to get off the trail, but I suspect they're pilgrims and will stay on the road so they don't get lost in the mountains."

"Are you familiar with this part of the Sangre de Cristo Mountains, Smoke?" Cal asked as they rode north, letting their horses find their own speed.

"Pretty much," Smoke answered. "Preacher and I used to hunt this area back in the old days pretty much. There were plenty of beaver and foxes back then, not like now when the miners have hunted them out."

"You think there are any mountain men still up here nowadays?" Cal asked.

Smoke glanced at the peaks, outlined against the evening sky in the distance. "I suppose there may be a few. Some of the younger men are left, but even they're getting on up there in age by now."

It was getting close to midnight when Smoke's horse pricked up its ears and snorted through its nose. Smoke reined to a halt and held up his hand. "Quiet, Cal. Joker smells someone coming."

Since they were heading northeast and the wind was out of the north, the smells of anyone on the trail ahead of them would be carried downwind toward them.

Smoke pulled Joker's head around and led Cal off the trail and into the heavy bushes nearby. Cal followed suit when he saw Smoke draw his pistol and sit calmly waiting for whoever was headed their way.

A few minutes later, a dark form, hunched over his horse's head, could be seen moving down the trail toward them. When he came abreast of them, Smoke spurred Joker out onto the trail.

"Holy shit!" Pearlie exclaimed at the sight of two men materializing out of the wind-driven snow in front of him.

"Evening, Pearlie," Smoke said, holstering his pistol.

"Howdy, Pearlie," Cal said.

"You boys 'bout scared me outta ten years' growth," Pearlie said, taking his hat off and using it to brush the accumulated snow and ice off his shoulders and legs.

"What news of the kidnappers?" Smoke asked.

Pearlie gestured over his shoulder. "They're camped for the night, 'bout five miles up the trail."

"And Sally?" Smoke asked, his voice hard.

"Looks like they're treatin' her all right, Smoke. I got close enough to make sure she was doin' all right, nobody botherin' her or nothin', and then I headed back this way to meet up with you and Cal."

"So they're not treating her badly then?"

Pearlie shook his head. "No. In fact, they even bought her some heavy clothes, coats and such, so she wouldn't get too cold on the trip through the mountains."

"I'll be sure and thank the bastards . . . right before I kill them," Smoke said dryly.

"You want me to lead you to 'em?" Pearlie asked.

"Do they have sentries out?" Smoke asked.

Pearlie nodded. "Yeah. Two men, one north and one south. The others are bundled up next to the largest fire I ever seen tryin' to keep from freezin'."

"Well, there's no hurry then," Smoke said, pulling Joker's head around and riding off the trail toward a group of boulders nearby. "Let's make a fire, heat some coffee, and give them time to get settled in and the sentries to get sleepy."

"A fire sounds damn good," Pearlie said. "You got any food to cook? I'm 'bout starved to death."

"No time for that," Smoke said, "but we do have some fried chicken, if you don't mind eating it cold."

"Cold, hell," Pearlie replied. "I'll eat it raw if it's all you got."

After Smoke built a hat-sized fire up next to the boulders where the light couldn't be seen from more than a few feet away, Cal filled the coffeepot with snow and melted it on the fire, adding a double handful of Arbuckle's coffee once the water was boiling. After a few minutes, the delightful aroma of fresh-boiled coffee swirled in the air.

Pearlie was so hungry that he couldn't wait for the coffee to be ready. He dug into Cal's saddlebags and pulled out one of the packets of fried chicken wrapped in waxed paper. He carried it over to the tiny fire and sat cross-legged on a stone nearby while he unwrapped the food and began to eat.

When Cal handed him a tin cup full to the brim with the strong coffee, he said, "Hey, Pearlie, save a little of that chicken for Smoke and me."

"Hand me a couple of those legs, will you?" Smoke said. He preferred the legs to the white meat since he was used to eating game birds that were almost all dark meat.

"I'll take a breast," Cal said, reaching for the package.

Pearlie, who would eat any part of a chicken except the feathers and feet, pulled the package back and handed out the meat, preferring to remain in control of the delicious food.

After he took a few bites and washed them down with the coffee, he looked over at Smoke. "This is right good chicken, but it don't compare to Miss Sally's."

Smoke nodded his agreement while he gnawed on a chicken leg and drank his coffee.

"It sure would be nice to have a handful of Miss Sally's bear sign for desert," Cal observed, his mood falling as he thought about the situation Sally was in.

"It would be even nicer to have Sally here with us now," Smoke said, his eyes moving off to the north where the outlaws were camped.

When they'd finished eating and had built cigarettes to enjoy with the last of the coffee, Smoke began to outline his plan of attack on the kidnappers.

"First thing we're going to do is find their camp. We shouldn't have to worry too much about noise since the snow will muffle the horses' hoofbeats, but we'll need to make sure anything we're carrying is tied down tight so it won't clatter when we ride up close."

"After we find 'em, what do you want us to do?" Cal asked.

"I'm going to go in close while you boys hang back. I want to make sure Sally's all right. If I see she's in no danger of being treated badly, then I'll come back out to you and we'll see if we can take out the sentries without risking any noise."

Pearlie pulled out his skinning knife and held it up so the fire reflected off the blade. "That shouldn't be a problem," he said with a dark look.

Smoke shook his head. "No, Pearlie. I want to take them alive if we can."

"Why?" Cal asked.

"Because I want to ask them some questions about exactly where the outlaws are headed and why they decided to take her in the first place."

He pulled out his pocket watch, glanced at the time, and got to his feet. "Put out the fire, boys. It's time we get back on the trail."

It was almost midnight by the time Smoke and the boys approached the kidnappers' camp. Smoke could see and smell the huge campfire from over a mile away, so he knew they were getting close. When he saw the glow of the fire over a ridge, he told Cal and Pearlie to stay with the horses, and he got down out of the saddle and crept over the ridge on foot, keeping well off the trail and into the brush surrounding the camp.

As he got closer, he got down on his belly and crawled through the forest until he was no more than thirty yards from the fire. He counted nine bodies sprawled close to the fire, bundled up in blankets and lying on rubber groundsheets to keep dry. One of the figures was a little away from the others, and he could tell it was Sally by the long, dark hair spilling out from under the blankets, which she had up to her forehead to keep warm.

He saw a rope leading out from under the blankets that was tied to a nearby tree. Evidently the bastards had tied Sally's hand or arm to the tree to keep her from trying to escape during the night. Actually, he thought, that was a good sign. If they'd harmed her significantly, they wouldn't be worried about her being able to make an escape, so she must be in pretty good shape, considering what she'd been through.

He lay perfectly still, not moving at all. He knew from the number of bodies he counted that there were probably two sentries somewhere near the camp. He figured sooner or later they would make some movement showing him where they were. Pilgrims, in cold like this, were unable to stay perfectly still while sitting sentry duty and would eventually move around to try and keep warm.

Sure enough, in a short while, he saw the flare of a lucifer off to one side as one of the sentries lit a cigarette or cigar. He made a mental note of his location and continued to let his eyes move around the periphery of the camp, searching for the other sentry's location.

His patience was rewarded after a few minutes when a moving shadow on the other side of the camp caught his eye. The man was walking in short circles, flapping his arms to his chest to get them warm.

Smoke shook his head and grinned to himself. The men were obviously dumber than dirt. The only value of a sentry is stealth. If the enemy knows the sentry's location, then he's worthless; a fact that was either not known by these men or that was being ignored out of a sense of security or boredom.

With their positions fixed firmly in his mind, Smoke slowly crawled back away from the camp until it was safe for him to get to his feet, and then he jogged back to where he'd left Cal and Pearlie and the horses.

When he got there, he drew a crude map of the camp in the snow with a stick, marking the positions of the sentries. "Now, here's what we're going to do," he said. "Cal, you and Pearlie will ease up on the man on this side of the camp, 'cause he'll be the easiest to get to without making any noise. Once you get to him, take him down with the butt of your pistol and make sure he doesn't make any noise when he falls. Then you bring him back here and make him comfortable until I get back."

"You gonna take out the other guard by yourself?" Cal asked.

Smoke nodded. "Yeah. It's going to be a little more difficult to get to him without him hearing me because of his position, but I think I can do it. If it looks like it'll make too much noise for me to take him, I'll just come back here and we'll try to get our information from the man you two get."

He stood up and put his hands on their shoulders. "Good luck, boys, and remember, Sally's life depends on you not letting them hear you."

FIFTEEN

Sam Kane felt as if his feet and hands were frozen blocks of ice. Even though he'd had some experience with blue northers down in Texas, he'd never seen weather so cold as this before. He pulled the cork from his canteen with shaking hands and took a swallow of the coffee he'd filled it with earlier. It was only lukewarm now and did little to warm his insides. It was definitely time for stronger medicine to ward off the chilly night air.

Looking around to make sure Bill Pike wasn't checking on him, he pulled a small bottle of whiskey from under his coat and upended it, swallowing deeply. Almost immediately, he felt the warmth of the liquor spread through his stomach and out into his limbs. Jesus, that tasted good, he thought.

He set the whiskey down on a rock next to him, being careful not to spill any, and took out his makings. He tried to build himself a cigarette, but his hands were shaking so much he spilled more tobacco than he got in the paper. He twisted the ends of the paper and stuck the butt in his mouth. Bending over against the wind, he struck a lucifer and lit the cigarette, gratefully filling his lungs with the warm smoke.

He jumped when he thought he heard a twig break

behind him, but when he turned and looked, he saw no signs of movement.

He shook his head. Must've been the wind, he thought. The spooky darkness and cold must be getting to him for him to be so jumpy.

He finished the cigarette and flipped the butt out into the snow, grinning as it sizzled in the wetness. Leaning over, he picked up the whiskey and leaned his head back to take another drink.

He caught a movement out of the corner of his eye, and turned his head just as the butt of a pistol crashed down onto his skull. The darkness opened up in front of him and he tumbled in.

Billy Gatsby, the youngest of Bill Pike's band of raiders, was lucky. He'd been given the sentry post that was partially sheltered by a large group of boulders and was back up against the side of a hillock, so most of the north wind was blocked.

Still, he was about as cold as he could ever remember being. In spite of the fact that he had on three shirts and a heavy coat over his long handles, he was still shivering and shaking like he had the fever. Don't know why Bill thinks we have to stand sentry duty way out here in the mountains, he thought. Ain't nobody within fifty miles gonna be crazy enough to be out in this storm this time of night.

He, like Sam Kane, had filled his canteen with coffee, but he'd been smarter than Kane. When Bill wasn't looking, he'd added a generous measure of rye whiskey to the canteen before filling it with coffee. His coffee wasn't as warm as Kane's was, but it packed a helluva lot more kick than Kane's did.

The night was only half over, and Billy had already just about emptied the canteen. As he took the last swallow, he debated whether he ought to go back over to the fire and fill it up again with the coffee that'd been left warming by the fire.

He shook his head and clamped his jaw tight. No, better not do that. Bill would have a fit if he left his position just to get some coffee. Not that he was afraid of Bill Pike. Billy was young and dumb enough not to be afraid of anybody, but he figured there was no need of pissing Pike off when they stood to make such a good payday off this Jensen fellow.

He wriggled his toes inside his boots, wishing he'd put on an extra pair of socks. He could barely feel his feet and they were beginning to burn. Wondering if they were getting frostbitten, he decided to walk around a little to get the blood flowing.

Slapping his arms against his chest, he stepped out from his sheltered place among the boulders, and almost ran into a shadowy figure standing just around the corner.

He grinned for a moment, thinking at first it was Bill Pike coming to check on him. And then he realized the man was much bigger than anyone in their group.

"Son of a bitch!" he started to say, grabbing for his side arm.

The big man's fist crashed into his jaw, dislocating it and knocking out three of his front teeth as it drove him down into unconsciousness.

When Smoke got back to the horses, carrying Billy Gatsby over his shoulder, he found Cal and Pearlie sitting on their groundsheets in front of an unconscious man propped up against a boulder in a copse of pine trees.

"Did you have any trouble?" he asked as he dropped his man on the ground next to theirs.

"Naw," Pearlie drawled. "This'n was too busy drinkin' whiskey to be payin' any attention to what he was doin'."

Smoke squatted in front of the men. "Rub a little snow on their faces and see if we can wake them up."

As Cal began to rub snow on the men's faces, he looked back over his shoulder at Smoke. "Jiminy, Smoke. This one's jaw looks like it's broken. What'd you hit him with?"

Smoke grinned. "My fist."

Cal grimaced at the misshapen appearance of the man's face. "Well, that was enough, I guess."

A few minutes later, both men sputtered and came awake. Billy was groaning and slobbering blood from his ruined mouth, while Sam just held his head in both hands and kept his mouth shut, glaring at Smoke and the boys with hate-filled eyes.

Smoke, still squatting in front of the men, said quietly, "You boys know who I am?" he asked.

Kane's eyes narrowed and he shook his head. "Nope. Never seen you before in my life," he said, his voice whiskey-rough.

"I'm Smoke Jensen," Smoke said, noticing how the men's eyes changed at the mention of his name. "And that's my wife you men kidnapped, and it was my hands you killed at my ranch."

"I don't know what you're talking about," Kane said sullenly, his eyes dropping, unable to meet Smoke's.

Smoke sighed and stood up, towering over the men. "Boys," he said calmly, "we can do this one of two ways: the hard way or the easy way, and trust me, you don't want to know what the hard way is."

Kane didn't answer, but his eyes filled with fear when he saw Pearlie take out his skinning knife and slowly rub it back and forth on his pants, his eyes fixed on Kane like a snake eyeing a rabbit.

"All right," he said grudgingly, "what do you want to know?"

"First, why did your leader pick my ranch to raid?" Smoke asked.

"He found a wanted poster on you up in Utah," Kane answered. "It offered a ten-thousand-dollar reward for you dead or alive."

Smoke snorted through his nose. "That poster's over ten years old," he said. "There isn't any price on my head anymore."

Kane glanced at Billy, lying next to him, his eyes puzzled. "Then why would he do all this?" he asked.

Smoke pursed his lips, thinking. "Tell me the names of all of the gang."

After Kane told him, Smoke nodded. "This Zeke Thompson, he any kin to Pike?"

"I reckon so. They got the same mother."

"Does he have a bum leg?" Smoke asked.

Kane nodded. "Yeah, an' his arm's messed up too."

Smoke looked at Cal and Pearlie. "It's just as I thought. Pike and Thompson are after me because I killed their brother up in Utah a while back. I shot up Thompson but let him live. My mistake, I guess."

"How about Miss Sally, you pond scum?" Pearlie asked, holding the knife in front of Kane's eyes. "Have you bastards hurt her in any way?"

Kane shook his head vigorously. "No, I swear we haven't. Bill said we couldn't do nothin' to her till he had Jensen prisoner. Then he was gonna make you watch what we did."

Smoke's hands clenched at his sides. "I hope you're telling me the truth, mister."

"Ask Billy if'n you don't believe me," Kane said.

Smoke glanced at Billy, who mumbled something

they couldn't understand since he couldn't talk, then nodded his head indicating Kane was telling the truth.

Smoke took a deep breath. "In that case, I'm going to let you live . . . for a while."

"What do you mean?" Kane asked.

"I'm going to take you up the mountain a ways and let you go."

"What do you mean, let us go?" Kane asked. "You mean, without no horses or nothin'?"

"That's right," Smoke said. "If you're smart and careful, you just might be able to survive until you can find some miners who'll take mercy on you. I will leave you with a knife so you can cut some trees for shelter, but that's about it."

"But we'll freeze to death up there," Kane pleaded.

Smoke shrugged. "At least you'll have a chance to live. That's more than you gave the men you killed at my ranch."

He turned to Pearlie. "Put them on your horse. I'll take them a couple of miles up the mountain and then I'll meet you back here."

Pearlie put his skinning knife away and walked over to where the two men were propped up against a boulder. He bent over to reach down and help Billy Gatsby to his feet. Billy moaned and spat out some blood from his mouth as Pearlie grabbed him under the arms.

Just as Pearlie straightened up with the young man in his arms, Sam Kane jumped to his feet, drawing a long knife with a skinny blade from his boot. He threw his left arm around Pearlie's face and stuck the point of the knife up against his throat, whirling around until he was facing Smoke and Cal.

Billy tried to grin but stopped when he realized it hurt too much. He reached down and pulled Pearlie's pistol from his holster and stood next to them, pointing the gun at Cal and Smoke.

Smoke sighed, squaring his body so he was facing the two men full on. "Are you boys sure you want to play it out this way?" Smoke asked.

"We ain't got no choice, Jensen," Zane said. "I can't let you take us up into the mountains to freeze to death or to be eaten by wild animals."

Smoke nodded. "I guess you're right, son," he said. "It might be more humane to just kill you both now, so you'll die quick and easy."

Zane grinned nastily. "I think you're forgetting who has the upper hand here, Jensen."

Billy mumbled something through his ruined mouth that sounded like "Yeah."

Smoke shrugged and glanced at Cal, who nodded grimly.

Quick as a rattlesnake striking, Smoke and Cal drew their pistols and fired, Cal's shot coming an instant later than Smoke's.

A tiny hole appeared in Zane's forehead from the slug Smoke fired, whipping his head back and flinging him spread-eagled on his back across the boulder behind him and Pearlie.

Cal's slug took Billy in the neck, snapping it and almost taking his head off before he crumpled to the ground, dead in his boots.

Pearlie reached up and fingered the thin red line on his throat where Zane's knife slid across it after he'd been hit. Pearlie smiled. "I thought you boys was gonna jaw all night 'fore you took them pond scum out."

He glanced down at Billy, noted the wound in his neck, and then he looked back over at Cal. "You a mite off on your aim there, Cal boy. Guess we're gonna have to see that you practice a bit more in the future."

Cal smiled and nodded. "Yeah, I was aiming for his heart, but I guess I rushed the shot a little since he already had his gun drawn and pointed."

Smoke holstered his pistol. "You did mighty good, Cal, especially in knowing I wanted you to take the one with the gun instead of the one with the knife."

"Yeah," Pearlie said, a puzzled look on his face. "I didn't see you pass no signals, so how'd you know which one to shoot, Cal?"

Cal spun his gun once and let it drop into his holster. "I knew Smoke would take the harder shot, so I took the easier one." He smiled at Cal. "Besides, I didn't want to risk hitting you 'stead of that bastard there, 'cause I knew I'd never hear the end of it if I did."

Pearlie and Smoke both laughed. "You got that right," Pearlie agreed.

Smoke pulled out the large bowie knife he carried in a scabbard on his belt and walked over to the dead bodies. "I think we ought to leave a little message for Mr. Pike now that these boys have forced our hand."

SIXTEEN

Bill Pike woke up just as the morning sun was peeking over the mountain peaks to the east. He yawned and stretched and climbed out of his blankets, noticing the fire had burned down to just coals.

He walked over to the bundle of blankets that covered Rufus Gordon and kicked it with his boot. "Rufus, wake your lazy ass up and put some wood on that fire," he said.

Rufus groaned. "Aw, Bill, you know I can't hardly use my right hand. Get somebody else to do it."

Pike looked surprised. "I thought that doc over in Canyon City fixed your hand up pretty good."

Rufus held up his right hand, totally encased in new bandages. "He did, but the damn thing's so wrapped up I can't use my fingers."

"Must make pickin' your nose a real chore," Hank Snow called from across the fire, laughing at his own joke.

"Glad you spoke up, Hank," Bill Pike said, turning to him. "Just for that, you can get the wood for the fire 'stead of Rufe."

As Snow got slowly to his feet, grumbling about no one having a sense of humor, Pike nudged Blackie Johnson with his boot. "Blackie, get up and fix us some coffee and breakfast 'fore it's time for lunch."

While Hank Snow got the fire going, Blackie

pulled the cooking utensils out of the bag on the back of one of the packhorses and began to make coffee and prepared to fry some bacon and boil some beans. He still had some biscuits he'd cooked the night before, and put them on a pan near the fire to warm up.

The rest of the gang began to get their blankets and groundsheets folded and packed on their horses. Sally sat up in her blankets and held up her hand with the rope still tied to it. "If you'll take this off," she said to Pike, "I'll put my blankets on my horse."

Pike walked over, squatted down, and untied the knots in the rope. "Did you sleep well, Mrs. Jensen?" he asked, a slight smile on his face.

"Yes, thank you, Mr. Pike," she answered. "But I'll feel a lot better after some coffee."

Pike looked over at Blackie. "That coffee ready yet, Blackie?"

Blackie nodded, poured some into a tin mug, and brought it over to Sally. "I'll have some biscuits and bacon and beans ready in about five minutes, Mrs. Jensen," he said, his eyes narrowing at the red rash the rope had made on her wrist. "And I'll get you some lard to smooth on that rash on your wrist."

Pike scowled at Johnson. "Don't go gettin' too kindly to the lady, Blackie. It ain't gonna do you no good."

Blackie stared at Pike for a moment, and then he just shook his head and went back to the fire to finish cooking breakfast.

Pike looked around at his men. "Where the hell are Billy and Sam?" he asked.

Rufus Gordon sat up in his blankets and glanced around, and then he shrugged. "They ain't here yet, Boss."

"If those lazy bastards fell asleep on guard duty, I'm gonna kick their asses!" Pike growled.

"Hank, you and Sarge go get 'em and bring 'em back here pronto," Pike ordered.

As Snow and Rutledge walked off toward the two sentries' posts, Pike squatted down, picked a piece of bacon out of the frying pan, and began to munch on it while he waited to see what was keeping the guards.

A few minutes later, both Rutledge and Snow came running back into the camp, their faces pale and sweating in spite of the frigid temperatures of the morning air. Snow looked as if he was going to throw up.

"What is it? What's the matter with you two?" Pike asked, his brow furrowed with worry.

"You . . . you better come on over here and take a look for yourself," Snow managed as he bent over, his hands on his knees, and dry-heaved.

Pike and the other men moved through the brush to the place where Sam Kane had been stationed. Lying on a boulder was a bloody scalp, two ears, and a tongue, arranged in a grotesque parody of a face on the bloody rock.

"Jesus!" Pike said, his stomach turning until he too thought he was going to be sick.

Sally Jensen pushed a couple of the men aside and stood before the boulder, a sympathetic look on her face for the dead men. "Oh, Mr. Pike," she said quietly. "I believe you've now seen some of my husband's handiwork."

Pike whirled around and glared at her. "Ain't no white man done this!" he shouted. "It must've been Indians."

Sally shook her head. "No, Mr. Pike. I'm afraid you're mistaken."

"What do you mean?" he asked, his voice a dry croak.

"In the first place, Indians wouldn't have left the scalps or the . . . other trophies," she explained. "And in the second place, if the Indians had killed your men, why do you think they would not have come on into camp and finished the rest of you off while you were sleeping?"

Pike looked at Rutledge. "What about Billy?" he asked, his eyes wide.

Rutledge shook his head. "Worse than this. You'd better come look."

The entire group moved across the camp, breakfast forgotten, and approached the sentry post of Billy Gatsby. They found his entire head stuck on a pole in the ground, his eyes open and staring at them as if in reproach, his swollen tongue protruding from an obviously broken jaw.

Pike whirled around, grabbed Sally by the shoulders, and shouted into her face. "What kind of man is your husband?"

She smiled back, unaffected by his display of temper. "He is a man of the old school, Mr. Pike. An eye for an eye and all of that."

"But we ain't harmed you none," Pike said, his voice becoming more normal as he got control of himself.

"You kidnapped me against my will, Mr. Pike, and you killed two of our friends back at the ranch. That's enough for Smoke." She turned her head to look at Billy. "I'm afraid this is what you've all got to look forward to for what you've done."

Pike jerked his gun out and pointed it at Sally. "Then it won't make any difference if I kill you now, will it?"

Sally showed no fear. "Not in the end result perhaps. You are all going to die, that is as certain as the fact that the sun will rise tomorrow. However, the manner in which you die *will* be determined by how you treat me."

Pike gritted his teeth, pulled back the hammer on his pistol, and stuck the barrel under Sally's chin.

She stared back at him with clear eyes and did not flinch in the slightest.

Blackie Johnson stepped over and put his hand on Pike's arm. "Maybe we'd better listen to what she says, Boss. If we kill her now, we won't have any hold over Jensen to make him come to us in Pueblo."

"Blackie's right, Bill," Zeke Thompson said. "I haven't waited all these years to be cheated out of my chance at Jensen 'cause you get pissed off."

Blackie glanced back over his shoulder at Zeke. "What do you mean, waited all these years, Zeke?" he asked. "I thought this was about the reward on Jensen's head."

Thompson blushed and stammered, "It was just a figure of speech, Blackie. What I meant to say was, I been waiting for a score like this for a lotta years and I don't want to blow it now."

Pike took a deep breath and let the hammer down on his gun. He holstered it and then he pointed at Sally with his finger. "You get a second chance, Mrs. Jensen, but if that crazy husband of yours does something like this again, I'll make you suffer like you've never even dreamed of."

Sally gave him a half smile and turned and made her way back to the camp, where she calmly poured herself another cup of coffee and sat there staring at the forgotten frying pan as the bacon strips slowly turned to charcoal.

Smoke, who'd been watching the scene below from a vantage point on a ledge fifteen hundred yards up the mountain, gently let the hammer down on the Sharps buffalo rifle he was holding. When Pike had put the pistol under Sally's chin, Smoke had drawn a bead on the man's head. He'd had the trigger half-depressed when Pike lowered his gun, saving his life.

Smoke took a deep breath. He knew how close he'd come to losing Sally, and the feeling made him weak with unaccustomed fear.

Time to back off for a while and let the situation simmer down, he thought to himself. As he moved down the mountain to where Cal and Pearlie were waiting for him, he began to make plans for his meeting with the outlaws in Pueblo and how he was going to handle it.

He knew it was going to take all of his skill to meet with Pike and not let the man get the upper hand.

The main thing he had to do was to stall the kidnappers along until he could get Sally out from under their control, which meant he'd have to leave the rest of them alive until he could figure out a way to do that without getting her killed by the desperados.

When he arrived back at the place where Cal and Pearlie were holding the horses, he put the Sharps in its rifle boot and climbed into the saddle.

"Did our little show have the desired effect?" Pearlie asked.

Smoke nodded. "It sure got them to thinking," he replied. He sat on his horse and built himself a cigarette. When he was done, he stuck the butt in the corner of his mouth, struck a lucifer on his pants leg, and lit the cigarette. As smoke trailed from his nostrils, he said, "Now, here's what we're going to do when we get to Pueblo."

When he was finished explaining his plan, they rode off after the outlaws.

SEVENTEEN

As Pike led his men through mountain passes toward Pueblo, Colorado Territory, he began to leave two men a slight distance behind to watch their backtrail. With what had happened to Sam and Billy, he now knew Smoke Jensen was in the vicinity, and he wasn't going to take any chances of Jensen sneaking up on them while they were riding.

When they got close to the town of Pueblo, he checked a map he'd been given while in Utah by a man who used to mine the area. The man had told him of a played-out mining camp north of Pueblo up in the mountain range that had some shacks and a couple of old mine shafts that would be perfect for what Pike had in mind.

The trail from Canyon City to Pueblo followed the course of the Arkansas River as it meandered southeast through the foothills of the mountains. The map indicated that just before reaching Pueblo, Pike should turn north and circle around the city until he came to a creek named Fountain Creek, which ran straight south toward Pueblo, where it then joined the Arkansas River. The deserted mining camp would be found about five miles north of the city on the banks of the creek.

As the group of outlaws rode single file down the trail, their horses moving slowly as they plowed through knee-deep snow, Sally slowed her horse until she was abreast of Blackie Johnson. She'd picked him to talk to because of all the men in the gang he seemed the least hostile toward her.

"Mr. Johnson," she said in a low voice that couldn't be heard more than a few feet away.

Johnson looked at her and nodded, but didn't speak.

"What was that you were saying back at the camp about a wanted poster on Smoke?"

Johnson glanced up at the head of the line of men, making sure Pike couldn't hear him. "Bill has a poster we picked up in Utah that says your husband is worth ten thousand dollars, dead or alive," he answered, also speaking in a low voice.

"So," Sally said, "that's why you're riding with these men?"

Johnson gave her a look. "Mrs. Jensen, no matter what you think of us, we wouldn't be out here waiting for your husband to come so we can kill him if he didn't deserve it. Men don't get ten-thousand-dollar rewards put on them if they haven't done some pretty bad things. We're Regulators, not bandits."

Sally looked puzzled. "Well, no matter what you call yourselves, there can't be a wanted poster out on Smoke. Smoke hasn't been wanted by the law for over ten years. All of the posters were recalled years ago by the governor of the territory."

Johnson slowed his horse and stared at her. "Are you sure about that?" he asked.

Sally smiled slightly. "Of course I'm sure. Smoke is in no trouble with the law, Mr. Johnson, and hasn't been for some years." She sighed deeply. "Think about it. With that much money at stake, you would have had to stand in line behind other bounty hunters to get at Smoke if it was true. After all, we weren't exactly living in hiding in Colorado."

Johnson's eyes narrowed and he stared at Pike's back. "I'll admit, Mrs. Jensen, I've been having my doubts. I thought it might be something like that. I couldn't figure why a man with such a price on his head would be living openly on a ranch in Colorado Territory so close to Utah."

Sally gave a low laugh. "That's simple. It's because he's not wanted and hasn't been for some time."

Johnson nodded slowly. "That figures," he said, disgust in his voice. He gave Pike, riding up ahead of them, a speculative look. "Bill must have some other reason for coming after your husband, something he didn't tell us about."

Sally gave him a close look. "You really don't know what all this is about, do you?" she asked.

Johnson turned his head to look her in the eyes. "No. The only reason Pike gave us was the money we'd make if we killed Jensen. Do you have any idea what's going on?" he asked, still speaking in a low voice so those in front of and behind them couldn't hear his words.

"Yes. It seems some years ago, Smoke shot and killed Mr. Pike's brother, and he wounded his half brother, Zeke. It must have been a severe wound, resulting in the problems he now has with his arm and leg."

Johnson's lips turned white as he pressed them together. "So, all this is about him getting even with your husband for something he did to his family a long time ago?"

Sally nodded.

Johnson lifted his reins and sat up straighter in his saddle. "That son of a bitch just got Billy and Sam killed, and there isn't even going to be any money in it for us."

He rested his right hand on the butt of his pistol. "I think I'll go call him on it right now."

Sally shook her head. "No, Mr. Johnson, I wouldn't do that if I were you."

"Why not?" he asked, relaxing a little.

"Because you have no proof, other than my word, and I do not think the men will believe me."

"You're right. These stupid galoots won't want to think they've come all this way for nothing."

"And killed two innocent men and gotten two of your friends killed all because Mr. Pike and Mr. Thompson want revenge against my husband," Sally added.

"What do you suggest I do?"

"Bide your time, Mr. Johnson, bide your time. Pike will give himself away sooner or later, and then you'll have the rest of the men with you instead of against you when you confront him."

"That's sound advice, Mrs. Jensen. I'm obliged," Johnson said, taking his hand off his pistol and sitting back in his saddle.

Just before noon, Pike and his men came to the stream running north and south that he figured must be Fountain Creek. They turned north and rode for another three hours, and finally came to a collection of old, weather-beaten clapboard cabins arranged in a semicircle on the banks of the river. There were well-worn paths from each of the houses down to the water's edge and to a pit dug in the middle of the open ground in between the cabins. There were even a couple of old privies that were still standing out behind the houses and away from the stream.

Pike rode into the center of the small camp and got down off his horse. "This must be the place that old miner told us about, boys," he said. "Get your gear together and see if any of these cabins are in good enough shape to bunk down in."

He stood in the center of the open area among the houses and stared up at the mountains that rose on steep slopes on all sides of them. "Hank, while the boys unpack our supplies, why don't you take a ride up the slope over there and see if you can find the mine entrance the old fool told us about?"

"All right, Boss," Snow said, and he jerked his reins around and walked his horse up the side of the mountain.

Sergeant Rutledge came riding up with the other man Pike had assigned to watch their backtrail. "All clear to the rear, Boss," he said. "If anyone's following us, they're staying well back and out of sight."

Pike moved to a circular area in the middle of the open area where dozens of small stones were arranged around a fire pit about two feet deep. "Sarge, take a couple of men and gather up some wood for a fire, and Blackie can fix us our noon meal while the rest of you unpack."

As the men bent to their tasks, Pike walked over to Sally and helped her down off her horse. Once she was on the ground, he untied the ropes he had around her wrists. "I'm gonna untie you, Mrs. Jensen, but I warn you again, don't try to escape or it'll go hard on you."

Sally glanced around at the surrounding mountains on all sides of them and decided to once again play the helpless female. "Why, where on earth would I go, Mr. Pike? I'd never find my way out of this wilderness by myself."

Pike gave her a long look, and for a moment Sally wondered if she'd overplayed her role.

"That's right, Mrs. Jensen," he finally said, beginning to turn away from her. "These mountains are no place for a woman on her own."

Sally bit her lip to keep from smiling. Truth was, with all Smoke had taught her about the High Lonesome over the years, she was far better equipped to deal with the wilderness than any of these flatlander pilgrims were.

She followed Pike over to where Blackie Johnson was struggling to get a fire going with wood that was wet from the snow on the ground.

She stood near him and talked out of the side of her mouth so the others wouldn't know they were communicating. "Mr. Johnson, if you'll use that little hatchet to split the wood open, you'll find it is dry on the inside and will make a much better fire," she whispered, her head turned away. "I'd start with some dry grass from up close to the trees where the snow hasn't gotten to it, and then use some pine cones on top of that. It'll make the fire start a lot easier."

"You seem to know a lot about living in the open, Mrs. Jensen," he said to her as he began to split the wood with his small ax.

Sally didn't answer, but she thought to herself, a woman learns a lot married to a mountain man, including how to outsmart galoots like this bunch.

Cal and Pearlie, who'd been keeping pace with the outlaws by riding up higher in the mountains, had been surprised when the gang had made a turn to the north and headed away from Pueblo, where they were supposed to meet with Smoke.

Smoke had circled around the men, and rode hard

to get to Pueblo ahead of the man he was supposed to meet there. He wanted to be waiting for him so he wouldn't know Smoke knew where his camp was.

Cal and Pearlie, from their vantage point on a slope high above the outlaws' camp, watched the men unpack their supplies and settle into the cabins near the stream.

"Looks like they're gonna make this their camp," Pearlie said.

Cal, who'd been watching Sally as she moved around the camp, nodded. "They seem to be treating Miss Sally all right," he observed. "At least, they're givin' her the run of the place an' not keepin' her tied up or anything."

Pearlie smiled grimly. "They'd better not do her no harm, if'n they know what's good for 'em.

"We'll watch them a mite longer an' then you can ride on into town and tell Smoke where they're stayin'," he added.

EIGHTEEN

When Smoke followed the trail into the city of Pueblo, he was surprised at how much the town had grown. He'd been through the area years ago when he was riding with Preacher, but the town seemed to have tripled in size and population since then.

Back when he and Preacher had passed through, Pueblo had been a sleepy little village built on the bank of the Arkansas River. Now the town straddled the river and was built up all along both sides of the slowly flowing body of water. The buildings weren't too close to the edge of the river because in the spring, when the snow and ice in the mountains above and all around the city melted, the river would more than double in size and speed of flow.

There was a wooden bridge built across the narrowest part of the river that allowed the inhabitants to move back and forth along both sides of it. Back when Smoke was first here, there had only been a flat raft that a couple of men pulled back and forth by means of a rope tied to trees on either side of the river.

As Smoke rode Joker across the bridge, he noticed there was now a fort occupying the north end of town. A sign on the periphery of the fort read FORT PUEBLO, and a small group of soldiers could be seen moving about within the confines of the structure.

"They must be here to maintain order among the miners, since there hasn't been any trouble with the Indians for some years," Smoke said to the back of Joker's head, a habit he'd picked up long ago when he'd spend half a year or more without laying eyes on another white man. He'd always felt talking to a horse was less troublesome than talking to oneself when alone up in the mountains.

The town was fairly busy, what with a lot of the miners coming down from their mountain camps to gather up supplies for the winter before the snows blocked the passes down to town. Along with the miners was a conglomeration of the people that invariably congregated around men with too much money in their pockets and too little civilizing influences: prostitutes, gamblers, footpads, thieves, and other assorted rowdy characters of an unsavory nature.

Now all Smoke had to do was to pick out a saloon out of the many that lined Court Street and grab himself a table. Today was the day he was supposed to meet the man who'd kidnapped Sally, and he couldn't wait to look the bastard in the eyes.

Back at the outlaws' camp, Bill Pike finished his meal and got to his feet. He checked his watch and then he looked out over the mountains thinking. It was about time for him to head into Pueblo to meet with Smoke Jensen and discuss the present situation and how they were going to deal with it. He realized he'd gotten himself between a rock and a hard place. On the one hand, he and Zeke needed to get Smoke out of Pueblo so they could wreak their vengeance upon him for killing their kin, but on the other hand, if he brought Smoke up here now, it was likely the other members of his band of cutthroats would soon learn that there was in fact no price on Smoke's head, and there was no telling how they would react to the news that they'd come all this way without a ten-thousand-dollar payday in the offing.

If they'd killed Smoke at the ranch, it wouldn't have been as bad. He could have said anything to his men. Hell, he could have waited a day or two, pretended to go to a sheriff, and then come back and told his men that the poster had been recalled. Maybe a few would have raised a fuss. But he and Zeke could have handled that. And meanwhile, Smoke would be dead.

But now, after all this time, after all they'd been through, his men needed something more. A payday, preferably a big one.

The only way out of this quandary that Pike could see would be to put Smoke off another day, and then have Smoke meet him and Zeke somewhere else with the promise to trade Mrs. Jensen for money. Hopefully, that would put Jensen's suspicions to rest and at that meeting Zeke and Pike could kill the son of a bitch.

When Zeke got in touch with Pike with the idea of getting revenge on Smoke Jensen for killing their brother and crippling Zeke, Pike had began his search for where Smoke might be living now. As famous as Smoke was, it didn't take Pike long to discover his whereabouts in Big Rock, Colorado. He'd also discovered that Smoke Jensen had become both respectable and rich.

Thinking on this, Pike chuckled to himself, seeing a way out of his predicament. He'd have Jensen wire the bank at Big Rock and have a letter of credit wired to the bank at Pueblo for ten thousand dollars as ransom for his wife.

After he and Zeke killed Jensen, Pike would simply tell the men that they had killed Smoke, taken his body to Pueblo, and gotten the ten thousand dollars reward as he'd promised. That should satisfy the men as far as the money was concerned.

To make them even happier, once he and Zeke were done with Smoke, he would give the men Mrs. Jensen as an added prize to make up for the hardships they'd faced in the frigid weather. He could then sweeten the pot by arranging to use the men to rob some of the miners in the area and make enough money to enable them to live for years on the proceeds of this little trip.

This seemed to Pike like the best way to keep everyone happy and for him and Zeke to get the revenge they craved against Jensen.

On the way into Pueblo, he would keep a sharp lookout for a place suitable for the meeting with Jensen. It would have to be isolated and yet easy enough to describe to the man so he could find it the next day.

Pike called the men together near the fire. "Blackie," he said, "take Mrs. Jensen to one of those cabins and tie her up good and tight. We've got some business to discuss."

Blackie nodded and walked over to help Sally to her feet. He led her to the cabin he'd put his things in, and told her to lie down on the bed.

Once she was lying down, he bent over her. "Mrs. Jensen, I'm going to put some ropes on your hands and feet, but I'm not gonna tie 'em real tight so they won't dig into your skin."

Sally nodded as he wrapped the ropes around her wrists and ankles. He straightened up. "Now, you got to promise me not to try and escape, or it'll go hard on me."

Sally took a deep breath. "Thank you for you kindness, Mr. Johnson. I will promise not to try and escape right now, but I won't promise not to try later on."

Johnson gave a short laugh. "That's good enough for me, Mrs. Jensen. I'll come in and untie you as soon as Pike's through with his talk."

He walked out the door and went over to the fire, where the other men were standing, warming their hands against the chill of the cold, mountain air.

Pike looked around at his men. "Boys, I'm going to go into Pueblo and see if Jensen showed up like I told him to in that letter we left at his ranch. If he's there, I'll get him to come back to camp with me by promising to let him go if he pays us for his wife."

"What's gonna happen when he gets here?" Hank Snow asked, picking his teeth with a stick.

Pike spread his hands. "Why, we'll kill him, of course, and then take his body to the nearest marshal's office and collect our ten thousand dollar reward."

Rufus Gordon rubbed the bandages on his ruined hand, hate filling his eyes. "And what's gonna happen to that bitch what shot off my fingers after we're done with Jensen?" he asked, letting his eyes go to the cabin where Sally was.

Pike shrugged. "I guess that'll be up to you boys. As cold as it is up here, maybe you can figure out some way for her to keep you warm for a spell."

Rufus jerked a long-bladed knife out of a scabbard on his belt and held it up. "That's fine with me, so long as I get her when everybody else is through with her. I owe her big for what she done to my hand."

"Rufe," Pike said, "personally, I don't give a damn what you do with her after we've gotten Jensen, but until that happens, she is not to be touched."

"Why not, Boss?" Sergeant Rutledge asked. "If we're gonna kill the son of a bitch anyway?"

Pike sighed. "Because I don't know if Jensen will agree to come into camp unless he sees that she is all right first. We may have to show her to him to get him in here."

Rutledge shrugged. "Oh," he said, "I never thought of that."

"That's why I do the thinking for this group, Sarge," Pike said, grinning. "Now, you boys get the camp straightened up and try and get some fires in those stoves in the cabins. I don't want to freeze my ass off tonight when I get back."

As the men left the fire and moved toward the cabins, Pike pulled Zeke to the side and explained his plan to him in low tones so no one else would overhear.

Zeke's eyes glittered with anticipated bloodlust. "I can't wait to get my hands on that bastard, Bill," he said. "I'm gonna make sure he's a long time dyin'."

"Me too, Zeke," Pike said as he swung up into his saddle and walked the horse down the trail toward Pueblo.

About halfway to the town, Pike came to a bend in Fountain Creek and saw a clearing on the other side of the stream with a ramshackle cabin in it that was leaning heavily to one side as if it were about to fall down. This is a good place to tell Jensen to meet me tomorrow, he thought. He won't have no trouble finding it, and it's far enough away from the camp so the boys won't hear any gunshots when we take Jensen out.

Going over in his mind what he was going to tell Jensen, and how much money he should ask for to make the man think the ransom demand was on the level, Pike moved down the trail toward Pueblo thinking how clever he was.

NINETEEN

After walking up and down Court Street a couple of times, Smoke decided to enter a saloon named the Dog Hole. He smiled when he read the sign over the saloon, since out West *dog hole* was a generic name for any bar or saloon, especially one that was dirty or unclean. He thought it would take a man with a special sense of humor to use the term as a name for his establishment, and he looked forward to meeting him.

As was his usual custom when Smoke first pushed through the batwings, he immediately stepped to one side with his back against the wall and his right hand hanging near his pistol butt. He let his eyes become accustomed to the relatively dark room while he looked over the occupants of the fifteen or so tables scattered around the place.

He saw no familiar faces from his past, and so he walked slowly to the bar, where he took up station at the end nearest another wall. He never stood with his back to the room or where people were sitting behind him. It was a habit that had saved his life on more than one occasion and the practice had become second nature to him now.

The bartender ambled over, wiping out a glass with a dirty-looking cloth rag, as bartenders always seemed to be doing.

"What can I getcha?" he asked, his eyes dull with boredom and disinterest.

Though Smoke was normally not a drinking man, when in such places he would order a drink so as not to stand out from the usual crowd. "A shot of whiskey with a beer chaser," Smoke answered.

When the man bent over and pulled out a bottle with no label on it, Smoke held up his hand. "I don't want that," he said in a friendly tone. "Give me some of the good stuff off that back shelf."

"It'll cost you extra," the man said sullenly.

Smoke shrugged. "That's not a problem," he said, still keeping his voice amiable.

The barman turned and took a dusty bottle off the rear shelf with a label that read OLD KENTUCKY on it. Smoke doubted if any part of the bottle or the liquor within had ever been within a thousand miles of Kentucky, but he kept his mouth shut.

The bartender pulled the cork and slapped a glass down in front of Smoke that was so dirty it was almost black.

Just as the man started to pour, Smoke put his hand over the rim of the glass. "And I'd appreciate a clean glass," he said, his voice getting a little harder this time.

The bartender raised his eyebrows. "Am I gonna have trouble with you, mister?" he asked, pulling a three foot long wooden stake that was three inches in diameter from under the bar and slapping his open palm with it.

Smoke's eyes grew flat and dangerous. "The only trouble you're going to have is trying to take a shit with that pole stuck up your ass!" Smoke growled, letting his voice grow deeper and harsher.

"Why you . . . " the barman began as he raised the large stick.

Before he got the words out or moved the pole more than a couple of inches, Smoke's pistol was drawn, cocked, and the barrel was against the man's nose.

"You want to get that glass, or do I pull this trigger and decorate the mirror behind you with what little brains you have?" Smoke asked, a grim smile on his lips.

When the barman looked into Smoke's eyes, he knew he was seconds away from death and his bladder let loose.

He groaned and glanced down at his urine-soaked trousers, and his face paled.

"What the hell's going on here?" a deep, gravely voice that had suffered too much tobacco and too many glasses of whiskey intoned from the other end of the bar.

Smoke holstered his pistol and smiled nicely at the heavyset man who was approaching behind the bar. The man had salt-and-pepper hair and a dark mustache whose ends hung down to the bottom of his chin, but his eyes were the blue of wildflowers and seemed to shine with amusement at his barman's state.

"Uh, this here man's causin' some trouble, Mr. Gooch," the bartender said, backing away from the bar but keeping his eyes on Smoke.

"That true, mister?" Gooch asked, moving between Smoke and the barman.

Smoke inclined his head at the dirty glass in front of him. "All I did was request the good whiskey and a clean glass," Smoke said. "If that is too much for this establishment, I will be happy to take my business elsewhere."

Gooch glanced at the glass, frowned, and whirled around to confront the bartender. "I've told you about this before, Jack," he said angrily. "Now, get out. You're fired."

"But . . ."

"No buts, you lazy shit. Get out and you can come back later for what I owe you."

After Jack left, holding his hands in front of his stained pants, Gooch turned back to Smoke, shaking his head. "Damn," he said. "It's the gold fever."

"Oh?" Smoke asked.

"Yeah. Every able-bodied man who's not afraid of a little work is out in the mountains digging for gold. What's left in town for me to hire are the ones too lazy to work or who are looking to steal what they need instead of earning it."

Smoke nodded. "I've seen it before," he said.

Gooch took the glass and replaced it with a clean one. As he poured the whiskey, he grinned at Smoke. "This one's on the house, 'cause of the trouble with my man, but you're gonna have to pay for the next one."

Smoke smiled. "Pour two and I'll treat you to one."

"Damn," Gooch exclaimed, "I don't get an offer like that too often."

He poured himself a drink and held up his glass to Smoke. "To happier days," he said.

"I'll drink to that," Smoke said, and took a sip of his drink while Gooch emptied his own glass in one long drink.

Smoke glanced at the sign over the bar. "I like the name of your place," he said. "It indicates an owner with a sense of humor."

Gooch grinned at him and topped off Smoke's glass and refilled his own. "My name's Homer Gooch," he said. "Growing up with a name like that, you either have to learn to be a good fighter or have a good sense of humor. I ain't much of a fighter, but I don't mind the occasional laugh at my expense."

"That's a sound philosophy," Smoke said.

Gooch stuck his hand across the bar, "And what's your handle, mister?"

Smoke shook his hand. "Smoke Jensen."

Gooch's eyes opened wide and he burst out laughing. "*The* Smoke Jensen?"

Smoke smiled back and nodded. "The only one I know of."

Gooch continued to chuckle. "Old Jack would have shit himself in addition to pissing himself if he'd known who he braced with that little stick he kept under the bar."

Smoke just grinned and took another small sip of his whiskey, following it with a drink of beer.

"What brings you to our neck of the woods, Mr. Jensen?" Gooch asked. "You're not about to try your hand at mining, are you?"

"Call me Smoke, and no, I'm not here looking for gold. I'm supposed to meet someone here today."

Gooch raised his eyebrows. "A friend?"

Smoke's smile faded. "Not exactly."

Gooch shook his head and glanced at the five-foot-long mirror behind the bar. "Well, Smoke, if it comes down to gunplay, would you try not to hit that mirror? It cost me two hundred dollars to have it shipped here from St. Louis."

Smoke laughed. "I'll do my best, Homer."

Gooch looked around the room. "I bet you'll be wanting a table in a corner so's you can keep your eye on the door. Am I right?"

"Yes," Smoke answered.

Gooch came out from behind the bar and walked over to a corner table where three men wearing the canvas pants of miners sat getting quietly drunk.

"You men are going to have to move," Gooch said. "I need this table."

One of the men glanced up, his eyes red and bloodshot. "I ain't movin' fer nobody. We was here first."

Gooch leaned down, both hands flat on the table as he stared at the man. "It's worth a free bottle of whiskey if you'll take another table," he said.

The man who'd objected jumped to his feet and looked around at his friends. "What the hell are we sittin' here for, boys. Let's do what the man says."

Gooch smiled at Smoke and waved his hand at the now empty table. "I'll send a bottle over, Smoke."

Smoke shook his head. "No, thanks, Homer. I need to keep a clear head."

Gooch winked at him. "How about I fill a whiskey bottle with sarsaparilla? It looks like whiskey but it won't get you drunk."

"Helluva good idea, Homer," Smoke said. "I'm obliged."

Gooch pointed a finger at him. "Just remember to miss the mirror and we'll call it even," he said good-naturedly.

TWENTY

Smoke settled into his chair in the saloon, sipping his sarsaparilla and smoking an occasional cigarette as he waited for Pike or one of his men to show up. He had the hammer thong on his Colts undone just in case whoever showed up started blasting instead of talking.

Smoke had no illusions; he knew Pike's ultimate desire was to see him dead, and Sally was just an instrument in that final outcome. Smoke's problem was to try and avoid killing Pike or his men until Cal and Pearlie could report back to him as to where they were keeping her. He refused to entertain any thoughts that she might already be dead or injured.

After a while, Homer Gooch walked over to his table. "Smoke, you haven't told me exactly what's going on here, but if you need some backup, I'll be over there behind the bar with a ten-gauge sawed-off express gun handy. You give the word and I'll blast shit out of anyone giving you trouble."

Smoke found he liked this man more and more. "Thanks, Homer. I don't think that will be necessary, but I appreciate the thought and the help."

Gooch nodded and made his way back behind the bar, where he leaned on it, his eyes searching the room for possible trouble. Smoke smiled to himself at the man's offer. He'd discovered over the years that once people found out who he was, they generally reacted in one of two ways: They either feared him and tended to avoid his company, or they liked what they'd heard about him and wanted to be friends and help him out if they could. Such was both the penalty and the benefit of being a celebrity among common folks.

The Dog Hole was the fourth saloon Bill Pike entered while searching for Smoke Jensen. He'd never laid eyes on the man before, but he thought he'd probably recognize him when he saw him.

He walked into the Dog Hole and stepped up to the bar. He ordered a shot of whiskey and after the heavyset man behind the counter gave it to him, he turned and leaned back against the bar on his elbows, sipping his drink and letting his eyes roam around the room.

He knew Smoke immediately when his eyes fell on the man sitting at the corner table. Damn, he thought, he's a dangerous-looking son of a bitch. Several inches over six feet tall, with shoulders as wide as an ax handle, Smoke dressed in buckskins. He must be in his forties by now, Pike thought, but his hair is still coal black, like his eyes, and there isn't a trace of softness about his body. Muscles bulged in his forearms where they rested on the table, and his expression looked as if it were cast in stone.

"You looking for somebody, mister?" Homer Gooch asked, noticing the way Pike scanned the room with his eyes.

"Yeah, but I think I just found him," Pike answered, emptying his glass and slowly moving toward the man in the corner. He kept his hands out from his sides, well away from the pistol on his hip. From what he'd heard, Jensen was snake-quick with a short gun, and Pike didn't intend to find out for sure when he was by himself.

As Pike walked toward Smoke, Homer Gooch got Smoke's attention and winked, pointing under the bar to indicate the shotgun was ready and waiting if Smoke got into trouble.

Pike stopped in front of Smoke's table and stared down at him. "You Jensen?" he asked, trying to make his voice low and hard.

Smoke looked up at him, a tiny smile curling the corners of his lips. "Yes. Are you Pike?" Smoke answered, his voice level and smooth without a trace of fear in it.

Pike nodded and pulled out a chair across the table from Smoke. He pushed his empty glass across the table. "How about a refill?"

"Get your own whiskey," Smoke said, all trace of good humor gone from his tone. "This isn't a social call."

Pike's face paled slightly at the insult, but he turned his head and waved to Gooch. "Another bottle of whiskey over here," he called.

After Gooch had delivered one of the cheap bottles with no label on it, Pike filled his glass and took a deep drink.

"You called this meeting, Pike," Smoke said. "Say your piece."

Pike's eyes narrowed to slits. "You're talkin' awful brave for a man who's lost his wife."

"I didn't lose her, you scum," Smoke said, leaning forward but keeping his right hand on his thigh near the butt of his pistol. "You and your men took her."

"Nevertheless," Pike said, trying to get the upper

hand in the conversation, "we've got her and you don't. You want her back?"

Now Smoke smiled. He screwed the butt of a cigarette into the corner of his mouth, lit it, and tilted smoke out of his nostrils, his face hard and set. "Oh, I'm going to get her back, Mr. Pike. There is no doubt of that. The only question is how you and your men are going to die . . . slow and painful or fast and easy."

"That ain't no way to . . ." Pike began, but Smoke interrupted him.

"Make your offer, Pike. I assume that's what you came here for."

Pike took a deep breath, trying to calm his nerves. This wasn't going at all the way he'd pictured it in his mind on the way here from the camp.

"You can have her back, unharmed and untouched, for ten thousand dollars," he said, attempting to make his voice firm and hard.

Smoke took the half-smoked butt from his lips and tapped it out in an ashtray. "That all you want?" he asked, knowing full well that it wasn't.

"I figure you can go to the bank here and have a letter of credit wired from your bank in Big Rock. Once you have the money in hand, we can make the trade and nobody has to get hurt," Pike said, his eyes shifting from the dangerous look on Smoke's face.

Smoke pretended to think the offer over for a few minutes, slowly sipping his sarsaparilla and staring at Pike.

"Oh, I know all about your reputation, Jensen," Pike said, "and if you're as good as they say you are, you may be able to take out me and my men like you're thinking you can. But"—Pike leaned forward as he spoke—"in the process of doin' all this, you wife is bound to get hurt, maybe even kilt."

"There is some truth in what you say," Smoke said, letting Pike think he was considering his offer.

"From what I hear, you won't have any trouble raisin' the money," Pike added, pouring himself another drink as he watched Smoke to see his reaction.

"The money is no problem," Smoke said. "I'm just trying to figure out how we can make the trade so everyone's happy and no one gets the idea of taking the money and not delivering my wife to me."

Pike held up his hands. "Hey, we know how dangerous you are, Jensen. And since there's only three of us, we wouldn't stand a chance against you if we went back on the deal," Pike lied.

Smoke smiled. He knew Pike had at least seven or eight men left in his gang and was lying through his teeth, but Pike didn't know he knew this.

Smoke got to his feet. "Come on with me," he said, throwing a couple of bills on the table and walking toward the door. "Homer," Smoke called, "save my table for me, would you?"

"Yes, sir," Gooch replied.

Pike hastily emptied his glass and followed.

Smoke walked down the street about fifty yards and entered a building with a sign on it that read PUEBLO BANK. He walked up to a teller and asked to see the manager.

A few minutes later, a portly man dressed in a black suit and a boiled white shirt with a string tie walked out of his office. "I'm Jedidiah Morgan," the man said. "What can I do for you gentlemen?"

Smoke handed him a piece of paper. "I'm Smoke Jensen, from Big Rock Colorado. I own the bank there. I want you to wire the bank for a letter of credit for ten thousand dollars, plus whatever fee you charge for the transfer. I'll want to pick up the money tomorrow morning."

"Why, yes, sir, Mr. Jensen," Morgan said. "That should be no problem at all."

Smoke turned on his heel without another word, walked back to the Dog Hole, and sat at his same table. Pike remained standing on the other side of the table.

"As you can see, I'll have the money tomorrow morning. How do you want to handle the trade?" Smoke asked.

"There's a small clearing about three miles up Fountain Creek. It has an old cabin in it. I'll meet you there at noon tomorrow. Bring the cash. My men will be out in the woods with your wife. Any sign of a double cross, and they'll put a bullet between her eyes 'fore you can sneeze."

"I'll need to see her and see that she's all right before I turn the money over," Smoke said.

"Of course," Pike said. "I wouldn't want you to take my word for it."

Smoke smiled. "See you tomorrow, Pike."

"So long," Pike said, tipping his hat and turning to walk out the door.

"Oh, Pike," Smoke called to his back.

Pike glanced back over his shoulder. "Yeah?"

"Best say your prayers tonight that I find Sally in perfect shape. If one hair on her head is out of place, you will find yourself begging me to kill you before I'm through with you."

Pike tried to grin as he turned and walked out the door, but his stomach knotted at the expression on Smoke's face. He was looking death in the eye as sure as he was standing there. He felt sweat break out under his armpits and on his forehead, and he began to wonder if his dead brother was worth all this trouble.

Hell, he hadn't been lying to Mrs. Jensen when he

said he hadn't particularly liked the bastard any way. If it weren't for Zeke and his big mouth, he wouldn't be up here in this godforsaken frozen country worrying about getting his ass shot off.

TWENTY-ONE

A few minutes after Pike left the Dog Hole, the batwings swung open and Pearlie walked in. He took one look around the place and began to move directly toward Smoke. Evidently, his rather disheveled appearance, the way he wore his pistol tied down low on his right leg, and his determined expression worried Homer Gooch.

Homer pulled the sawed-off shotgun from under the bar and rested it on top, his eyes watching Pearlie for any false moves. Smoke grinned and waved at Homer. "It's all right, Homer," he called. "This one's a friend of mine."

Homer relaxed and put the shotgun away. He raised his eyebrows and pointed at the good bottle of whiskey Smoke had been drinking from when he first arrived.

Smoke nodded and waited for Pearlie to take a seat across the table from him. After Pearlie sat down, he looked around the room and smiled. "This place is right nice," Pearlie said, grinning. "When I saw the name on the sign outside, I thought it was gonna be a dive."

Smoke laughed. "Yeah, Mr. Gooch has quite a sense of humor," he said, also looking around.

The saloon was large and well lighted, with fresh paint on the walls, and the floor was clean and well swept. The tables were placed so that everyone had plenty of room to move around without being too crowded. In one corner, a piano sat facing the room with several bar stools in front of it. There was no one playing presently, and Smoke figured it was used mainly at night. Another thing he liked was that there were no "saloon girls" hanging around to cadge drinks from the miners who frequented the place. It was just another indication of Mr. Gooch's class.

Smoke finally looked back at Pearlie. "Did you find their camp?" he asked.

Pearlie turned his attention from the decor of the room and nodded. "Yep. Cal's got 'em all staked out now. He'll tail 'em if they try to move."

Homer stepped up to the table and put the whiskey bottle down in the center of the table along with a glass for Pearlie. He picked up the bottle of rotgut Pike had left behind and the bottle of sarsaparilla and grinned. "Wouldn't want you gentlemen to get sick drinking this horse piss," he said.

"Thanks, Homer," Smoke said. "I owe you one for all you've done."

Homer waved a hand and blushed slightly. "It's the least I could do, Smoke," he said as he moved back behind his bar.

"What about Sally?" Smoke asked. "Did you see her and is she all right?"

Pearlie nodded. "She seems right as rain, Smoke. They're camped in this clearin' that has five or six old cabins scattered around. They got her stashed in one most of the time, but they seem to be leaving her alone an' not botherin' her none. They let her out to eat with them when they have a meal, but they make her sit off to one side by herself."

Smoke's face wrinkled as he concentrated on the

mental picture Pearlie had painted. "So, they don't leave anyone in the cabin with her as a guard?"

Pearlie shook his head. "No, at least they didn't the night I watched 'em bed down. I think they must tie her up to the bed or to a post in there or somethin', 'cause when she comes out she's usually rubbing her wrists like they maybe were raw from the ropes."

Smoke nodded. "That's good for us," he said. "That'll make it easier for us to get her out of there without them realizing it and starting to throw lead around."

"I noticed that big man comin' out of here when I was comin' in," Pearlie said. "I seen him out at the camp yesterday and I think he must be head honcho out there 'cause everybody listens when he talks."

"Yeah. That's Bill Pike, brother to the Pike I killed years ago. He and his half brother named Thompson are the cause of this mess."

Pearlie leaned forward. "You know, Smoke, there's only about eight or nine of them galoots out at the camp. If you and me and Cal lined 'em up in our sights, we could probably get them all 'fore they knew what was happening."

Smoke shook his head. "No, Pearlie, I don't want to do it that way for two reasons. One, we might miss one and give him time to hurt Sally. Two, that'd be too easy for these bastards. I don't want to just kill them, I want to make their lives miserable with fear before I let the hammer down on them and end it all."

Just as Smoke finished talking, Pearlie's stomach growled loudly, causing Smoke to break out in a wide grin. "Sounds like you're a mite hungry, partner," Smoke said.

Pearlie blushed and rubbed his stomach to try and make it quit howling. "Yeah. Cal and I didn't want to risk building a fire while we watched those assholes, so about all we've had for two days has been old cold biscuits and water."

"Well, I can fix that," Smoke said. "Hey, Homer," he called, "you got a good place to eat in this town?"

Homer nodded and pointed to the left. "You bet, Smoke. The Shorthorn Diner right down the street. Has the best steaks this side of the mountains."

While Smoke and Pearlie ate their late lunch, with Pearlie of course eating enough for two men, they discussed Smoke's plans for the outlaws.

"After we finish eating, I want you to buy an extra horse with saddle and all the gear to take back up the mountain with us."

When Pearlie looked puzzled, Smoke explained, "We may need it for Sally. When I take her out of the gang's camp, I may not have time to get her horse and she'll need it to ride out on."

"What about the packhorse we got up there?" Pearlie asked around a mouthful of steak.

"It doesn't have a saddle on it, and we may need it for our supplies," Smoke answered. "Besides, we may lose a horse in the battle and it's always better to have too many horses than not enough, especially up in the High Lonesome in winter."

Pearlie nodded as he continued to stuff food into his mouth as if he hadn't eaten in weeks instead of just two days.

"Now," Smoke continued, sitting back and lighting a cigarette since he was already finished with his meal, "Pike is expecting me to meet him at noon tomorrow at a small clearing a few miles up Fountain Creek, but we're not going to wait that long. As soon as you finish your meal and get the horse for Sally, we're going to head up there and get Cal."

Pearlie pointed his fork at the remains of his steak. "Don't let me forget to take him some food with us."

Smoke smiled. "All right, but we're going to be plenty busy setting up some surprises for those bastards. I'm going to use those supplies you and Cal bought for me to set some traps on the trails around their camp and on the slopes up above it. As soon as Sally's safely away from them, we're going to show them just how stupid they were to mess with us."

Pearlie grinned as he stuffed a gravy-soaked roll into his mouth. "Damn right!" he agreed.

As he rode back toward his camp, Pike kept looking back over his shoulder. His meeting with Smoke Jensen had spooked him pretty bad. He didn't think he'd ever met anyone who looked as downright dangerous as the mountain man. He recalled stories he'd heard about Jensen back when he was tracking him down in preparation for his revenge. Stories of how he'd dealt with men who'd crossed him—stories that made a man's blood run cold.

As he thought about this, his mind went back to the bloody scalp and the pieces of Sam Kane's face that someone had left for them as a warning. Now, he had no doubt it had been done by Smoke Jensen.

He knew he was riding a thin line, and if he made one false step, Jensen would exact a terrible retribution. He was going to have to make sure he and his men were on their guard at all times, or they'd never live to spend the money Jensen was getting together.

When he finally got back to the camp, he saw Mrs. Jensen sitting near the fire, her face turned away from

Hank Snow, who was standing next to her. Mrs. Jensen's expression was shocked and her face was blushing a bright red. From the stiffness of her back and neck, Pike knew something was wrong.

He got down off his horse and walked rapidly over to the couple. As he got there, Snow turned and gave him a smirk.

"What's going on here?" Pike asked.

Sally cut her eyes at him and then she looked away, as if he didn't deserve her attention.

"I was just tellin' this little lady what I plan to do to her after we kill her husband," Snow said, a husky tone to his voice.

Pike stepped around so Sally would have to look at him. "Has he been bothering you, Mrs. Jensen?" he asked in a kind voice.

"What do you think, Mr. Pike?" she asked scornfully. "He is an animal and no matter what happens to my husband, he will have to kill me before I will allow him to lay a hand on me!"

"You stupid bastard!" Pike said angrily as he moved toward Hank Snow. "Didn't I tell you to leave Mrs. Jensen alone?"

"But Boss," Snow began, a puzzled look on his face.

Before he could finish, Pike reared back and smashed him in the face with his fist, knocking him down flat onto his back.

Snow grimaced in pain and his hand went toward his gun on his hip.

Pike drew and pointed his pistol at the man's face and growled, "Go on, Hank, just give me one more reason to blow your fool head off!"

Snow slowly moved his hand away from his gun and said, "Jesus, Boss. I didn't mean nothin' by it. I was just havin' a little fun with her is all."

Pike looked up at the men who'd gathered around

to see the fight. "Let this be a lesson to you," he said in a harsh voice. "I'm still the ramrod of this outfit, and anyone who crosses me is going to get this, or worse."

When no one said anything, Pike holstered his pistol and took Sally by the arm, helping her to her feet. "Why don't you go into your cabin and I'll have someone bring you some coffee, Mrs. Jensen?" he asked.

Sally gave him a slight nod. "Thank you, Mr. Pike," she said, and moved off toward the cabin they'd put her in the day before.

"What's the problem, Boss?" Rufus Gordon asked. "Why are you treatin' her with kid gloves all of a sudden?"

"Because she's worth ten thousand dollars to us, Rufe," Pike explained. "If she's hurt or messed up, Jensen ain't gonna take the bait."

"Oh," Gordon said.

"I just met with him in Pueblo," Pike said. "I convinced him we just wanted some money and we'd let her go."

"That's a good idea, Boss," Sergeant Rutledge said.

"He's gonna get the money from the bank tomorrow and meet me at a place about halfway here from Pueblo at noon."

"How much money we talkin' about?" Gordon asked.

"Ten thousand dollars," Pike answered.

"Holy shit!" Gordon whooped. "That means with the reward money, we'll be getting twenty thousand!"

Pike decided now was the time to break the bad news about the reward to the men, before they found out about it on their own.

"Uh, there's not gonna be any reward, boys," he said.

"What?" several of them exclaimed in unison.

He held up both hands. "That's right. While I was in Pueblo, I checked with the sheriff's office and found out that wanted poster was recalled some years ago."

As his men glowered at him angrily, Pike continued. "But the good news is, we're gonna be getting it anyway. The only difference is, it's gonna be comin' outta Jensen's own bank."

This last seemed to mollify the men, and Pike said, "I think this news deserves a drink, what do you say?"

The men grinned, their anger of a moment before forgotten, and they all went to get their bottles of whiskey. Any excuse for a drink was a good excuse to them.

Once they all had bottles in their hands, Pike held his up and gave a toast, "To ten thousand dollars, and what it can buy."

Gordon added, "And to the little lady over there, and all the fun we're gonna have with her after we kill her man!"

TWENTY-TWO

After Smoke and Pearlie got an extra horse and tack for Sally and some food for Cal, they proceeded northward up Fountain Creek. Smoke made sure to stay off the trail in case Pike checked his backtrail to see if he was being followed, though Smoke doubted the man bothered—from their meeting at the saloon, Smoke figured he was a mite slow when it came to thinking.

A few miles out of Pueblo, they came to the small clearing with the ramshackle shack that Pike had designated for their meeting the next day.

"Hold on a minute, Pearlie," Smoke said. "I want to check this place out a little before we head on up the mountain."

Since the clearing was on the other side of the stream, Smoke turned Joker's head toward it and gently spurred the horse out into the water. Though the current was moving fairly quickly, he found the water level to be only a couple of feet deep at this time of the year.

He glanced to the sides and saw the banks of the river were several feet higher than the water level, indicating that when the spring thaws came, the stream would turn into a raging torrent unsafe to cross at any place.

Pearlie followed him across the creek and they rode

around the clearing, checking for places to set traps and such. The ground rose sharply on three sides of the clearing, with assorted boulders and outcroppings of granite at many different levels. Smoke pointed these out to Pearlie.

"Pike told me he only had two or three men with him, so I'll bet he'll have the others hidden up behind those rocks, ready to fire down on me if he gives the signal," Smoke said.

Pearlie glanced back across the creek to where the trail passed the clearing. "Yeah, Smoke. It'd have to be up there 'cause there ain't much cover on the other side of the crick," he observed.

Smoke followed his gaze and saw that the nearest heavy cover was a copse of pine trees with some low brush about four hundred yards away. Other than that, the trail was pretty much open for the next quarter mile.

Smoke smiled. The setting gave him an idea if he ended up having to meet with Pike here the next day. Of course, if things go well tonight, he thought, we'll have Sally out of their camp safe and sound and I can deal with them on my own terms after that.

A couple of hours later, Pearlie slowed his mount. "The gang's camp is about another quarter mile up the trail, Smoke, so we'd better move on up the side of the mountain to get around them in case they got some sentries out watchin' the trail."

Smoke nodded, and let Pearlie lead the way off into the bushes off to the side of the trail. He found his heart was beating faster and his mouth was dry in anticipation of seeing his wife again. Even though Pearlie had assured him Sally was all right and being treated good, he wanted to see for himself, and God help any man who'd bothered her.

It took them another hour of moving slowly through dense underbrush and ravines where melting snow had washed out the side of the mountain before they got to the place where Cal was keeping watch over the gang.

Just before riding into the area, Pearlie cupped his hands around his mouth and gave a short cry like that of a bobcat on the hunt.

Smoke smiled. "You did that pretty well, Pearlie," he said. "I couldn't tell it from the real thing."

This was a high compliment from the mountain man, and Pearlie grinned back. "I had a good teacher, Smoke. You showed Cal and me how to do all the calls of the mountain critters a couple of years back, remember?"

Smoke nodded. "Yeah, but you seem to have gotten better at it than you used to be."

Pearlie shrugged, blushing at the compliment. "Well, when Cal and I are out on the trail with the beeves at the ranch, we practice a bit." He gave a low laugh. "Hell, anything's better than having Cal sing."

Seconds later, an answering cry came from the slope just ahead of them, signaling Cal knew they were coming and wouldn't shoot them when they rode into his camp.

A few minutes later, Smoke and Pearlie, along with the extra horse for Sally, pulled into a small clearing just back from a ledge that looked down on the outlaws' camp.

Cal was there to greet them. Smoke noticed he had a bandanna tied over his horse's mouth and nose to keep it from whinnying to the horses in the camp below. Smoke nodded, pleased that Cal had remembered what he'd taught him in the past about tracking men in the High Lonesome.

Cal grinned and shook Smoke's hand. "Jiminy, but I'm glad to see you, Smoke," he said.

"Everything going all right?" Smoke asked, anxious to get a look down into the camp below the ridge.

"Yes, sir. They've been sitting around the fire and drinking all afternoon."

"Is Sally there?"

"Come on and you can see for yourself," Cal said, bending down and moving low as he moved toward the ridge.

Smoke followed, crawling the last few feet on hands and knees so they couldn't be seen from below in case any of the gang happened to look up.

Smoke eased his head over the ledge just enough to look below. He saw the outlaws sitting in various positions around a roaring fire, talking and laughing and drinking from bottles of whiskey. Off to one side, a cup of coffee in her hands, Sally was sitting by herself near the far edge of the fire. Her head was down and she looked tired, but otherwise all right.

Smoke thought his heart was going to break seeing her sitting alone and in such danger. He didn't know what he would do if he ever lost her. She was his entire reason for living, and nothing would ever be the same if something happened to take her from him.

Suddenly, he had an idea of how to make her feel better. He moved back from the ledge until he could stand up and see her through a stand of hackberry bushes. He cupped his hands around his mouth and gave the whooping call a coyote would make when calling to his mate in the wild. It was a sharp barking sound followed by a mournful wail.

At the sound, he saw Sally's back stiffen and her head come up. He was too far away to see her eyes, but he knew they were looking in his direction. In their years together, Sally had spent a lot of time with Smoke up in the mountains, and she knew his calls as well as he did. She also knew that coyotes never barked or called in the middle of the afternoon, only at dawn and dusk and in the middle of the night.

The outlaws all looked up too, and one or two of them shivered at the ghostly sound Smoke made.

Sally got to her feet and moved to the fire to refill her coffee cup from the pot sitting at the edge of the coals. As she straightened up, she briefly let her right hand cross over her heart, a sign that she'd heard and recognized Smoke's call to her.

She went back to her place and as she drank her coffee, she sat straighter and more confident now that she knew her man was nearby.

When Smoke gave the coyote call, Pike lowered his bottle and looked around, clearly spooked by the mournful cry coming from the slopes above the camp.

He got to his feet and moved slowly around the campfire, his eyes on the ledges around them, his hand hovering near his pistol butt.

"What's the matter, Boss?" Rufus Gordon said, more than a little drunk. "You're not afraid of a little ol' coyote, are you?" he asked, his voice slurred.

Pike answered with his eyes still on the mountainside. "I didn't know they had coyotes up here in the mountains," he said warily.

"Well, it can't be Indians, Boss," Sergeant Rutledge

said, "The man in Canyon City said they ain't given no trouble around here in years."

"It's not Indians I'm worried about," Pike said. He took a short drink from his bottle and moved over to stand next to Sally, staring down at her.

"You hear that, Mrs. Jensen?" he asked.

She stared up at him. "Of course, Mr. Pike. It was a coyote calling to its mate. Fall is the rutting season for coyotes in the mountains," she added, hoping he didn't know anything about coyotes, which mated all year long.

"Is that so?" he asked suspiciously. "It wouldn't be your husband out there signaling to you, would it?"

Sally smiled sweetly. "Mr. Pike, if my husband were out there that close, you would already have a bullet between your eyes and would be lying flat on your back."

Pike grunted as if he didn't believe her.

Sally looked around at the men lying sprawled around the fire. "You said you met with Smoke today, Mr. Pike. Did he impress you as a man who would be afraid of a bunch of men who are so drunk they couldn't hit the side of a barn with a shotgun right now?"

Pike followed her gaze and realized she was right. His men were in no condition to fight anyone right now. He decided enough was enough.

"All right, men," he called, moving back over to the fire. "Put the liquor away and get ready for nightfall. I want two men to stay in the cabin with Mrs. Jensen tonight, just in case Jensen decides to try and take her without paying the money."

He looked up at the mountains around them, which were turning slowly darker as dusk approached. "You hear that, Jensen?" he hollered. "If you're out there and you try anything, the first thing my men are going to do is put a bullet in your wife!"

Gordon looked around at the men, who were getting worried that their boss had lost his nerve. "Boss, take it easy," he said. "It was just a coyote, that's all."

"Nevertheless," Pike said, remembering the look in Jensen's eyes when they talked in Pueblo. "We're gonna post a couple of sentries and we're gonna keep a close eye on Mrs. Jensen tonight. I don't want anything goin' wrong until we get that money tomorrow."

Gordon got clumsily to his feet and stuffed the cork back in his bottle. "Whatever you say, Boss."

As the outlaws began to get to their feet and two men escorted Sally into her cabin, Smoke moved back from the ledge. "Damn," he said, "I guess that means we don't try and get Sally out tonight."

"So, what are we gonna do?" Pearlie asked.

Smoke's eyes were hard as flint. "We're going to set up some surprises for those men back down the trail so when I meet with them tomorrow, we'll have the upper hand."

As they moved away from the ledge, he relaxed a little. "But first, I'm going to make us a fire and we're going to eat some food and drink some coffee." He smiled at Cal, who was grinning in relief. "Preacher always said you can't do battle on an empty stomach."

Pearlie looked at Cal. "We brung you some steaks and biscuits and beans from town."

"Right now, I'd settle for some rawhide to chew on I'm so hungry," Cal said.

Smoke gave a low chuckle. "Now you're starting to sound like Pearlie."

TWENTY-THREE

Smoke and the boys gathered up all their supplies and the packhorse and horse they'd brought for Sally, and they moved off down the mountain about a quarter of a mile. It was fairly easy going as the night was one of those only seen in early winter: crystal-clear skies, bright starlight, and a crescent moon shedding just enough light so the path through the high mountain forest could be easily seen.

Smoke pulled his fur-lined buckskin coat tight around him. "It's gonna get mighty chilly tonight, boys," he said. "With no cloud cover or snow, the temperature is going to drop like a stone."

Once they'd circled around the slope of the mountain so as to be away from where the outlaws might spot their campfire glow, Smoke dismounted. "Cal, see if you can find some really dry wood, the kind that doesn't make much smoke," he said.

While Smoke was arranging some stones in a small circle next to a large outcropping of boulders so the fire would be out of the wind, Pearlie got the cooking gear off the packhorse along with the food he and Smoke had gotten in Pueblo.

Before long, coffee was brewing, steaks were sizzling in one pan, day-old biscuits steaming in another, while beans were heating in a kettle. When he poured the coffee in their tin mugs, Pearlie looked at Cal and smiled as he pulled a small paper bag out of his pocket. "I brung you somethin' special, Cal, 'cause of how you had to starve yourself watchin' those outlaws."

He handed the paper bag to Cal, who immediately opened it. "Jiminy," he said, "real sugar for my coffee."

Though on the trail Cal often had to drink his coffee black, Pearlie knew he much preferred to lace it with generous amounts of sugar, changing it into what Pearlie called black syrup.

As Smoke poured coffee all around, being up in the High Lonesome brought thoughts of Puma Buck to mind. The old mountain man, a decades-long friend of Smoke's, had been killed some years earlier while helping Smoke out of a jam.

He filled Cal's cup, saying, "Remember what Puma Buck said about coffee, boys?"

"Sure do," Cal replied with a nostalgic smile. "The thing 'bout makin' good mountain coffee is it don't take near as much water as you think it do."

Pearlie chuckled at the memory. The boys had only known Puma for a short while, but had come to love him as much as Smoke did. "He also said," Pearlie added, "that coffee that wouldn't float a horseshoe wasn't worth drinkin'."

"I think them steaks are 'bout ready," Cal said, eyeing the pan with the steaks in it hungrily. "At least, they've quit moving."

Cal liked his steaks rare.

Smoke picked one of the pieces of meat out of the pan with the point of his bowie knife and placed it on a plate on Cal's lap. "You'll have to get your own biscuit and beans," he said, picking out another steak for Pearlie.

Soon, they were all chowing down, relishing the flavor of food cooked outdoors under a starry sky.

After a while, their talk turned to what Smoke proposed to do about the men who held Sally prisoner.

"You know if'n you go to that meeting with Pike carryin' ten thousand dollars, he's just gonna kill you and steal the money and then do no telling what to Miss Sally," Pearlie said around a mouthful of biscuit soaked in steak juice.

"That's right, Smoke," Cal agreed. "If what you say 'bout this hombre is true, he didn't take Sally for the money, but to draw you out where he could take you down."

Smoke nodded. "I know that's his plan, boys, but planning on killing me and actually doing it are two very different things."

"If you go in there by yourself, with eight of his men drawing down on you, how are you going to keep him from killing you, Smoke?" Cal asked. "Heck fire, you won't even be able to see most of 'em."

Smoke grinned. "Easy," he answered. "I'm going to have two aces up my sleeve."

"I take it by that you mean Cal and me?" Pearlie asked after washing down his food with a drink of coffee and glancing around to make sure he hadn't missed any tasty morsels.

"That's right, Pearlie. And when the time comes, both my life and Sally's will depend on you two doing exactly what we've planned."

Cal and Pearlie glanced at each other, sobered by this responsibility. After a moment, Pearlie inclined his head. "Then let's get down to the plannin'," he said seriously.

"All right," Smoke said. He moved off a short distance from the fire and picked up a stick. Using the flat of his hand, he smoothed out the dirt in front of where he was squatting. He drew a crude map in the dust and dirt, indicating the position of the outlaws' camp, the trail down the mountain alongside Fountain Creek, and the proposed meeting place.

"Now," he said after they'd had a chance to look at the map, "Pike and his men are going to have to head down to the meeting place at least a few hours before noon."

"Why is that, Smoke?" Cal asked, clearly puzzled about how Smoke knew what Pike was going to do.

Smoke looked at him and smiled, thinking sometimes he forgot just how young and inexperienced in such matters Cal was. "They're going to have to get there early because Pike figures I'm going to be there early to check the area out," Smoke said. "He'll also need to send a couple of men ahead to make sure I don't show up with reinforcements intending to overpower them and take Sally by force."

"So, he'll want to have his men in place a good while before you get there so you won't know where they're hiding," Pearlie observed.

"Exactly," Smoke answered. "Once they've come down the mountain from their camp to the meeting place, that will give us some time to work on the trail, both above and below the meeting place, to set some traps I have in mind for them."

"Then what're we gonna do after we've set all the traps an' such?" Cal asked.

"You and Pearlie will set up where I tell you, where you'll have a good line of fire down on the clearing where I'll be meeting with Pike and on the places where we figure his men will be stationed."

"What do we do then?" Pearlie asked.

Smoke got to his feet. "Come on, and I'll show you. We've got to set some surprises around the meeting place tonight, before they go there tomorrow morning. Once that's done, I have a feeling you'll know what I want you to do."

* * *

While Pike was in the cabin where Sally was to be kept for the night, under continuous guard, the rest of the men gathered around the fire, speaking in low tones so he couldn't hear them.

Sergeant Rutledge was angry and let everyone in the gang know it. "I think that son of a bitch Pike lied to us about the reward money just to get us to come along on this trip. You can't tell me he didn't know all along Jensen wasn't really wanted."

Rufus Gordon looked down at his ruined hand and then up at Rutledge. "So what, Sarge? He told us we'd be splittin' up ten thousand dollars, an' that's exactly what we're gonna be doin'. What the hell do you care if it's reward money or money we get from Jensen?"

"It's the principle of the thing, Rufe," Rutledge answered angrily. "Why didn't he just tell us the real plan to begin with?"

Zeke Thompson, heavily into his bottle of whiskey, glanced up from the far end of the fire. "Quit your bellyaching, Rutledge," he growled, clearly more drunk than sober. "Would you have come if Bill told you he intended to try and get the money from Jensen himself in trade for his wife?"

Hank Snow laughed sourly. "Hell, no!" He shook his head. "I don't know nobody who'd pay that kinda money to get their wife back." He hesitated and then with a chuckle, he added, "Most of the men I know would more likely pay it to get someone to take their wife away 'stead of bringin' 'em back."

Zeke nodded and took another drink. "And that's exactly why Bill kept his plan to himself. He'd been askin' around about Jensen, and he knew the man had plenty of cash and that he loved his wife more than he loved the money, but Bill knew you boys wouldn't believe that, so he made up a little story to get you here. It don't matter a damn where the money's comin' from long as you get your share, right?" he asked.

Slim Cartwright, a cattle thief and footpad from Galveston nodded his head. "I do believe Jensen's money will spend just as good as the sheriff's, boys."

Larry Jackson, nicknamed Razor because of the straight razor he carried in his boot and enjoyed using on dance hall girls, agreed. "Yeah. And the best part of the whole deal is after we kill Jensen, we get the woman too."

Blackie Johnson's head came up at that remark and he winced. He was no angel and he'd done his share of bad things, but raping and killing women wasn't one of them. Besides, he'd come to like Mrs. Jensen and he hated to think of what was going to happen to her after her husband was killed. Trouble was, he didn't have the faintest idea of what he could do to prevent it, if anything.

Sally was half-sitting and half-reclining on the bed in "her" cabin, her left wrist and ankle tied to a post, while Bill Pike was sitting across the room at a broken-down table. He was leaning back in an old handmade chair, smoking a long black cigar and drinking coffee. He'd offered a cup to Sally but she'd declined, thinking she needed a good night's sleep to be able to deal with what was going to happen the next day.

"You don't seem particularly worried about tomorrow, Mrs. Jensen," Pike said in a conversational tone of voice, sounding extremely confident.

Sally's hazel eyes stared into his, her expression

bland and unconcerned. "I'm not, Mr. Pike," she answered calmly, pulling her heavy coat close around her against the chill in the room. It was so cold in the cabin they could see their breath as they talked.

Pike held the cup in both hands to gather the warmth from the scalding coffee. He cocked his head. "Oh? I would think the prospect of losing your husband might concern you, not to mention what we have planned for you afterwards," he said, trying to get a rise out of her. The calmness of her demeanor was starting to get to him and he wanted to shake her up a little.

Sally straightened up in the bed and smiled slightly, almost sadly at Pike. "Mr. Pike, when you were planning this assault on my family, did you take the time to find anything out about Smoke Jensen?"

Pike shrugged. "Well, I figured out he could afford to try and buy you back." He grinned. "I don't care a whit about the money, Mrs. Jensen, it's killing your husband that's my goal, but I need something for my men."

"You really should have paid more attention to the stories I'm sure you heard about Smoke, Mr. Pike."

"Why is that, Mrs. Jensen?"

"Then you would have learned that Smoke came out here when he was just a boy. He lived up in these mountains when there wasn't more than one white man per thousand square miles and the Indians were thicker than fleas on a hound dog. Do you have any idea why Smoke not only survived this wilderness but thrived when hundreds of other men died in the attempt?"

"I hadn't really thought much about it, Mrs. Jensen," Pike answered as if he could care less.

"You should, Mr. Pike. Smoke survived when many others didn't because he is smart, tough, and when he sets his mind to do something, heaven help those who stand in his way, be it Indians or criminals."

"Well, back then he didn't have you to worry about, did he, Mrs. Jensen. Oh, I'll agree that he might get the best of us if it were just him and us up here in the mountains. But we have you and your husband knows I'll kill you if he doesn't agree to my conditions."

Sally smiled and lay back against the wall at the head of the bed and closed her eyes. "I hope you will remember, in those seconds before Smoke cuts your heart out, that I *did* warn you, Mr. Pike," she said, and then she turned on her side with her back to him.

Pike felt his heart flutter with fear at her words and the confidence with which she spoke them. He'd never met a woman as strong and as loyal to her man as this one, and he gave a short prayer that he hadn't underestimated Smoke Jensen.

TWENTY-FOUR

While Pike and his men sat around their fire drinking whiskey and telling each other lies, Smoke and the boys traveled back down the mountain toward the rendezvous place so Smoke could set up some surprises for their meeting the next day.

Once they arrived across the creek from the clearing, Smoke had Pearlie bring the packhorse across the water and into the clearing. The moon had become slightly larger over the past week and there were only ragged bunches of snow clouds to hide the brilliant starlight.

Smoke unpacked the pony carrying the supplies he'd had Pearlie and Cal buy and laid them out on the ground. He used a small hammer to break the top of the keg of horseshoe nails that had so puzzled Pearlie when he obtained them. He then opened a keg of gunpowder and laid out several empty Arbuckle's coffee cans in a row. One by one, he filled the cans with a mixture of gunpowder and horseshoe nails, and then he sealed the tops of the cans. Once that was done, he took an old white shirt of his out of his saddlebag and stuck it under his belt.

Picking up a can under each arm, he indicated Cal and Pearlie should do the same thing and for them to follow him. He walked up the steep slope at the rear of the clearing until he came to one of the larger boulders sticking out of the side of the mountain. Looking for the exact right spot, he finally stooped down and placed the can up next to the boulder where it could be seen from across the creek. He shoveled a mixture of dirt and pine needles over the can until it could barely be seen, and then he ripped off a piece of the shirt and stuck it in the dirt just over the can.

He straightened up and dusted off his hands. Looking at Cal and Pearlie he asked, "Do you think you can see that from that grove of trees where you're going to be hiding?"

Pearlie looked back across the creek and then down at the white scrap of cloth in the ground. After a few seconds, he nodded. "Yep, an' the next question you're gonna ask is can I hit it with that Sharps, ain't it?"

Smoke nodded. "Yeah, and both Sally's and my life depends on your being able to plug it dead center."

Pearlie slowly nodded. "All right, no problem. How about you, Cal?" he asked, turning to Cal.

Cal grinned. "You may be a mite faster on the draw and a little more accurate with a handgun than me, Pearlie, but you know I'm miles better'n you with a long gun." He looked up at Smoke. "Don't worry, Smoke, when you give the signal, we'll get the job done."

Smoke smiled. "I know you will, boys, or I wouldn't put Sally's life in your hands. Now all we have to do is figure out all the likely places those bastards will pick to hide in and we'll plant us some more Arbuckle's cans nearby."

They spent the next hour and a half walking around the clearing and looking at it from all angles. They found several more boulders and outcroppings of rock that looked like likely candidates for hiding places, and even put one can in front of a small group of misshapen trees and brush just in case one of the men tried to lie down in it. They even put one can on top of the roof of the small, dilapidated cabin in the clearing just in case some of the men tried to take refuge in it.

Finally, Smoke was satisfied with their efforts in the area around the clearing. "Now we get to work on the trails to and from this place," he said, leading them back across Fountain Creek.

"First, we'll go down the mountain a ways and get things ready there," he said once they were on the trail. After he was about fifty yards past the clearing, he got down off Joker, took the pick and shovel he'd had Pearlie buy off the packhorse, and began to dig up a hole in the center of the trail. While he was digging, he looked up and said, "Get me some of those tent stakes out of the pack, Cal, and bring 'em over here."

In the soft gravely sand and dirt of the mountainside, it only took him a few minutes to dig a pit two feet deep and four feet wide. He took the tent stakes from Cal and kneeled down next to the pit. One by one, he stuck them down into the ground at the bottom of the pit with their sharp ends up, until he had the entire bottom of the pit covered with sharpened stakes pointing upward. Pointing to the sides of the trail, which had thick layers of pine boughs and needles lying on the ground, he told Cal and Pearlie to gather some up and to fill in the pit, and then to scatter dirt around so it looked like a normal part of the trail.

"Jiminy, I'd hate to be ridin' the bronc that steps in that hole," Cal said, rubbing his jaw.

"The stakes are in case the hole itself doesn't break

the horse's legs," Smoke said. He shook his head. "I hate like hell to do that to any animal, but sometimes when you're dealing with pond scum you have to do things you don't like.

"We'll dig a couple more of these at fifty-yard intervals down the trail, and there are a couple of other things I want to do in between the pits," he added.

He rode down the trail with Cal and Pearlie following for another twenty yards, until he came to a place where there were trees close on either side of the trail. He got down and pulled the bail of barbed wire off the back of the packhorse along with some wire cutters.

He went to one of the trees on the left side of the trail, wrapped the barbed wire around it about six and a half feet off the ground, and twisted the ends together. Then, unrolling the barbed wire as he went, he crossed the trail and did the same thing on the other side, clipping the bale off the end as he twisted it.

Pearlie shook his head. "Damn, that's gonna take a man's head plumb off if'n he rides into it at speed."

Smoke's lips turned up in a nasty grin, but his eyes were flat and without any trace of humor at all. "That's the idea, Pearlie."

They followed him down the trail as he dug more pits and wired more trees, sometimes stepping off the trail and booby-trapping the area alongside just in case the outlaws got smart and got their horses off the trail.

At each of the pits and on each of the trees he rigged, Smoke hung a small piece of white cloth.

"Why for are you doin' that, Smoke?" Cal asked, a puzzled look on his face. "We ain't gonna have to shoot these traps to make 'em work."

Smoke cocked his head at Cal and frowned. "Come on, Cal," he said patiently. "You're smarter than that."

Cal looked over at Pearlie, who shrugged. "I ain't tellin' you, Cal boy. Figure it out for yourself."

Cal thought for a moment, and then he snapped his fingers. "I got it. If'n we're riding down the trail with them galoots on our heels, we'll know where the traps are when we see the white pieces of shirt."

Smoke smiled, this time for real, and nodded. "That's right, Cal. If our little surprises up at the clearing don't kill all of the sons of bitches, we may have to make a run for it to get Sally out of danger. This way, we won't get hurt by one of our own traps."

Finished with their preparations on the lower part of the trail, Smoke and the boys headed back up the mountain toward the outlaws' camp.

"One thing's botherin' me, Smoke," Cal said.

"What's that?"

"What if in the mornin' those galoots start to go down the trail past the clearin'. Won't they come upon our traps and know somethin's wrong?"

"Good question, Cal," Smoke said. "I'm glad to see you're thinking of things that can go wrong with our plan. That is one of the most important things to do when you're trying to trap something, figure out what may go wrong and allow the animal to escape. To keep them from finding our traps below the clearing, I'm going to be in the brush just below the clearing in the morning. If they start to ride down that way, I'll come out and tell them I got there early."

"How about the trail above the camp, Smoke?" Pearlie asked. "We can't set any traps there or they'll find them on their way down."

"I know," Smoke said. "What we're going to do tonight is find the right places for the traps and mark them with white cloth. In the morning, after the outlaws come down the trail and head to the clearing, you and Cal should have time to prepare the pits and wire up above just as we've done below before the meeting takes place."

"But why are we doing both sides of the clearing, Smoke?" Cal asked. "If we do have to make a run for it, won't we be going down the mountain toward Pueblo?"

Smoke looked at him and shrugged. "Probably, Cal, but I don't want to bet my life and Sally's life on a probably. Depending on how things break, we may have to head up the mountain instead of down. Much better to make too many traps than not enough."

"You got that right," Pearlie said, "though it plumb galls me to think we may have to run from these bastards 'stead of stayin' and fightin' it out face-to-face."

"Me too, Pearlie," Smoke said. "But my first obligation is to get Sally out of danger. Once that's done, believe me, there won't be a hole deep enough for them to crawl into to escape what I have planned for them."

It took them until almost midnight for Smoke to find and mark the various places he wanted the pits dug and the trees wired and to leave small patches of cloth on the areas for the boys to find the next day.

By then, they were all dog-tired, and Smoke insisted they go back to their camp near the outlaws and get some shut-eye. "Like Puma Buck used to say," Smoke told them, "it plumb don't make no sense to go into a battle sleepy or hungry. Two things a man don't do good on an empty stomach or on too little sleep: fight or make love to a woman. You need all your wits about you to do either one right."

The boys laughed at the old mountain man's wisdom and humor and as they rode up the trail, they asked Smoke to tell them more mountain man lore.

By the time they got to their camp, he'd told several stories of how he and Puma Buck and Preacher had pulled some tricks on the Indians that were a constant menace to mountain men in the old days.

Once at their camp, he built a very small fire and heated up some more steaks and some coffee that was quite a bit weaker than what they'd had for supper.

"Probably won't have time for breakfast in the morning, so we'd better fill our bellies now," he advised.

Pearlie grunted around a mouthful of steak. "You don't have to tell me that twice," he said.

TWENTY-FIVE

Before falling asleep the night before, Smoke had set his internal alarm to awaken him before dawn. Over many years of living in the High Lonesome without alarm clocks to keep him on schedule, he'd acquired the ability to make himself awaken at just about any time he wanted. Then it had been an essential survival skill, but now it was Sally's life that depended on this ability.

He blinked awake about an hour prior to sunrise and, as was his long habit, he surveyed his surroundings carefully before moving or making a sound. The forest around his camp was very quiet. The night hunters and predators had long since found their evening meals and were preparing for a day of sleep, and the daytime hunters had yet to awaken. Even the hoot owls were quiet and had ceased asking their eternal question, "Who?"

Smoke eased out of his sleeping blankets and built a small, hat-sized fire in the corner of some boulders to heat some water for coffee. Once the water was boiling, he threw in a couple of handfuls of Arbuckle's and roused the boys.

Like Smoke, years on the trail herding cattle had taught them to come instantly awake. They drank their coffee as they broke camp, cleaning up all evidence of their presence and making sure the fire was completely out before they headed down the trail to prepare for their confrontation with Pike and his men later in the day.

A light dusting of snow had fallen during the night, so they had to stay well off the trail on their way down the mountain lest their horses' hoofprints in the snow give their presence away to the outlaws.

Once they were opposite the clearing where the meeting was to take place, Smoke had Cal and Pearlie move the horses well off the trail so they wouldn't nicker when they smelled the gang's animals, and then he showed them where to set up their line of fire into the clearing.

The copse of trees he'd picked had enough underbrush scattered around to hide their position, and there was a fallen pine log behind which they could lay and rest their rifles on for better aim.

"Remember, don't dig the pits or fix the barbed wire to the trees until you are sure all of the outlaws have moved down to the clearing area," Smoke advised. "After the two dead men we left them as a warning, Pike may be worried enough to have a man hang behind to watch their backtrail, so be careful."

As the boys nodded their understanding of his warning, Smoke put his two good pistols in Pearlie's saddlebag and took out a couple of older, less accurate weapons to put in his holsters.

"Why're you doin' that?" Cal asked.

"First thing Pike's going to do when I ride up is take my weapons," Smoke said, "and I don't want to give him my good ones."

Smoke then took a small folding knife from his saddlebags and put it in the inside of his right boot, along with a .44-caliber two-shot derringer. After he'd done this, he took his large bowie knife out of the scabbard on his belt and stuck it in the outside of his right boot, leaving it where the handle could plainly be seen.

When Cal raised his eyebrows at this, Smoke explained, "I'm leaving the big knife where they can find it in my boot," he said. "That way, they'll hopefully be satisfied they've got all my weapons and won't search any farther and find the other knife or the derringer."

Once Cal and Pearlie's weapons were laid out behind the pine log, along with extra ammunition, Smoke told them to head on up the mountain so they could prepare the other traps as soon as the gang came down.

He shook each of their hands solemnly, knowing it might well be the last time he saw them, for he was taking an awful risk in putting himself in Pike's hands. He just hoped the man would want to talk and brag and gloat before deciding to shoot him. He knew if the man were smart, he'd kill Smoke as soon as he was disarmed, but he'd never yet met an outlaw who was smart. He prayed this wouldn't be the first time.

Pike and his men began to come awake as the sun rose over the eastern peaks and warmed up the air a few degrees. Most of the men were heavy-lidded and groggy after a night of too much whiskey and too little sleep, but before long the fire was rebuilt, food and coffee prepared, and they began to feel as if they might actually survive the morning, headaches and all.

Sally woke up in the cabin to find both the men assigned to guard her fast asleep, snoring loudly. For a moment, she debated whether to try and undo her ropes and make her escape, but in the end she decided to trust in Smoke and to let things play out the way he'd planned. She was afraid if she tried to escape and was caught, it would put Pike on alert and spoil whatever Smoke had in mind for the man, so she just lay there in her bed, missing Smoke and wishing the day would hurry up and begin.

"Grub's ready," Blackie Johnson announced from his place next to the fire.

Pike looked up over the rim of his coffee mug and told Rufus Gordon to go and get Mrs. Jensen from her cabin so they could feed her.

"Why're we wastin' good food on a dead woman, Boss?" he asked, his eyes glittering with hate at the thought of the woman who'd blown half his hand off.

Pike scowled at him. "The important question you should be asking yourself, Rufe, is why are you questioning my orders all of a sudden. Are you trying to get yourself killed before we collect that ten thousand dollars of Jensen's?"

"Uh, no . . . of course not, Boss. I was just . . ."

"Shut up and get Mrs. Jensen like I told you," Pike growled grumpily. He hadn't slept well the night before. Mrs. Jensen's warnings and apparent confidence in her husband's ability had worried him much more than he'd let on to her. He'd dreamed that just as he was facing Jensen the man's face had turned into a snarling, growling mountain lion. Pike woke in a sweat just as the man/lion's long, gleaming teeth were tearing into his neck. The rest of the night had been spent tossing and turning in his blankets, his nostrils full of the sour stench of his own fear-sweat. It wasn't the booze he'd drunk the night before that was making his mood foul this morning, but the fact that the mountain man's reputation had caused him such fear.

When Rufus Gordon brought Sally out of the cabin

and over to the fire, Pike noticed she looked refreshed and clear-eyed, as if she'd slept like a baby. In fact, he thought, she looked about as beautiful as any woman he'd met his entire life. He shook his head to clear such thoughts from his mind. He couldn't afford to feel anything for this woman, considering what was going to happen to her after he'd killed her husband.

"Good morning, Mrs. Jensen," he said, trying to screw his face up into an expression of confidence he didn't feel about the upcoming confrontation.

Sally smiled sweetly, as if she hadn't a care in the world. "Good morning, Mr. Pike," she replied as Blackie Johnson handed her a mug of coffee and a tin plate with two biscuits and some pieces of bacon on it.

She glanced at the sky, which had dawned clear and cloudless after the snows of the night before had blown through. "It looks to be a lovely day today," she added as she drank her coffee and split the biscuits and put the bacon between them, making sandwiches of her breakfast.

Pike glanced skyward and grunted. "You think it's a good day to die, Mrs. Jensen?" he asked, again trying to rattle her out of her good mood.

She shrugged. "Any day is a good day to die, Mr. Pike, if you've lived a full and happy life," she said agreeably. "When my time comes, whether it is today or in the future, I won't regret it because I've been lucky enough to have had everything in life I always wanted."

"Well, enjoy the dawn, Mrs. Jensen, 'cause it's probably the last one you'll ever see," Pike grunted, and he turned back to his own food and coffee, trying to ignore the burning in his gut at the thought of meeting up with Smoke Jensen later in the day.

Blackie Johnson's lips were tight and his eyes were narrow. He too didn't want to think about what the men had planned for this lady. He'd come to respect and even to like her for her courage and loyalty to her husband. He thought he'd never met anyone like her before in his life, and even mused that if he had, things might have turned out differently for him.

After a moment, Pike looked around at his men, eating and drinking their coffee. A few of the men had laced the dark brew with dollops of whiskey, the hair of the dog and all that. "Hurry up with the grub, men," he groused. "We've got to get going before long."

"What's the hurry, Boss?" Hank Snow asked. "We ain't supposed to meet up with Jensen until noon."

Pike sighed. Snow was a capable gunny and as mean as a snake, but he was also dumb as a doorknob. "Hank, we got to get there and get set up long before Jensen arrives," Pike tried to explain patiently. "Far as he knows, I've only got three men with me. I don't want him to know about the rest of you, so we got to get you hidden 'fore he gets there."

Sally lowered her head to her plate at this comment to hide her knowing smile. Pike was really dumb if he thought Smoke didn't know to the man what he was up against, she thought.

Thirty minutes later, the gang had finished breakfast, packed their gear, and were headed down the mountain trail toward the meeting place Pike had told Smoke about.

"Keep your eyes open, men," Pike warned. "Jensen might have come early hoping to surprise us, so ride with your guns loose and loaded up six and six."

As they moved down the trail, Pike kept his eyes on the ground, making sure there were no fresh tracks in the snow to indicate Jensen had been there before them.

Sally, on the other hand, noticed the small pieces of white cloth stuck on various trees and bushes along the way. She'd been with Smoke long enough to know his habits and realized this was his doing. She didn't know exactly what he had planned for Pike and his gang, but she breathed easier at this sign of her husband's presence in the area.

When they got to the clearing, Pike pointed at the boulders and outcroppings on the slopes that rose from the edges of the area. He pointed to his men one at a time, showing them where he wanted them to station themselves so they had clear lines of fire down on the clearing.

"Keep a sharp lookout, men," he said to the ones he sent up the slope. "Don't fire unless Jensen tries something or you see something going wrong, and for God's sake, try not to hit me or any of the other men."

He went to the ramshackle cabin in the clearing and brought out an old stool and a rickety handmade chair, which he sat in the center of the open space in front of the cabin. He set Sally on the stool and had Blackie Johnson tie her hands in front of her.

"Zeke," he said, "you hide yourself in the cabin. I don't want Jensen to see you 'cause he might remember your face from the last time he seen you."

Zeke nodded, his eyes staring holes in Sally as he licked his lips. Before he moved off to the cabin, he leaned down and whispered, "I can't hardly wait till I'm done with your man, Missus, and then it'll be your turn."

"Rufus, you stay here in the clearing with me and Blackie. That scattergun you use won't be any good from more'n fifteen yards so I want you at my back."

Rufus and Blackie nodded and took up station behind the chair that Pike placed ten feet from Sally's stool. He took a seat facing her, leaned back and crossed his legs, and built himself a cigarette. He struck a lucifer on his pants leg and lit the butt, exhaling a long cloud of smoke into the chilly air.

Sally watched him, her eyes steady and unafraid as he sat and smoked. She saw a thin trickle of sweat form on his forehead and run down onto his cheek, even though the temperature was in the forties.

"You know, Mr. Pike," she said easily, "it's not to late to stop this thing you're doing. If you quit now, Smoke might even let you live."

Pike's eyes darted to her and then away, as if he didn't want her to see the fear in them. "It's gone too far to stop now, Mrs. Jensen," he replied in a low voice so his men behind him couldn't hear. "Even if I wanted to, which I don't, it's much too late."

"Do you have any family you want me to notify about your death then?" Sally asked, sounding as if she were truly concerned about it.

Pike stared at her, amazed at her faith in her husband's ability to conquer all of his men. He sighed and shook his head. "If you don't shut up with that kind of talk, Mrs. Jensen, I'll have Blackie tie a gag on you."

"All right, Mr. Pike. I'll be quiet and leave you to your thoughts," she said calmly.

TWENTY-SIX

Smoke observed the activity around the clearing from a bluff up on the mountainside a quarter of a mile down the trail through his binoculars. He saw the various positions that Pike stationed his men in, and fixed them firmly in his memory. He knew that even with Cal and Pearlie covering his back, it was going to be a close thing to get both Sally and himself out of the trap without either of them catching some lead.

He waited patiently, smoking a couple of cigarettes to help keep his nerves under control. He'd faced many such situations in the past and had never worried about his ability to come out on top, but this time the most precious thing in his life hung in the balance and his gut was in knots.

Finally, he turned his binoculars to the position Cal and Pearlie were to take, and saw the brief flash of a mirror reflecting sunlight from the copse of trees across the creek from the clearing, Pearlie's signal that they were ready for him to appear.

Smoke stubbed out his cigarette, took a deep breath, and climbed into the saddle. He pulled Joker's head around and made his way down the side of the mountain until he was on the trail so it'd look like he just came up from Pueblo.

He let Joker walk the quarter mile up the trail until

he was across from the clearing. He saw Pike and the two men behind him pull their weapons at his approach. Pike and one of the men held pistols, while the other, the one with a dirty bandage on his right hand, held a sawed-off shotgun cradled in his arms, the twin barrels pointing directly at Sally.

Shit, Smoke thought, he hadn't counted on the shotgun. That was going to make it even tougher to extricate Sally unharmed from the outlaws. A man under attack that's holding a pistol often can't count on his aim being accurate, but a man with an express gun doesn't have to be dead on to do considerable damage.

Breathing slowly to slow his racing heart, Smoke walked Joker across the creek and climbed down out of the saddle, holding his hands out from his body well away from the two pistols on his belt.

"Keep her covered, boys," Pike said as he got up off his chair and holstered his gun.

He walked over to stand in front of Smoke, looking him up and down with a smirk on his face, but his forehead was covered with sweat, indicating he wasn't as sure of himself as he was trying to appear.

"Give me your weapons," Pike ordered, holding out his hand.

Smoke took his pistols out, being careful to handle them with only two fingers so as not to provoke the men holding their guns on Sally.

He handed the Colts to Pike, who stuck them in his belt. Pike's eyes roamed over Smoke's body and he spied the knife handle in his right boot.

"The pig-sticker too, Jensen," he said.

Smoke bent down, pulled the bowie knife out of his boot, and handed it butt-first to Pike, who smiled evilly.

"Thought you could put one over on old Bill, huh?" he asked, testing the razor-sharp blade with his finger.

"If I was trying to trick you, Pike," Smoke said evenly, "I wouldn't have had it sticking out in plain sight."

Pike grinned. "Nevertheless, I'm gonna have to check you to make sure you don't have anymore up your sleeves," he grunted.

Smoke held his hands out from his body and Pike moved closer. He ran his hands around Smoke's waist and up along his shirt, and then he bent and felt around the left boot, ignoring the right boot as Smoke had hoped he would do.

After a couple of minutes, Pike stepped back and moved over toward the chair in front of Sally.

"You got the money?" he asked, seemingly more at ease now that Smoke had been disarmed.

"Maybe," Smoke said, letting his eyes cut to Sally and giving her a wink where Pike couldn't see it.

"What do you mean, maybe?" Pike asked, his voice becoming hard.

"I need to see if Sally is all right before I give it to you," Smoke said.

Pike grinned. "I could just take it," he said.

Smoke's face smoothed and his eyes grew flat. "That might be harder than you think," he said, his voice as low and hard as Pike's.

"Come on, Boss," Blackie Johnson said from behind him. "Let him check her out. There's no need for any rough stuff since she ain't been hurt."

Pike's shoulders relaxed and he stepped to the side. "You're right, Blackie. No need to make this any tougher than it already is. Go on, Jensen, check her all you want," he said, spreading his arms wide.

Smoke moved over to squat in front of Sally, using his body to block the outlaws' view of her. "How are you doing, sweetheart?" he asked.

Sally smiled. "Better, now that you are here," she said, though her voice croaked from the dryness in her throat.

Smoke leaned forward to give her a hug. As his lips moved next to her ear, he whispered. "There's a knife and a derringer in my right boot. Slip them out and hide them under your hands until I give the signal."

She gave a barely perceptible nod against his cheek and he felt her fingers dip into his boot and then withdraw.

"That's enough, Jensen," Pike called from a dozen yards away. "Let's see the money and then you can kiss her all you want."

"Take Pike and the shotgun man first," he whispered before he moved, "I'll take the other one."

"I love you," Sally whispered back, knowing that in the next few moments she might lose him forever, one way or the other.

Smoke leaned back and kissed her lightly on the lips. "I love you too, wife," he said.

He slowly stood up and turned around facing Pike. As he moved toward him, he pulled a thick wad of bills from inside his shirt just below his belt, moving slowly so as not to alarm the men holding the guns.

He waved the bills in the air to get their attention off Sally so she could open the knife and cut the ropes holding her hands without them noticing it.

Smoke and Pike moved closer, and Smoke held the wad of greenbacks out in front of him as if to give them to the outlaw when he got close enough.

Suddenly, Smoke threw the bills in Pike's face and dove to the side toward Blackie Johnson. As he swung his fist as hard as he could against the man's jaw, Smoke heard two quick pops behind him so close together they sounded almost as one report.

His fist connected with Johnson's jaw, snapping his head to the side and putting his lights out instantly.

Smoke whirled around in time to see Pike grab his stomach and double over as he toppled to the ground.

The man with the shotgun stood there, his mouth open and his eyes wide with surprise as he glanced down at the small hole in the center of his chest and watched blood spurt from the wound.

Smoke took two quick strides and jerked the express gun out of his hands just as the cabin door on the far side of the clearing splintered open and Zeke Thompson limped out, pistols in both hands firing wildly as he screamed, "Jensen, you bastard!"

Smoke dove onto his stomach as bullets pocked the sand and gravel in front of his face and let go with both barrels of the shotgun at Thompson.

Thompson was picked up off the ground and blown backward by the ten-gauge buckshot loads in the shotgun, blood coming from a dozen wounds in his chest and abdomen.

Smoke didn't wait to see if he was alive or dead, but rolled to his feet and ran in a crouch toward Sally, who still stood there with the smoking derringer held out in front of her.

The entire episode had taken only thirty seconds, but Smoke knew the men on the slopes above them would be standing up to fire momentarily.

Smoke grabbed Sally at a dead run and got her behind Joker, who was rearing his head and whinnying at the sound of gunfire and the smell of cordite that filled the air.

"There's men on the hillside," Sally yelled at him as he grabbed Joker's reins and pulled the horse along with them toward the creek. He didn't dare try to get into the saddle, but used the animal as a shield for him and Sally.

The distinctive crack of a Henry rifle came from behind them and the pommel of Joker's saddle exploded.

Then, like music to Smoke's ears, the deep, booming report of a Sharps fifty-caliber came from across the creek, followed almost instantly by an explosion on the mountainside and the high-pitched scream of a man shredded by high explosives and hundreds of horseshoe nails.

The Sharps boomed again, and was accompanied this time by the higher-pitched crack of Cal's Winchester rifle as the boys began to lay down a covering fire against the men on the slopes above them.

The outlaws managed to get off several shots, which smacked into the creek with tiny splashes as Sally and Smoke ran through the freezing water toward the forest on the other side of the trail.

Another explosion boomed from behind them, and Smoke and Sally were both hit with several horseshoe nails, though at this distance they did little damage. Joker reared and bucked against the reins as three of the nails dug into his flanks, but Smoke held onto the reins for dear life and forced him to go with them across the trail.

As soon as they were across the trail and into the thick forest of ponderosa pines on the other side, Smoke threw Sally to the ground and covered her body with his just as several shots ricocheted off the trees, sending splinters of bark flying through the air.

Sally grunted and pulled Smoke close, kissing his neck and laughing. "Oh, darling, it feels like you've gained weight," she said.

TWENTY-SEVEN

When they saw Smoke walking Joker up the trail toward the clearing, Pearlie and Cal lay down behind the large ponderosa pine log on the ground and rested their rifles on it, aiming at the area across Fountain Creek.

"I'm gonna draw a bead on that white cloth just beside that outcropping of boulders just above the clearing," Pearlie said. "That's the galoot that's closest to where Smoke and Sally are gonna be standin'."

Cal nodded. "What about the two men down in the clearing? It looks like one of 'em has a shotgun," Cal asked.

Pearlie shook his head. "Smoke said he an' Sally would take care of anyone in the clearing an' for us to concentrate on the men up on the ridges above 'em," Pearlie replied.

"All right," Cal said. "I'll try and take out any men who stand up off to the right when Smoke makes his move. I don't know if I can hit any of those cans of gunpowder from this distance, but I oughta be able to get close enough to make the men duck for cover," he said.

"You keep their heads down an' I'll use this buffalo gun to hit the explosives," Pearlie answered, shoving his hat back on his head so it wouldn't interfere with his aiming. "We'll just have to trust Smoke to do the rest."

They watched as Smoke handed his guns over to the big man who seemed to be in charge and then moved over to squat before Sally and give her a hug.

As Smoke stood up and pulled out his wad of greenbacks and moved toward Pike, Pearlie whispered, "He'll make his move any minute now. Get ready."

When Pearlie saw Smoke throw the bills in Pike's face and dive to the side, he gently squeezed the trigger on the Sharps Big Fifty, the front sight about an inch above the white patch of cloth just next to a group of boulders on the ridge.

The rifle butt slammed back against his shoulder, turning him half around from the force of the recoil. An instant later, a tremendous explosion boomed across the valley and he could see a man blown into the air, parts of his body twisting and whirling in the air like candy out of a busted piñata. Clouds of white smoke billowed into the clear air as branches from nearby trees were shredded by hundreds of horseshoe nails zinging through their limbs.

In spite of Smoke's assurances he would take care of the men in the clearing, Cal kept his eyes on Smoke and Sally to make sure it went as planned. As soon as he saw Sally stand up and fire two quick shots into the men and Smoke knock the other one's lights out, he shifted his gaze to the slope above the clearing and eared back the hammer on his Winchester.

He saw a couple of heads pop up and took dead aim at the first one, who was aiming a rifle down at Smoke. He squeezed off a shot, hitting the man just below his neck, and saw him flung backward, screaming as his hands dropped the rifle and grabbed at his throat.

Cal's second shot missed, but it hit the rock in front of the second man and showered his face with needle-like shards of granite, making him duck back down.

Two other men, slightly above these and off to the

side, managed to get off a few rounds before Cal could lever another bullet into the firing chamber of the Winchester. Unable to work the gun fast enough lying down, Cal raised up on his knees and began to fire and reload and fire again as fast as he could, not trying to aim accurately but just to lay down enough lead to keep the men across the way from being able to get set when they fired.

Pearlie fired again, pocking dirt next to the white cloth of the second can of explosives. He levered another cartridge into the Sharps, adjusted his aim, and pulled the trigger again.

This time he was dead on and the can exploded, blowing a door-sized boulder into the air and shredding the man behind it into mush.

By now, Smoke and Sally had crossed the creek and made it to cover in the pine trees and brush on their side of the creek.

"Keep 'em pinned down," Pearlie said. "I'll grab the mounts and take 'em down to Sally and Smoke."

Cal didn't have time to answer. He was firing and levering and firing over and over. As soon as he saw heads rise above cover across the way, he'd fire a couple of quick shots close enough to make them duck down again.

Pearlie backed up into the brush and ran to where he'd ground-reined the horses. He jumped up into his saddle and grabbed the reins of the horse they'd gotten for Sally. As he rode down the hill through heavy underbrush, he pulled Smoke's gunbelt and holsters out of his saddlebags.

Smoke eased off Sally and took her hand. Scrabbling on hands and knees, he led her back through the brush away from the trail.

He looked up as he heard horses, and drew a breath of relief when he saw Pearlie coming toward them. He stood up just as Pearlie flipped him his belt and guns.

Smoke buckled the belt on and then he lifted Sally up into the saddle. He slapped the horse's rump to get it into a lope back up the hill, and then he swung up into the saddle on Joker and raced after her. Pearlie followed, keeping a close watch behind them to make sure none of the outlaws were trying to cross the creek and follow them.

Smoke jerked the reins, pulling Joker to a halt when he got to Cal's horse. He gave a shrill whistle, and grinned when Cal burst out of heavy brush running toward them.

"Good job, boys," he said as Cal jumped into the saddle. "Now, let's shag our mounts out of here," he yelled, and they took off down the mountain.

As they galloped down the hillside, Sally turned her head and yelled, "What about the money?"

"I'll come back for it later," he answered, not telling her he wanted to get her down to Pueblo and safety before he came back for the outlaws. He knew if he told her that, she'd resist and want to go back with him right now and finish the job. Sally could shoot and ride as well as most men, but Smoke didn't want her in any more danger. He'd almost lost her and he wasn't about to take another chance on her life, not even for ten thousand dollars.

When they'd gone far enough to cut over and ride to the trail, Smoke slowed the horses to let them catch their wind.

As they neared Pueblo, Sally asked, "What now?"

"I'm going to pay the sheriff a visit and tell him what's going on," Smoke said. "I'll leave you in his care and then Cal and Pearlie and I will ride back up the mountain and finish what we started."

Sally shook her head violently. "Not without me, you won't!"

Smoke almost flinched from the fire in her eyes. "Now, Sally, don't argue," he pleaded. "You've been through enough in the past few days. Why don't you just take it easy and let me take care of this?"

Sally took a deep breath before answering. After a moment spent collecting her thoughts, she said, "Smoke, I had to stand there and watch those bastards shoot two of our friends down in cold blood, and then put up with being taken captive and held against my will for days on end. Don't you think I have a right to be in on it when you end it?"

Smoke sighed and looked over at Cal and Pearlie for support. Pearlie shrugged. "She's got a point, Smoke," he said.

Cal nodded. "I agree, Smoke. Besides, it looks like we only got three or four of 'em back there. Probably still another four or five left. Since Sally's as good with a gun as any man I know, it wouldn't hurt to have her along."

Smoke grinned and held up his hands in surrender. "All right, I give up. But I still want to go to town and let the sheriff know what's going on, just in case some of those men circle around and get down to Pueblo before we can find them."

Sally cleared her throat. "Uh, Smoke."

"Yes, dear?" he asked.

"Do you think I'd have time to take a bath and change clothes while you talk to the sheriff? I'm filthy."

Smoke and the boys laughed out loud.

TWENTY-EIGHT

The afternoon sun was almost obscured by the heavy cloud of cordite and gunpowder smoke that hung over the clearing on Fountain Creek like a morning fog.

As the frigid north wind slowly pushed the smoke away, Blackie Johnson groaned and tried to sit up. Pain from his swollen jaw coursed through his head like a lightning bolt, and he moaned again as he gingerly probed his face with his hands.

He tasted blood, and spat out two teeth and ran his tongue over two others that felt as if they'd been broken in half.

Jesus, he thought groggily, what the hell did he hit me with? He knew Jensen's hands had been empty, but he'd never been hit so hard in his life before and shook his head, thinking Jensen's fists must be as hard as rocks to do so much damage so quickly.

Johnson struggled to his feet and glanced around the clearing to see if anyone else was still alive. Bill Pike was lying a few feet away from him, still doubled over with his hands covering his stomach.

Blackie squatted and gently rolled his boss over onto his back, expecting to see a pool of blood underneath him. Instead, to his amazement, Pike groaned and opened his eyes.

Pike moved his hands away from his stomach, and

Blackie saw the handle of the Colt Pike had taken away from Jensen sticking up out of his belt with a lead slug imbedded in the wood of the handle.

Pike shook his head and pulled the pistol out, staring at the slug in its handle with wide eyes. "Jesus, that little derringer kicked like a mule," he said.

Blackie grunted. "I don't know, Boss. All I saw was Jensen throwing that money in the air in your face, and the next thing I know I'm waking up with a jaw that feels like it's broken in two. What happened?"

Pike gave him a sardonic grin. "You wouldn't believe it," he said. "I ain't never seen nobody move that fast in my whole life. The bastard must've slipped his wife a purse gun an' a knife when he was talking to her. After he slugged you, she shot Rufe an' me an' that's the last I remember."

"Let's go see where the hell the rest of the men are and maybe they can tell us what went on," Pike suggested.

He turned to walk to the cabin and he saw Rufus Gordon lying on his back, pink froth and bubbles coming out of his mouth as he gasped for breath like a fish out of water.

They moved quickly to his side and Pike knelt and cradled the wounded man's head in his hands. "Rufe, you still with us?" he asked.

Gordon's eyes opened and he tried to speak, but all that came out was a gurgle, followed by a moan of pain as he tried to get his breath.

The hole in his chest was still slowly oozing blood, and it was clear from the froth on his lips and the sound his breath made when he breathed that he had a lung wound.

Blackie whispered, "He's lung-shot, Boss. He ain't gonna make it."

Pike nodded, and laid Gordon's head back down on

the ground and stood up. He looked around the clearing and saw Zeke Thompson sprawled on his back just in front of the cabin, bleeding from what looked like a dozen wounds in his chest, arms, and legs.

"Jesus," Pike grunted. "Look at Zeke."

Blackie nodded. "Looks like he got in the way of an express gun." He looked back at Rufus and noticed his shotgun was missing. "Probably Rufe's."

"Come on, let's see if he's still alive," Pike said, and they walked toward the wounded man.

As the moved across the clearing, a movement on the slopes above them caught Pike's eye and he crouched, drawing his pistol and pointing it upward.

"Hold on there, Boss," Hank Snow called. "It's just us."

Several of Pike's men began to appear from their hiding places on the side of the mountain above the clearing, moving slowly and looking back and forth to make sure they weren't going to be fired on again.

Pike holstered his gun and squatted next to Zeke, shaking his shoulder with his hand.

"Goddamn!" Thompson exclaimed, coming awake and grabbing for his holster with his good hand.

"Hold it, Zeke," Pike said, grabbing his arm. "It's me an' Blackie."

Thompson shook his head and pushed himself up to a sitting position in the dirt. He looked down at the numerous patches of blood on his shirt and pants and began to gingerly feel of each and every one.

"What happened, Zeke?" Pike asked. "I'm a little hazy on the details after I was shot."

Thompson didn't answer for a moment, being busy making sure none of his wounds were serious. After a few minutes, he looked up, his face a mask of hate. "Jensen threw the money in the air to distract you and then he knocked Blackie on his ass. While he was doin' that, his bitch of a wife shot you and Rufus with that little peashooter Jensen slipped her while he was hugging her."

Pike's eyes narrowed as he pictured it in his mind, again remembering how fast Jensen had moved.

"I came out of the cabin when I saw what was goin' down, both my guns blazin', and Jensen grabbed Rufus's scattergun and let me have it with both barrels." His lips curled in a sarcastic grin. "Good thing Rufe made his own loads, 'cause they must've been light. The buckshot just barely went under my skin 'stead of clear through me."

Blackie was puzzled and he frowned. "But Zeke, why didn't the rest of the men blow Jensen to hell and gone after he made his move?"

Thompson shrugged. "I don't know. Maybe you'd better ask them. That shotgun plumb knocked me on my ass, even though the loads were light, I took both barrels at one time, and it put my lights out."

"I guess I'll do that," Pike answered, standing up and turning to face the men coming down the slope.

Hank Snow was leading the way, his left arm cradled in his right hand, blood smeared on his shirt from an arm wound.

Sergeant Joe Rutledge was limping along behind him, his hand holding his right flank where a bullet had pierced his side.

Slim Cartwright was alongside Rutledge, his face covered with blood where stone splinters had peppered it and shredded the skin. Luckily, his eyes had been spared.

Pike took in their condition with a glance and then he looked back up the slope.

"Where's Johnny Wright and Razor Jackson?" he asked.

Hank Snow grimaced. "They're both still up there,

Boss. Johnny looks like he's been through a meat grinder, an' all we could find of Razor is about eight pieces, none much bigger'n my hand."

"What the hell happened up there?" Pike asked, shaking his head. "How come you boys didn't take Jensen and his wife out when he started this ruckus?"

"We were too busy ducking to do much good, Boss," Snow answered. "Jensen must've had lots of help, 'cause soon as he hit Blackie and his wife shot you an' Rufe, we came under a shitload of fire from across the way over there," he said, pointing to the area where Cal and Pearlie had been lying.

"What about Johnny and Razor?" Pike asked. "How'd Jensen manage to blow 'em up like that?"

"This is how," Sergeant Rutledge said, holding up an Arbuckle's can he was carrying. "I found this over by one of the boulders we was hiding behind. It was half-buried and the spot was marked with a piece of white cloth." His eyes moved toward the place Snow had pointed out. "Jensen must've had somebody over there with a long rifle, an' when the fight started he just shot the cloth, blowing up the cans."

He put the can down and pried off the top, showing the horseshoe nails and gunpowder inside.

He looked up. "As you can see, somethin' like this explode under your feet, it'll mess up your entire day."

"How long ago did all this happen?" Pike asked, glancing at his pocket watch.

"They pulled out 'bout thirty minutes ago," Hank Snow said, "Leastways, it's been that long since they done any shooting at us."

"Then we've still got a chance to catch them and kill the sons of bitches," Zeke Thompson growled, snapping open the loading chamber on his pistol and reloading.

Pike nodded. "Sarge, you get over there where they

were firing from and see if you can tell how many we're dealin' with. I'll gather up the money an' we'll take off down the mountain after 'em."

"We got the money, Boss," Blackie Johnson said. "Why not just let it go?" He glanced around at the wounded men. "After all, most of us ain't exactly in the best shape for another gunfight."

"Let 'em go, hell!" Thompson yelled. "They kilt Johnny and Razor and Rufe an' you want to let the bastards go?"

Pike held **up** his hand to silence Zeke and he turned to Blackie. "Son, if we let them get down to Pueblo, they're gonna go straight to the sheriff an' he'll wire every federal marshal between here and Texas. It won't be much fun tryin' to spend this money with the marshals on our asses, will it?"

Johnson hung his head. "No, I guess not."

"Then get busy loading up our mounts," Pike said forcefully. "We got some people to catch."

When they were all mounted up and ready to go, Rutledge came out of the bushes where Cal and Pearlie had been stationed. "Looks like only four horses, Boss," he said, pointing to the tracks in the snow.

"And one of them is his wife," Pike said. "So we're only goin' up against three men."

Blackie grunted. "From what I could see, Mrs. Jensen could handle herself 'bout as good as most men."

Pike nodded. "That's why we're not going to show her any mercy. She goes down just like the rest of the bastards when we catch up to 'em." He jerked his horse's head around and pointed it down the trail. "Now, let's ride!"

* * *

They spurred their mounts down the trail, Pike in the lead, followed closely by Slim Cartwright and the others in single file behind him.

They'd only gone about fifty yards when Pike's mount stepped in one of the pits Smoke and the boys had dug. The horse screamed in agony as its right leg snapped and it swallowed its head in a tumbling somersault, throwing Pike headfirst into a thick snowbank alongside the trail.

Following too close to stop or turn, Cartwright jerked his horse's reins and had him jump Pike's horse in a running leap.

He'd only managed another fifteen yards when the barbed wire Smoke had strung across the trail caught him just under the chin. The razor-sharp barbs on the wire sliced through his neck like a hot knife through butter and took his head off just under the chin.

Cartwright's body continued in the saddle for another ten yards before it toppled lifelessly off the horse and sprawled onto the trail.

"Holy shit!" Hank Snow exclaimed, jerking his horse to a halt when he saw the mess of Cartwright's head hit the trail and bounce and roll like a child's ball, leaving splotches of blood in the white snow.

The rest of the men stopped their mounts and jumped down to see if Pike was still alive. All they could see of him were his boots sticking out of the pile of snow next to the trail.

Johnson and Rutledge each grabbed a boot and yanked, pulling a sputtering Bill Pike out of the snow.

He brushed himself off and moved over to stand next to his horse, which was snorting and gasping and trying to get to its feet. He pulled his pistol out when he saw the mangled leg and put a bullet in the horse's head, ending its misery.

Johnson stepped up next to him. "You're lucky you

hit that snowbank, Boss," he said, "or you'd've broken your neck."

Sergeant Rutledge moved over next to Johnson and Pike. "Looks like Jensen laid some traps along the trail, Boss. Maybe we'd better rethink our idea of chasin' him an' his friends down."

"You're right, Sarge. We're down to five men now, an' there's no tellin' what else that bastard has waitin' for us along the trail up ahead."

"So, we're gonna give up and head back to Texas?" Johnson asked.

Pike shook his head. "Not on your life, Blackie. But we are gonna be very careful the next time we go up against Jensen and his friends."

TWENTY-NINE

As they moved down the trail toward Pueblo, every so often Smoke would have either Cal or Pearlie hang back to watch their backtrail to make sure none of the outlaws were following them. He wanted to make sure they weren't surprised before they got to the town and told the sheriff what had happened.

While he was riding, Smoke found it difficult to keep his eyes off Sally. In spite of the fact that she'd not had a chance to do her hair or to bathe while a prisoner, and though she was still dressed in the over-sized men's clothing the gang had bought for her in Canyon City, he still felt she was the most beautiful woman in the world.

It was amazing to him that after all she'd been through the last couple of weeks, she seemed to be none the worse for wear. She still managed to laugh and joke with Cal and Pearlie, and in general acted as if they were out on a trip to see the country instead of fighting for their lives against a band of desperate criminals.

When they finally reached the outskirts of Pueblo and rode down along the main street toward the sheriff's office, they attracted stares from almost everyone they passed on the way. Like all mining towns in the mountains of Colorado Territory, there were few women residents other than prostitutes and a very few hardy wives of miners, none of whom even approached Sally's good looks and regal manner.

A few of the younger men on the dirt streets even whistled or gave appreciative catcalls when they saw Sally passing, acts that infuriated Cal and Pearlie, but merely amused Smoke and Sally.

When Pearlie almost went after a couple of the men, Sally laughed and calmed him down. "Take it easy, Pearlie," she said. "They don't mean any harm. It's just their way of letting off steam after being up in the mountains for a long time without female companionship."

"But Miss Sally," he said, glaring at the two miscreants with narrowed eyes, "they oughta show more respect for a lady."

Sally laughed again and looked down at the oversized men's pants and shirt and coat she was wearing. "And just how are they supposed to know what a 'lady' I am, Pearlie, dressed like this?"

Under Sally's calming influence, the group finally made it to the sheriff's office without being involved in any fights or other misadventures.

When they entered the door, they found a tall, lean man with a handlebar mustache sitting at a scarred wooden desk with his feet up on the corner. He was leaned back in his desk chair and had a cup of steaming coffee cradled in his hands.

A handmade sign on the desk informed them he was Sheriff John Ashby.

When Ashby saw Sally enter with the men, he immediately got to his feet and tipped his hat, a weather-beaten black Stetson. "Mornin', ma'am, gents," he said in a voice that had more than a little Texas twang to it.

Sally chuckled. "I can see you're not from around here, Sheriff," she said.

Ashby smiled. "No, ma'am. I came up here with my daddy a few years back from Galveston. He was seeking his fortune in the gold fields."

"Did he find it, Mr. Ashby?" Sally asked as she took a seat across from his desk.

Once she was seated, the sheriff also sat back down behind his desk. "Yes, ma'am. At least, we dug up enough gold for him to head back down to Texas and buy himself a cattle ranch over near Austin." He grinned. "But I never liked chasin' beeves around under the hot Texas sun, so I stayed up here and somehow got myself elected sheriff."

Sally nodded and Smoke spoke up. "Sheriff Ashby, we've come to report some killings up along Fountain Creek."

"'Fore we get down to business, I got some hot coffee brewin' on the stove over yonder," he said, indicating a large Franklin stove in the corner of the office. "You folks can help yourselves if you've a mind to."

"Would you like a cup, Miss Sally?" Cal asked as he headed toward the stove.

"Yes, please, Cal," she answered.

Once they all had mugs in their hands and had taken seats in front of his desk, Ashby crossed his legs and sat back in his chair. "Now, you want to tell me all about it?" he asked, his eyes centering on Smoke.

Smoke started at the beginning and told the sheriff how a band of men from Texas had gone to his ranch, killed two of his hands, and kidnapped Sally.

Ashby's eyes narrowed and he looked at Sally. "They mistreat you any, ma'am?" he asked, his voice softening with concern.

"No, not really," Sally answered. "Other than keeping me tied up at all times, they did nothing to harm me in any way."

Ashby's eyes went back to Smoke, who then told him about how he figured it was a revenge motive by Pike and Thompson for what he'd done years before in Idaho.

"What did you say your name was?" Ashby asked.

"I didn't say, but it's Smoke Jensen," Smoke replied. "This is my wife, Sally, and my friends Cal and Pearlie."

"The Smoke Jensen?" Ashby asked, sitting forward in his chair, clearly more interested now.

"I'm the only one I know of," Smoke answered.

"Last I heard, you was livin' over near Big Rock," Ashby said. "Settled down an' livin' the quiet life."

"That's where my ranch is," Smoke said. "And my life was quiet until Pike and his men interfered in it."

Ashby pursed his lips. "You say there were 'bout ten or so of 'em?"

"That's right, Sheriff," Smoke said, "though their numbers are considerably less now."

"Oh?"

"Yes. I killed a couple of them a few days ago on the trail and I figure we got another two or three this morning."

"That still leaves five or six to deal with then," Ashby said.

"I guess that's about right," Smoke said.

"Let me get some deputies together an' you can show me where all this took place."

"Before you do that, Sheriff," Smoke said, "my wife would like to clean up a bit and we all need to eat something. Can you give us a couple of hours?"

Ashby shrugged. "Sure. It'll take me that long to find some men to deputize to go with us anyway. We'll meet back here in two hours, all right?"

* * *

After they left the sheriff's office, Smoke asked Cal and Pearlie to get them rooms in the hotel while he and Sally made a couple of stops.

He and Sally went first to the local general store, since the town of Pueblo didn't have a woman's dress shop. In there, Sally picked out some clothes that fit her better than the ones the gang had bought. She bought some pants, boots, and several shirts that were in her size, along with a fur-lined leather coat. After that, Smoke took her to the local gunsmith's store down the street.

After browsing for a few moments, Sally picked out a Smith and Wesson .36-caliber short-barreled pistol and a gunbelt and holster in a small size for her tiny waist. Though Sally could shoot a .44 as well as any man Smoke knew, she preferred the .36-caliber with its lighter recoil.

When they got to the hotel, Smoke arranged for a hot bath for the two of them. Once the boy working for the hotel had the large tub filled with steaming hot water, Smoke shut the door and braced it closed by putting the back of a chair under the doorknob.

When he turned around, Sally was already undressed and slipping into the tub. Smoke had started to take a seat in a nearby chair to wait for Sally to finish when she smiled at him. "This tub seems big enough for two, Smoke," she said, lowering her eyes.

Smoke didn't need a second invitation. He shucked out of his buckskins and joined her, taking a long-handled brush off the wall as he walked to the tub. For the next twenty minutes, they took turns scrubbing the trail dirt off each other and generally getting reacquainted after their long absence from each other.

When the scrubbing threatened to lead to more serious play, Sally stopped him with a smile. "Why don't you wait until tonight, darling," she said. "It's been a long time since we stayed in a hotel together."

Disappointed, but looking forward to the upcoming evening, Smoke got out of the tub and then helped Sally out. She dressed in her new clothes and they went down the corridor to find Cal and Pearlie's room.

There was a note on the door that read, "Couldn't wait. We're in the hotel dining room."

Smoke and Sally laughed and went to join the boys for a late lunch.

When they got to the dining room, they found them at a table for four, with enough food in front of Pearlie to serve three people.

"I see you didn't waste any time finding the grub," Smoke said as he pulled out a chair for Sally.

"I told the cook to put on a few more steaks for you two," Pearlie said. He blushed. "I didn't know how long you were going to be, so I just told him to get them ready and keep them warm until you showed up."

Smoke called the waiter over and told him to keep bringing food out until they told him to stop.

Sheriff Ashby showed up just as the last bit of steak was consumed, and raised his eyebrows at Sally's new look. When she stood up from the table and he saw the pistol tied down low on her hip, he glanced at Smoke. "Is Missus Jensen gonna go with us?" he asked.

Smoke grinned. "You want to try and stop her, you're welcome to try."

Ashby inclined his head at her pistol. "She know how to use that?" he asked.

"Probably better than you, Sheriff," Smoke said.

The sheriff looked at Cal and Pearlie, who both nodded. "He's right, Sheriff," Pearlie said.

"Then let's shag our mounts," Ashby said. "I've got four men ready to ride up there with us an' check the place out."

THIRTY

Bill Pike led his men down the mountain, making sure to stay well off the trail that Smoke Jensen had booby-trapped. It was very slow going with the snowdrifts halfway up their mounts' legs in some areas, and they had to be careful not to let their horses break a leg on stones or gopher holes covered by the thick blanket of snow and ice that was everywhere.

As he rode, Pike looked back at his motley crew of men, ravaged by the encounter with Smoke Jensen and his friends. Hank Snow rode hunched over, his wounded left arm covered with a bandage made out of a couple of bandannas tied together; Zeke Thompson was wearing his usual scowl, still wearing his clothes with holes in them from the buckshot Smoke had peppered him with and with the balls he'd pried out of his skin with his skinning knife resting in his shirt pocket; Sergeant Joe Rutledge was riding cocked over to one side, favoring his right flank and keeping his right arm pressed tight against it to stop the bleeding; Blackie Johnson was nursing a bottle of whiskey to stop the throbbing in his swollen jaw and to ease the pain of his broken and missing teeth.

Pike shook his head. All in all, he'd made the one mistake he'd tried to avoid—underestimating Smoke Jensen. Well, he thought, that was one error he wasn't about to make twice. His plan was to circle around Pueblo and to head back to Canyon City. There, he would use some of the ten thousand dollars Jensen had thrown in his face to hire more men for his next foray against the mountain man, and this time he would make sure to plant the bastard forked end up.

Lost in his thoughts of revenge and death, Pike almost didn't hear the hoofbeats of the men riding up the trail in front of him. When he realized there were riders coming, he raised his hand and motioned for his men to move further into the brush, out of sight and hearing of the trail.

From deep in the forest, Pike could barely make out a band of eight or nine men, heavily armed, riding up the trail toward the clearing they'd just left. That son of a bitch Jensen had gotten the sheriff of Pueblo and he'd brought a posse up the mountain after him and his men.

Once the posse was past, Pike said, "Spur them mounts, boys, 'cause Johnny Law is gonna be on our tracks 'fore long and we'd better be shut of this place by then."

"I don't know if I can ride any faster, Boss," Rutledge moaned. "My side's about to kill me."

"Then I'll leave your worthless ass behind an' let Jensen finish what he started," Pike growled, putting the spurs to his horse.

Rutledge and the others gritted their teeth and followed, all of them wincing at the pain the faster pace caused to their wounds.

Smoke led the posse, along with Cal and Pearlie and Sally, up the trail toward the clearing. He was riding point so he could help the men avoid the traps he'd set for Pike and his men. As they came to the pits, he would have Cal and Pearlie take out the stakes and fill in the holes so no one else would inadvertently injure themselves or their horses in the traps he'd laid for Pike and his men. He also clipped the barbed wire off the trees as they passed so innocent miners or trappers wouldn't be injured.

Sheriff Ashby raised his eyebrows when he saw what Smoke had done to prevent their being followed. "Looks like you play pretty rough, Jensen," he observed while Cal and Pearlie filled in one of the pits.

Smoke looked at the sheriff, his face serious. "Man takes my wife and kills my hands, Sheriff, he deserves whatever happens to him," he said.

Then, Smoke's face softened as he remembered something Preacher had once told him. "A friend of mine once said any man who sticks his hand in a bees' nest trying to steal the honey has to expect to be stung a few times," he said.

Ashby laughed. "I can't hardly argue with that sentiment or with whatever happens to kidnappers or killers."

A few hundred yards farther along, just past a bend in the trail, the posse came upon a man sprawled on his back, his head torn off and lying ten yards from his body.

One of the posse members, a young man of no more than seventeen or eighteen years who wore his twin holsters tied down low on his hips like the gunfighters he'd read about in dime novels, leaned to the side after he saw the headless man and puked his guts out, retching and choking up his lunch.

Smoke, who'd seen many such men who fancied themselves gunnies, rode up next to the boy. "It isn't much like you thought it would be, is it?" he asked gently.

The boy sleeved vomit off his lips with his arm and

turned red, bloodshot eyes to Smoke. "No, sir, it ain't."

Smoke inclined his head at the dead man lying on the ground. "Take a good look at him, son," he said, leaning forward and crossing his arms over the pommel of his saddle. "When you kill a man, you take everything he ever was or ever will be from him. It's not a thing you should do lightly, or without good reason."

"Have you kilt many men, Mr. Jensen?" the boy asked.

"Yeah, I have," Smoke answered seriously. "But none that didn't deserve it, son, so I can live with that. The question you have to ask yourself is, can you live with pictures like this in your mind for the rest of your life? If you can't, then you'd better hang them guns up right now and think about a different way of life, 'cause if you keep wearing those six-killers, sooner or later you're either going to be looking down at a man you've killed, or a man who's just killed you will be staring down at your lifeless body."

"I can't believe his friends just left him here an' didn't take the time to bury him," one of the posse said.

"Just because killers ride together doesn't mean they're friends," Smoke said, and spurred Joker on up the trail.

Further up the trail was a dead horse lying over one of the pits, its front legs broken and a bullet hole in its head.

"The clearing is just up the way a bit," Smoke said as he led the posse forward.

When they arrived opposite the clearing, Smoke led them across Fountain Creek to the site of the gunfight.

"Jesus God Almighty," one of the posse exclaimed

when they saw a pack of timber wolves working on the remains of the outlaws that had been killed.

Sheriff Ashby pulled a Winchester rifle out of his saddle boot and started to take aim at the wolves. Smoke reached out and pushed the barrel of the rifle down. "Hold on, Sheriff," he said. "Wolves got to eat, same as worms. They're only doing what they have to in order to survive up here in the High Lonesome."

Smoke drew his pistol and fired a couple of shots into the air, scaring the wolves off without killing any of them.

The posse spread out and moved around the clearing and up the slopes around it, checking for bodies. When two of the men came upon what was left of the two men who'd been blown apart by the explosives, they too bent over, hands on knees, and gave up their lunch.

Sheriff Ashby shook his head at the scattered body parts lying around the area. "Like I said before, Jensen, when you go after somebody, you do it in a serious way."

Smoke was standing in the center of the clearing, his hands on his hips, staring down at the place where he'd left Pike's body. "Looks like the ringleader got away," Smoke said.

"But I shot him full in the stomach," Sally said.

Smoke nodded. "Well, I don't see any blood here where he was lying, Sally. If he was gut shot, he should've leaked some blood here and there."

"Maybe you missed, Mrs. Jensen," Sheriff Ashby said.

Smoke shook his head. "No, she hit him dead center and knocked him off his feet. The only thing I can figure is something must have deflected the bullet— either the gun he took from me and stuck in his belt or his belt buckle. Either way, he took the money I left and what was left of his gang and hightailed it somewhere else."

Pearlie, who'd been searching the area for tracks, found where the outlaws had left the trail and headed down the mountain. He gave a shrill whistle through his fingers and yelled, "Smoke, here's their tracks."

Smoke and the rest of the posse rode back across the creek and found the place where Pike and his men had left the trail and taken to the brush. It was right next to where the headless outlaw's body was lying.

"I guess after they lost this man to one of your traps, they decided the trail was not a healthy place to ride," Sheriff Ashby observed.

Smoke got down off his horse and knelt in the snow, examining the horses' tracks. "It looks like four or five horses, Sheriff, headed back down the mountain toward Pueblo," Smoke said.

"Damn!" Ashby said. "We'd better hightail it back down there."

"Ain't we gonna bury these men, Sheriff?" one of the posse asked.

"Hell, Jensen killed 'em, let him bury 'em," another posse member said.

Smoke climbed back in the saddle. "Like I said, boys, wolves and bears got to eat too. Let the bastards serve some purpose in death, 'cause they sure as hell didn't in life."

He took off down the trail, riding hard, followed by Cal and Pearlie and Sally. After a moment's hesitation, the sheriff grinned and said, "What the hell, let's go, boys!"

When they got to a fork in the trail, just outside the city limits of Pueblo, Smoke saw tracks coming out of the brush and going off on the side trail toward Canyon City.

He reincd his horse to a halt and sat staring down the trail. When the sheriff and his posse arrived a couple of minutes later, Smoke pointed at the tracks.

"Looks like Pike and his men headed back toward Canyon City instead of into Pueblo, Sheriff."

Ashby frowned, shaking his head. "I don't have any jurisdiction in Canyon City, Jensen. The county line is about a mile up that trail. Past that, it's the sheriff in Canyon City's problem."

"Can you wire him to be on the lookout for them, Sheriff?" Sally asked.

"I can, if the wire's not down," he answered. "Usually, it goes down after the first heavy snowfall and we don't bother to put it back up until spring."

Smoke shook his head. "Well, I don't intend to chase them any farther right now. Me and my friends are gonna ride back up the trail and take care of some traps we set between that clearing back there and the outlaws' old camp." He looked at Sally and winked where only she could see it. "After that I'm going back to Pueblo, have a good dinner, get a good night's sleep, and worry about those bastards tomorrow."

Pearlie smiled and nodded. "That part about the good dinner sure sounds good to me."

Smoke looked at him and grinned. "You might also want to consider a bath and a change of clothes while we're there, Pearlie."

Pearlie looked surprised. "Change my clothes? Heck, I've only been wearing these for a week now. They ain't hardly used at all."

THIRTY-ONE

When they arrived at the town of Pueblo, the sheriff dismissed his posse and turned to Smoke. "Mr. Jensen, I don't know much about this Bill Pike who started this vendetta against you, but if he did all this to get back at you for something you did ten or fifteen years ago, then he must be a mighty determined fellow."

Smoke smiled grimly. "I guess you could say that, Sheriff."

"I don't have either the manpower or the budget to post guards around your hotel tonight, but if I was you, I'd sleep with one eye open. Even though Pike's tracks seemed to head toward Canyon City, he might just decide to double back and try and finish what he started while you and your friends are here in Pueblo."

"Point taken, Sheriff," Smoke said. "Believe me, we're going to be very careful until we get back home or I plant Pike and his men six feet down."

Sheriff Ashby grinned and stuck out his hand. "Well, even under the circumstances, it was nice to meet you, Jensen. I been hearing about you for some time and I must say, the stories I heard weren't exaggerated."

"Thanks, Sheriff. We'll check in with you before we leave in the morning."

"Good night, Jensen, ma'am," Ashby said, tipping his hat and turning his horse's head toward his office.

"Come on, let's get these mounts to the livery so we can get to the hotel and get some dinner and then some shut-eye," Smoke said.

At the livery, he told the boy on duty to be sure and give their horses plenty of grain and a good rub-down so they'd be fit for the trip back to Big Rock the next day.

They walked back to the hotel and found they were just in time for the evening meal.

When the waiter came to their table and saw Pearlie, he broke out in a wide grin. "I hope your appetite is good, sir," he said. "I have a bet with the cook. He says you can't possibly eat as much for supper as you did this morning for lunch."

"How much did you wager?" Pearlie asked, pleased to be the center of attention.

"My tip, sir, and since you and your friends are so generous, it amounts to a lot of money for me."

Pearlie leaned back in his chair, grinning at Cal and Smoke and Sally, who were watching the byplay with smiles on their faces. "Well, son," Pearlie said, "bring on the grub, 'cause I got a powerful appetite that needs fixin'."

"Yes, sir!" the waiter said happily. "And for the rest of you?"

Smoke nodded at Pearlie. "He's right, just keep on bringing out the food until we say we've had enough. And son," he added, "don't cook those steaks too much. Just tell the cook to throw them on the fire until they quit moving and then bring 'em out here."

When they were done with dinner, Smoke left the happy waiter a large tip so he could win more money, and they moved to the lobby. When they got to the desk clerk, Smoke asked for their keys. As the man was getting them, Smoke asked, "Has anyone been inquiring as to our presence in your hotel?"

The clerk shook his head. "Why, no, sir. Are you expecting company?"

Smoke handed the man a ten-dollar bill. "No, but if someone should happen to stop by asking for us, you haven't seen us, all right?"

"Yes, sir!" the man said, making the bill disappear in his pants pocket.

"Oh, and my friends here are going to need plenty of hot water and some strong soap for their baths," Smoke said, glancing sideways at Cal and Pearlie.

"Aw, Smoke," Cal protested. "It's too cold for a bath. I'll catch my death."

Smoke put a serious expression on his face. "If you two want to ride the trail back home with Sally and me, you'll take a bath and get some clean clothes. I don't want to have to ride the whole way home staying upwind of you fellas."

As he and Sally started to go up the stairs, Sally turned and smiled at them. "And boys, no spit baths. Put your whole body in the tub, it'll be good for you."

"Yes, ma'am," they replied, glaring at the clerk when they saw him smiling.

When Smoke and Sally got to their room and began to undress, Smoke saw Sally digging in the valise she'd bought that morning.

"What are you doing, dear?" he asked, shucking his shirt off and dropping it on the floor.

She glanced back over her shoulder. "Why, I'm looking for the nightgown I bought this morning when we were shopping for my new clothes."

Smoke grinned and moved over to put his arms

around her. "Never mind," he said. "You won't be needing a nightgown to keep you warm tonight. I intend to do that all by myself."

She looked up into his eyes and pressed herself against him. "Are you sure you're up to it, sir?" she teased. "After all, you've been through a lot lately."

He pressed back against her. "I think I can manage," he said, his voice suddenly husky.

Her eyes opened wide and she moved back to look down. "Yes, I can see you're up to it after all, darling."

In the morning, Smoke and Sally were up early and dressed just as dawn was breaking. They walked down the stairs, arm in arm, intending to get breakfast before the boys woke up.

As they moved through the lobby, Smoke was surprised to find a bleary-eyed Pearlie sitting in a large chair, his Winchester across his thighs, facing the front door.

He and Sally looked at each other and then they moved over to stand next to Pearlie's chair. "Pearlie, what are you doing here?" Smoke asked.

Pearlie looked up and gave a half grin. "Cal and I wanted to make sure nobody disturbed you two. Like the sheriff said last night, there's no tellin' what that Pike feller might be up to."

"Did you sit there all night?" Sally asked.

"No, ma'am," he answered, getting to his feet. "Me an' Cal split the night up. Each of us took four-hour shifts."

Smoke put his arm around Pearlie's shoulder, touched by his concern for them. "Go on up and get Cal. It's time to eat."

Pearlie's face brightened immediately. "You don't have to tell me that twice."

* * *

After skirting the town of Pueblo, Pike and his men pushed their mounts as fast as they could toward Canyon City. He knew Smoke and whoever had been helping him would probably go to the sheriff in Pueblo and then come after them, but he didn't know if they would push the chase all the way to Canyon City or not.

Even so, he didn't plan to underestimate Smoke Jensen ever again, so he made the journey as fast as they could.

Blackie Johnson, Hank Snow, Zeke Thompson, and Sergeant Joe Rutledge didn't ask any questions along the way. They all knew the law would soon be on their trails and they too wanted to put as much distance between them and Pueblo as they possibly could.

Once they entered the city limits of Canyon City, they slowed their broncs and walked them down the main street, letting them blow a bit after being pushed so hard.

Johnson eased his horse up next to Pike's. "What's the plan now, Boss?" he asked. "We got the money from Jensen, so I guess you plan to divide it up and we can all go our separate ways, huh?"

Pike slowly turned to glare at Blackie. "You're right, Blackie, we got the money, but we didn't get Jensen. so the job ain't done yet."

"Wait a minute, Bill," Blackie protested. "We didn't sign on to this just to kill Jensen. The idea was he was wanted and we went after him in order to get the reward money. Now, we got the money and as far as I'm concerned, the job *is* over."

"Listen to me, you son of a bitch!" Pike growled, his face flushed with anger. "That bastard Jensen killed Rufe an' Johnny an' Razor an' Slim. and he mos' likely killed an' cut up Sam and Billy too. Now, I don't know about you, but I rode with them boys for a lotta years an' I don't intend to let Jensen go on home without his payin' for what he did."

Johnson gave a short laugh. "Jesus, Bill, what the hell are you talking about? Jensen killed those boys 'cause we stole his wife and killed two of his hands. What the blazes did you expect him to do? Thank us?"

Pike jerked his horse to a halt and turned in the saddle, pulling the edge of his coat back to uncover the butt of his pistol. "All that don't matter a damn, Blackie. The fact is Jensen is gonna be made to pay for killing our friends. Now, if you're too lily-livered to go along with that, you're welcome to ride on off." Pike paused and grinned nastily. "But I ain't dividin' up this money till that son of a bitch is in the ground."

Blackie took a deep breath, his hand itching to go for his gun, until Hank Snow moved up beside them, holding his hand up. "Hold on, boys," he said, trying to be reasonable. He looked around at the people moving up and down the boardwalks and along the street. "Try to keep it down, all right?" he said. "We don't want everybody in Canyon City to know our business, do we?"

Both Pike and Blackie realized this wasn't the time or the place for a confrontation, especially with the law back in Pueblo possibly on their trail.

Hank inclined his head toward a clapboard building just down the street. "There's a saloon just over there. What do you say to getting off these broncs an' downing a little whiskey to ward the chill off our bones while we discuss it?"

Pike and Blackie glared at each other for another moment, until Pike finally nodded and turned his horse up the street.

* * *

Once they were in the saloon and had downed several stiff drinks, the men finally persuaded Blackie to go along with them on a quest to go after Jensen.

Blackie reluctantly agreed, with the proviso that they wouldn't attempt to kill Mrs. Jensen. "After all," he reasoned, "she didn't do nothing but try to protect herself."

"I knew from the way you was hangin' around her with your tongue hangin' out, you was getting' sweet on her," Zeke said sourly.

Blackie flushed crimson at the suggestion. "That ain't so," he said heatedly. "But she didn't have nothing to do with killing your brothers nor any of our friends," he argued.

"She shot Rufe dead in the heart," Pike said, his eyes narrow.

Blackie stiffened. "Well, that's my offer," he said. "Take it or leave it."

Pike thought for a moment, and then he smiled and spread his hands. "All right. I don't really care what happens to that bitch anyway. It's Jensen an' the men who helped him shoot up our friends I want to see planted."

"Now that that's settled," Hank Snow said, "what are we gonna do about killin' Jensen? There's only the five of us left, an' I don't relish goin' up against him an' his men with just five guns."

Pike grinned and looked around the saloon. "Oh, I think we can find some men up here who'll be glad to ride with us for a share of the loot we took off Jensen. Hell," he said, "it's a lot easier than tryin' to dig gold outta these mountains in the winter."

"I hope you're not plannin' on offering them a full

share of our money, since they ain't exactly been in on this from the start," Sergeant Rutledge said.

Zeke Thompson leaned forward and smiled evilly. "It don't matter too much how much we promise them," he said. "When it's all over, who's to say they're gonna survive the trip anyway?"

As the other men laughed at this suggestion of a double cross, Blackie tried to hide his displeasure. He'd done a lot of bad things in his young life, but he'd never gone against his partners. Zeke's suggestion made him think about what might be planned for him once this was all over. He knew one thing—he was going to have to watch his own back in the future.

"Just where are you plannin' on staging this attack on Jensen?" Hank Snow asked. "On the trail on the way back to his ranch?"

Pike thought for a moment. "Naw," he said finally. "They're gonna be on their guard till they get back home. I think it'd be better for us to take a few days off 'fore we head out after 'em. Let 'em get good an' settled, thinking they're all safe an' sound back home, 'fore we take 'em out."

"You don't mean for us to hang around here waiting, do you?" Blackie said. "That sheriff over in Pueblo is bound to get word up here to be on the lookout for us."

"No, you're right for once, Blackie," Pike said. "We'll head on down toward Silver Cliff, get us some partners there. As I remember, it's a mite smaller than Canyon City an' it's on the way toward Jensen's ranch. It'll be the perfect place to lay low for a while till we get ready to go after him an' his men."

"Well, at least we got plenty of money to spend while we're waitin'," Hank Snow said, grinning. "And I'll just bet there are some women in Silver Cliff who'll be glad to help me get rid of some of it."

THIRTY-TWO

After they'd finished eating and gotten their horses packed for the journey back to Big Rock, Smoke and the others stopped by Sheriff Ashby's office.

"We're heading back home, Sheriff," Smoke said. He handed the sheriff a piece of paper. "That's where we live, and the name of our sheriff is Monte Carson. I'd appreciate it, if you hear anything about the outlaws, you send me a message care of the sheriff."

"Will do, Mr. Jensen," Ashby said. "And if any of the boys head over to Canyon City, I'll send a note to the sheriff over there to also be on the lookout for anyone matching the gang's descriptions. With any luck, they'll be caught before you get back home."

Smoke shook his head. "I don't think it'll be that easy, Sheriff, but I do thank you for your trouble and for all the help you've been."

Ashby smiled. "It comes with the badge, Mr. Jensen." He turned to Sally and stuck out his hand. When she took it, he said, "You held up real well under difficult circumstances, ma'am. It's been a pleasure to meet you."

"Thank you, Sheriff," she said, casting her eyes at Smoke. "I had a good teacher."

* * *

As they made their way down south toward home, Smoke decided to take a trail straight through the mountains to avoid going through Canyon City. He didn't want to risk running into the outlaws while he still had Sally with them. This way would take them a couple of days longer, but there was no way the outlaws would know which way they went, so it would be almost impossible for them to set up an ambush along the way.

Even so, while they rode, Smoke took turns with the boys riding point ahead of the group, just in case there was trouble.

Sometime later, when they finally arrived in Big Rock, they were surprised to see that the town was almost deserted, the streets practically devoid of citizens.

"That's strange," Smoke said. "I wonder where everyone is today."

"Smoke," Sally said, "could we stop at the undertaker's? I want to see where Sam and Will are buried."

"Certainly, dear," Smoke said.

They had the undertaker show them the graves of their two hired hands, buried while they were gone. They all stood around the still-fresh graves and Sally led them in a prayer for their departed friends.

She then arranged with the undertaker to have fresh flowers kept on their graves in season, and she paid him to carve granite headstones for their resting places with their names and the date of their deaths on it.

Afterwards, Smoke suggested they stop off at Monte Carson's office to let him know Sally was all right and that the sheriff of Pueblo might be wiring him with news of the outlaws.

They found Sheriff Carson in his usual spot, behind

his desk with his feet up on the corner and a steaming cup of coffee in his hands.

When they entered, he jumped to his feet and immediately gave Sally a hug. "Damn but it's good to see you're all right," he said happily.

Smoke smiled at the sheriff. He knew that Sally was everyone in town's best friend and that the townspeople would be as relieved and as happy as Monte to see that she had survived her ordeal intact and unharmed.

After he finished hugging Sally, Monte shook hands with Cal and Pearlie and Smoke, telling them all how glad he was to see them back.

"I can't hardly wait to hear the story of how you got Sally away from them desperados," he said, looking at Smoke.

"Well, we've been on the trail for several days now," Smoke said. "Why don't we go on over to Longmont's and get some food under our belts and we'll tell you all about it."

"Yeah," Pearlie said, grinning. "I'm sure Louis would like to say hello too."

"Smoke," Sally said, "I'm really not too hungry just now. Why don't I go on over to the hotel and make arrangements for us to stay there while you and the sheriff visit Louis?"

Before Smoke could reply, the sheriff asked, "Hotel? Why are you gonna stay there?"

Sally looked at him, surprised at his question. "Why, don't you remember, Monte? Our cabin was burned to the ground by the outlaws."

The sheriff blushed and stammered, "Well, Sally, first of all, Louis ain't at his place right now."

"I've been meaning to ask you, Monte," Smoke said. "Where is everyone? The town looks deserted."

The sheriff got an embarrassed look on his face.

"Uh, most of 'em are off working on something right now."

When he saw by their expressions his explanation really didn't answer Smoke's question, he leaned over and finished off his cup of coffee in one long drink. "I'll tell you what," he said, hitching up his pants. "Let's go on out to the Sugarloaf and then we'll talk."

Smoke looked at Sally and shrugged. "All right, Monte," he said, wondering why his friend was being so mysterious.

"Hold on a minute," Pearlie said. "I thought we were going to eat first."

Monte Carson glanced at him and gave him a wink where the others couldn't see it. "Pearlie," he said, "just this once, will you forget about your stomach for a while?"

"All right, but if I starve to death before we find some grub, you can just plant me out on the Sugarloaf somewheres. No need to buy me a fancy headstone, just put a batch of Miss Sally's bear sign in my casket an' I'll be happy."

On the way out to the Sugarloaf, Monte Carson refused to answer any more questions from the group, telling them it would all be clear to them once they got to the ranch.

As they rode up the final mile toward where their cabin used to be, Smoke saw dozens of buckboards and wagons and about thirty horses milling around their corral.

When they turned the final bend before arriving at the cabin, they saw most of the townspeople they'd come to call their friends busily engaged in building them a new house. Men and boys swarmed around the place on ladders and up on the roof, putting the final touches to a large, well-appointed log cabin with two stories on it instead of the original one.

The women of the town were busy cooking food and serving hot coffee and hot chocolate to the workers and fetching kegs of nails and spikes that were being driven into the walls.

Three large wagons stood off to one side filled with furniture, drapes, and even three trunks of clothes.

Sally put her hands to her mouth as her eyes filled with tears. "Oh, Monte," she gasped, "this is so wonderful!"

Louis Longmont, his sleeves rolled up and minus his usual trademark fancy coat, wiped his hands off on a rag and walked over to meet them.

"Howdy, folks," he said cheerfully. "We'd hoped to be finished before you got back, but we're awfully glad to see Sally is all right anyway."

Smoke jumped down off Joker and walked over to embrace his friend. "Louis, I can't believe you all have done this."

"Why not, partner?" he asked. "After all you and Sally have done for the town, we figured it was time to pay you back a little bit."

"I'm overwhelmed," Smoke said, blinking rapidly to hide the tears in his eyes.

Louis spread his arms. "Well, come on in and let me show you around your new home."

As they walked forward, the townspeople all stopped their work and clapped and yelled their hellos, the women rushing over to see how Sally was and to make her promise to tell them the "whole" story later.

Pearlie made straight for the table that was spread with fried chicken, steaks, rolls, corn, and just about every kind of pie he'd ever heard of. For Pearlie, sentimentality always came second to hunger.

* * *

By nightfall, all of the furniture and clothes were in the house and it was complete except for some minor things that Louis promised would be fixed within the week. Seeing how tired Smoke and Sally were from their long trip, everyone finally left for town, with promises to come back out to the house later in the week for a housewarming party.

Once they were alone, Smoke and Sally walked around their new home. Smoke stopping to admire the brand-new handmade gun cabinet that the owner of the local gun shop had filled with new rifles, shotguns, and pistols to replace those Smoke had lost in the fire.

He took Sally in his arms and smiled down at her. "It is good to be home, dear," he said.

"Yes," she said, wiping her eyes with the back of her hand, "it is." She took his hand and led him into the bedroom. She stood before the large double bed and handcrafted quilt that was covering it, thinking how comfortable it looked. "I think it's about time we tried out that new bed the townsfolk gave us," she said, looking at him out of the corner of her eye.

"Tired?" he asked.

She grinned and shook her head. "Not that tired," she said, laughing. "I said try it out, not go to sleep."

THIRTY-THREE

Bill Pike and his men spent almost two weeks hanging around Sliver Cliff, drinking, carousing, and getting to know some of the local toughs. Even with the inflated prices of a mining town, they couldn't manage to make a small dent in the ten thousand dollars Smoke had left for them.

Finally, Pike chose five men to make an offer to. Four accepted and one declined, not wanting to make the long journey to Big Rock no matter how much money Pike offered. It took him another day to find a fifth man to join their group, and they headed out to make their way south toward Big Rock and Smoke Jensen.

On the way, Pike avoided even the smallest towns in order to keep any word of their approach from getting back to Jensen. The men grumbled about having to camp out in the frigid weather, but Pike reminded them they were being well paid to do just that.

By the time they got to the outskirts of Big Rock, they were tired, half-frozen, and in need of more supplies, especially whiskey.

Pike decided to send one of the new men into town, figuring Jensen and his men hadn't seen his face, so it would be safe for him to go for what they needed.

He sent a man named Cutter Williams, so named

because of his penchant for slicing up anyone who disagreed with him with his twelve-inch Arkansas Toothpick knife. He had bright red, almost orange hair and a full beard, grown to cover a couple of jagged scars on his face from old knife fights.

Williams rode into town with a list of needed supplies in his saddlebags, and with orders to go directly to the general store and buy the goods and leave town without talking to anyone.

Williams intended to do just that, until his horse came abreast of Longmont's Saloon, where the delicious aroma of frying steaks and liquor changed his mind. *What the hell,* he thought, *nobody in this town knows me so it oughta be safe enough. Besides,* he reasoned to himself, *what Pike don't know won't hurt him.*

He tied his horse to the hitching rail in front of the saloon and swaggered inside, moving immediately to the bar area. When he cocked his foot up on the brass rail running along the bottom of the bar, Louis Longmont, who was sitting at his usual table having his morning coffee and cigar, noticed the handle of the wicked-looking blade in Williams's boot.

Louis's experienced eyes also took in the way Williams wore his Colt pistol tied down low on his thigh, a sure sign the man wasn't a stray cowboy stopping by for a quick drink before returning to the herd.

Though Big Rock occasionally had such men passing through, Louis was on alert because of the continued threat of the men that had kidnapped Sally. He'd discussed the possibility of them coming after Smoke with the Jensens, but this man didn't fit the descriptions of any of the outlaws Smoke had given him.

Still, better to be safe than sorry, Louis told himself. Anything out of the ordinary needed to be checked out.

He sat there, sipping his coffee and letting the smoke from his cigar curl up to be scattered by the wind through the windows and door, as he observed the man at the bar.

After the redhead downed two quick whiskeys, he took his glass and moved to a table next to Louis's. When the waiter came over, he ordered a large steak, fried potatoes, and sliced peaches.

As he sat back and sipped his third whiskey, Louis looked over at him and forced his face into a friendly smile. "Howdy, mister," Louis said, nodding his head at the man.

Williams looked at him suspiciously and slowly nodded back, the barest hint of a smile on his ugly face.

"I'm the owner of this establishment," Louis said, shifting his chair around to face the man. "I notice you're new in town and if you need it, I can recommend a good place to stay the night, and I can also tell you who's hiring hands in the area if you're looking for a job."

Williams's eyes narrowed. He wasn't used to men striking up conversations with him in saloons—his face didn't invite such friendliness.

"I ain't plannin' on stayin', mister, if it's any of your concern. I'm just passin' through."

This statement really raised Louis's concern. Not many men traveled across country this time of year. The winters here were just too difficult for casual travel.

"Oh, well, then, enjoy your meal and I'm sorry I bothered you," Louis said. He raised his hand to the waiter and signaled for him to bring the man another drink. "Have a drink on me for the intrusion," Louis said, and turned back to his table.

When the waiter poured the man another whiskey, his expression softened. "Hey, mister," Williams said, holding up the glass. "Thanks for the drink. I didn't mean to be ornery. It's just I been on the trail a long time and I ain't used to talkin' to other people much."

"That's all right," Louis said, trying not to seem too interested. "You come from up north?"

"Yeah," Williams replied, his voice starting to slur a bit from the amount of liquor he'd consumed. "I was minin' up in the Rockies till it got too cold. A man offered me a job down here an' I took it. Anything to get outta the mountains in the winter."

Louis figured he'd pressed the man all he could without raising his suspicions, so he just nodded and went back to his coffee and cigar.

After Williams finished his meal, he got up and walked unsteadily out the batwings. Louis watched him get on his horse and head down the street toward the general store.

Louis was still watching thirty minutes later when the man came out with a large burlap sack filled with supplies and headed back out of town the way he'd come in.

Once he was out of sight, Louis walked over to the general store and went inside.

Ed and Peg Jackson, the owners, were busy stacking shelves with goods that had just come in from Colorado Springs by wagon.

"Hey, Louis," Ed said, wiping his brow with the back of his sleeve. "You in need of some supplies for your restaurant? We just got some tins of tomatoes and peaches that'll get you through the winter."

Louis shook his head. "No, Ed, that's not why I'm here this time."

Ed's face looked puzzled. "What can I do for you, Louis?" he asked.

"I'm interested in that redheaded man that was just in here, and I was wondering just what he bought."

"Any particular reason?" Ed asked as Peg, wondering what was going on, joined him.

Louis shrugged. "It's probably nothing, but Smoke asked me to be on the lookout for any strangers that came to town, just in case those men who kidnapped Sally wanted another chance at him."

Ed scratched his chin. "Now let me see," he said, and then he told Louis about all the things the man had bought.

"That's strange," Louis said. "It sounds like he bought enough supplies for eight or ten men, and he told me he was traveling alone."

Ed shook his head. "That doesn't sound right, Louis. There's no way a single man could need all the food he bought. It'd go bad before he could finish half of it."

"That's what I thought. Maybe I'd better take a ride on out to the Sugarloaf and tell Smoke about this."

Ed started to untie his apron. "You need any help?"

Louis held up his hand. "No, Ed, but thanks anyway. I may just be jumping to conclusions. No need to get too worried just yet."

Louis got his horse out of the livery stable and rode as fast as he could out to Smoke's ranch.

When he got there, Sally immediately offered him breakfast.

"No, thanks, Sally," he said, "I've already eaten."

"Then, how about a cup of coffee and some of my bear sign?" she asked, pulling a dish towel off a platter covered with the doughnuts.

Louis smiled as he took off his hat. "Now, that I could go for." He hesitated. "Uh, Sally, is Smoke around?"

Her face sobered at his tone. "Yes. He and Cal and Pearlie are out in the front pasture working on some fences that needed mending."

"Maybe I'd better go get him," Louis said. "There's something I need to talk to you two about."

She held up her hand. "No need for that, Louis. Keep your seat." She walked out on the front porch and rang a large bell hanging there. When she came back in, she said, "He'll be here in a few minutes. He put that bell there so I could call him in if I needed anything or if anyone showed up who looked suspicious."

Sure enough, it wasn't five minutes before Smoke and Cal and Pearlie came galloping up to the house, pistols in their hands.

They relaxed and holstered their weapons when they saw Louis's horse tied up to the rail by the porch.

They entered the house, still breathing heavily from their rapid ride in from the pasture. "Howdy, Louis," Smoke said, his eyes going to Sally to make sure nothing was wrong.

She smiled. "Louis here has something he says he needs to talk to us about, and since the bear sign just came out of the oven, I thought you boys might like a break from working on that fence."

"Did you say bear sign?" Pearlie asked, grabbing a chair and sitting at the table, his eyes wide with anticipation.

Sally's bear sign were so famous, some neighbors had been known to ride twenty miles just to partake of them.

Sally put the platter on the table and said, "Dig in, men, while I pour some coffee all around."

Once they were eating bear sign and drinking coffee, Smoke glanced at Louis. "Well?" he said.

Between bites, Louis filled them in on what he'd seen in town and his suspicions about the redheaded stranger. "It may be nothing," he added, "but I thought you ought to know about it."

Smoke nodded gravely. "You did right, Louis. I don't believe in coincidence when it comes to pond scum like Bill Pike."

"But Smoke," Pearlie said around a mouthful of bear sign, "there weren't no redheads in that gang."

Smoke looked at him. "That means Pike has gotten some men to replace those we killed, Pearlie, so there's no telling how many men we're going up against."

"What do you want to do about it, Smoke?" Louis asked. "You know you can count on my guns, as well as any you need from town."

Smoke glanced out of the window at the darkening skies. "There's no time for that, Louis. If Pike is out there, he'll probably hit us tonight. That doesn't leave us enough time to go to town and round up any help."

"So, what's your plan?" Louis asked.

"First of all, I'm going to send the rest of the hands into town. They're not gunfighters and I don't want any more innocent men to die out here." He paused, glancing at Sally. "And I'd like you to go into town too, sweetheart."

Sally's lips pressed into a tight line. "No, sir, not on your life, Smoke," she said firmly. "I can handle a gun as well as most men and I don't intend to run away to town and leave you here to face those men by yourself."

"But . . ." Smoke began, until Sally put her hands on her hips.

"We are *not* going to argue about this, Smoke. My place is here with you and that's final."

Louis smiled and shook his head. "I think you're outgunned on this one, Smoke," he said.

Smoke slowly nodded. "I think you're right, Louis.

It's easier to throw a bull in heat than to change a woman's mind once it's made up."

"I'm glad you all agree," Sally said, her face softening now that she'd won her argument. "Now, what are we going to do?"

"Cal, you round up the hands and send them into town. Tell them once they get there to tell Monte Carson what's going on. I doubt he can get here before morning, but in case they don't make their move tonight, we'll have some backup for when they do."

"Yes, sir," Cal said, jumping to his feet and running out the door to round up the hands.

"What else, Smoke?" Pearlie asked.

"First of all, Sally's going to make us lots of coffee and food in case we come under siege, and then we're going to shut this house up tighter than a drum." He glanced around, glad that the townspeople, when they'd built the house, had thought to provide wooden shutters for the windows, with small gun ports in them, that could be shut against just such an attack.

Sally nodded and got to her feet, and began to prepare huge pots of coffee and to start to cook some steaks and biscuits that could be carried in bags for nourishment when needed.

Smoke leaned forward across the table. "As soon as it gets dark, we're going to leave one man here with Sally and the rest of us are going to spread out around the house in the woods and wait. When and if they come, we'll be ready for them."

THIRTY-FOUR

As dusk approached, Smoke had Pearlie take the horses up to a corral in a distant pasture to get them out of harm's way, and he closed up the house, closing all the shutters and placing rifles and shotguns next to them along with plenty of extra ammunition. Once that was done, he got an old Indian bow and quiver of arrows Cal had been trying to learn to use out of the bunkhouse. Smoke strapped the quiver on his own back.

"What do you want that old thing for?" Pearlie asked, eyeing the bow with a puzzled stare. "Don't a rifle or shotgun work better?"

"Not if you need to dispatch someone quietly and they're too far away to use a knife," Smoke answered, a deadly gleam in his eyes.

He stationed Cal in the house with Sally after pulling him to the side and telling him to make sure she didn't get hurt.

"Only way they'll get to Sally, Smoke," Cal said seriously, "is over my dead body."

Smoke then told Pearlie and Louis to take everything off their clothes that might make any noise. "Remember, sound carries a long way in cold night air," he cautioned. "The smallest clink or scrape might give your position away."

Taking his advice, Pearlie and Louis removed all

bits of metal from their clothes, and tied down their holsters tight so they wouldn't slap against their thighs when they moved or get caught on any branches in the brush.

As a final measure, Smoke got out a tin of bootblack and they each smeared it on all parts of their exposed skin, making them nearly invisible in the darkness.

When they got ready to head out into the night, Sally gave each of them a canteen filled with steaming coffee, a bag of steak sandwiches, and a couple of bear sign to help ward off the chill of the night.

"One thing we got going for us," Smoke said as they walked out of the door, "is that the moon is hidden by those snow clouds. It's going to be darker than a prostitute's heart out there tonight."

"Yeah," Pearlie added, "an' colder'n a well-digger's belt buckle."

After she closed and locked the door behind them, Sally went around the house, turning down all the lanterns so there was just enough light to see to move, but not enough to make them a target from outside.

As the three men moved off into the brush, Louis looked back at the cabin, thinking how well Smoke had planned the original site when he first built it. All the trees for a hundred yards in all directions had been cut down so there was a clear line of fire from the cabin. There was no way anyone could sneak up on it unobserved and there was no cover nearby for assassins to hide behind.

Louis smiled to himself. Smoke was a good man to have on your side, he thought, and a deadly adversary to have as an enemy.

* * *

Pike and his men moved across the nearby pastures toward the ranch house. When he saw the large house silhouetted against the night sky, Pike was surprised. Since they'd burned the cabin down when they were here before, he figured Smoke and his family would be living out of the bunkhouse. He couldn't believe the cabin had been rebuilt so fast.

"Hey, Boss," Sergeant Joe Rutledge said, "the house looks dark. Maybe they're not there."

Pike put his binoculars to his eyes, and didn't like what he saw. The windows were all covered, with only small points of dim light visible in them. "They're there all right," he said. "They just got the place buttoned up tight, like maybe they're expectin' us."

"But Bill," Zeke Thompson said, "there's no way they coulda know we was comin' tonight."

Pike grunted, staring at Cutter Williams. *The fool must've given us away somehow,* he thought.

"Yeah, well, don't count on it," he said. "You men split up and circle around the house. We'll just have to come at it from all sides and hope we can get close enough to set it afire an' burn 'em out."

Blackie Johnson didn't like the sound of that. "Remember, Bill, you said we weren't gonna kill the woman."

Pike glared at him. "Not on purpose, Blackie, but if she's in there and comes out shootin', then I can't be responsible for what the men do."

"Lyin' son of a bitch," Blackie muttered under his breath as he joined the others in circling around the house.

Smoke was squatting on his haunches, leaning back against a tall pine tree, when he heard the soft sound of a horse's hooves crunching through nearby snow.

He slowly stood up, keeping his back up against the tree, and fitted an arrow into his bow.

When he saw a dark figure leaning over the neck of a horse walking through the forest, he drew the bow-string back, took careful aim, and let go.

The arrow whispered through the air and embedded itself in the man's neck with a soft thud.

"Aieeee," the man screamed, clawing at his neck to try and stop the horrible pain.

Smoke bounded through the brush, somehow not making the slightest sound, and jerked the man off his horse, sticking his bowie knife up under his ribs to pierce his heart and kill him instantly.

Someone twenty yards off through the woods let go with a shotgun, the roar echoing among the trees. Smoke dove to the ground and rolled, feeling his shirt pelted by buckshot, but the range was too far for the slugs to do any real damage.

When Smoke rolled up onto his knees, his Colt was in his hand. He fired by blind instinct at the place where he'd seen the fire belch from the shotgun, pumping off three quick rounds a couple of feet apart.

The third one struck home and he heard a grunt and then a thud as the man toppled from his horse to land on a small bush.

Circling around, Smoke eased his way toward the man he'd shot to make sure he was dead and not just wounded. He eased around a tree and saw the man, dark blood staining his right shoulder, trying to re-load his shotgun.

Smoke didn't hesitate. These men who kidnapped women and hid behind them deserved no mercy. He flipped his bowie knife over to grab it by the point and flicked it at the man. It turned over the standard three times and hit the man squarely between the shoulder blades. He flopped forward without a sound. Smoke walked over, removed the knife, and wiped it off on the man's shirt before sticking it back into his scabbard.

Pearlie jumped when he heard the shotgun go off over to his right, and he felt his heart begin to beat rapidly. This was it. They were out there and on the move, he thought.

He eased the hammer back on his express gun, having chosen it because of the difficulty of aiming a rifle in the darkness.

Suddenly, the faint light of the night sky was obscured by the shadows of two men moving past him in the darkness. A slight twinkle of light showed him they had their guns out and were moving toward the house.

Pearlie, not quite as bloodthirsty as Smoke, felt he ought to give the men a chance to give themselves up. He whispered, "Drop them weapons!"

Instead of lowering their guns, the men turned toward him and he let go with both barrels, blowing the men out of their saddles and almost cutting them in two at such a close range.

As he moved past them, the coppery smell of blood and the acrid odor of cordite filled his nostrils. Before he could reload, a man on horseback charged him, firing a pistol wildly.

Pearlie dropped the shotgun and drew his pistol in one quick movement. Just as one slug tore through his coat and another grazed his neck, Pearlie returned fire. His second shot hit the man full in the chest, knocking him backward off his horse with a harsh grunt.

Hearing the gunfire in the woods, Pike screamed out as loud as he could, "Charge the house!"

Zeke Thompson bent over against the wind and struck a lucifer on his pants leg, and then he held it to the torch he was carrying. He was going to burn that bastard Smoke Jensen out of his house.

Just as he started to put the spurs to his mount, a man stepped out in front of him, his teeth gleaming whitely in the gentle light from the sky. "Don't you know a grown man shouldn't play with fire?" the cultured voice asked.

"Why you . . ." Zeke yelled as he pulled his pistol up.

The Colt in the dark man's hand exploded and Zeke felt as if he'd been kicked in the chest. The force of the gunshot rocked him back in his saddle, but he didn't fall.

He grunted with effort and looked down to see a fine stream of blood that looked black in the darkness pumping out of a hole in his chest.

"Son of a bitch!" he growled, trying to raise his pistol again.

Louis chuckled. "Leave my mother out of this," he remarked as he shot from the hip and put a bullet directly into the bridge of Zeke's nose, snapping his head back and putting out his lights forever.

Just as the moon came out from behind the clouds, Cutter Williams lit his torch and spurred his mount toward the house, yelling, "Burn the bastards out!"

Blackie Johnson, outraged by this tactic, which would surely mean the death of Mrs. Jensen, kicked his horse forward after Williams. When he saw he couldn't catch him, Blackie drew his pistol and shot him in the back, knocking him off his horse.

Sally, in the house and fixing to shoot Williams, saw what Blackie did and a small smile creased her lips.

She knew he wasn't as bad as the others, she thought, lowering her rifle.

Just then, Bill Pike and Sergeant Joe Rutledge rode out of the forest toward the house, each carrying torches. When Pike saw what Blackie did, his aimed his pistol at him and fired twice, knocking Blackie to the ground.

Rutledge was almost to the front porch when the door opened and Cal stepped out, his hands full of iron. He fired from the hips with both guns, hitting Rutledge in the chest and stomach three times before the man flopped off his horse and fell across the hitching rail in front of the house.

He looked up, his hand rising with a gun in it. "You don't have to do that," Cal said, hoping the man would drop the pistol.

Rutledge grinned through bloodstained teeth. "Yes, I do."

Cal fired once more and blew the back of Joe's head off.

Pike jerked on his reins and snapped off a shot at the man standing on the porch, grinning tightly when he saw the man go down.

Hell with this, he thought, jerking his reins around and galloping across the pasture away from the house.

Smoke ran out of the woods and over to the porch to kneel beside Cal.

Cal was doubled over, his hands pressed against his side, trying to stop the flow of blood from a wound in his flank.

"Sally, get me a hot iron!" Smoke yelled as he cradled Cal's head in his arms.

In preparation for the upcoming fight, Smoke had told Sally to keep a couple of pokers ready in the stove in case a wound needed cauterizing.

Just as Sally appeared on the porch with the iron,

Pearlie and Louis came running out of the woods. Louis stood on the porch facing outward in case of another attack, both hands filled with Colts.

Pearlie squatted down next to Cal. "Damn it, Cal!" he groused, his eyes filled with worry. "You just can't seem to join in a fight without getting shot up."

Cal grinned weakly, still in shock from the bullet wound. "I didn't want to disappoint you, podnah," he croaked.

As Sally bent over and Smoke pulled the shirt back to expose the wound, Pearlie took a bear sign out of his sack. "Here, pal, chomp on this. It'll help ease the pain."

Sally, who'd been through this many times with Smoke, put the red-hot end of the poker against the bleeding hole. Cal grunted and bucked against the pain, but didn't yell.

After the hole sizzled and smoked until it was cauterized shut, Sally threw the poker aside and eased Smoke out of the way as she sat down and took Cal's head into her arms, holding him tight.

"Hold the fort, boys," Smoke growled, with one last look at Cal. "I'm going after that bastard."

He took a running jump, vaulted up on the back of Rutledge's horse, and took off after Pike.

When he was gone, Sally looked up at Pearlie. "Pearlie, would you go and check on that man lying over there?" she said, indicating the place where Blackie Johnson had fallen. "That man helped save us tonight."

Pearlie nodded and walked over to check on Blackie Johnson and see if he was still alive.

It took Smoke almost five miles to catch up to Pike. As Smoke neared the man's horse, Pike reached back and took several shots at Smoke with his pistol, missing narrowly a couple of times.

When his gun was empty, he threw it at Smoke, also missing his mark.

Smoke pulled his horse up next to Pike's and dove across the mount, knocking Pike to the ground.

When they'd both stopped rolling and tumbling across the snow, each man got to his feet, facing the other.

Pike jerked a long, thin knife from his boot and crouched in the typical knife-fighter's stance.

Smoke bared his teeth in a savage grin, pulling out his bowie knife and beginning to circle the other man.

Suddenly, Pike dropped his knife and stood up straight, seeing something in Smoke's eyes that scared the shit out of him.

"All right, Jensen, you got me. I give up," he said, raising his hands.

Smoke slowly shook his head. "No, Pike. You don't get off that easy. I'm going to cut you into little pieces, knife or no knife."

"But you can't kill an unarmed man," Pike protested.

"Then arm yourself, coward," Smoke spat.

Reluctantly, Pike picked up his knife and moved quickly toward Smoke, slashing wildly back and forth.

Smoke leaned to the side, Pike's knife so close to him that it sliced through his shirt.

Smoke made a lightning-quick move with his hand and his bowie knife cut the tendons in Pike's right hand down to the bone, causing him to drop the knife.

Pike grabbed his right arm with his left. "All right, I'm done."

Again Smoke shook his head. "Pick up the knife, Pike," he ordered.

Pike shook his head. "No."

Smoke grinned. "You ever seen a man scalped alive, Pike. It is not a pretty sight."

"You wouldn't . . ."

"Remember your two men in the mountains, Pike?" Smoke asked. "That's how you're going to look in a few minutes."

Pike screamed in fear and frustration, grabbed the knife off the ground with his left hand, and ran at Smoke.

Smoke stepped to the side and as Pike passed he backhanded him across the throat with the edge of his Bowie knife, slicing through his larynx as if it were butter.

Pike dropped to his knees and grabbed at his throat, trying to stop the bleeding.

Smoke stepped around and squatted in front of him. "I'm going to sit here and watch you drown on your own blood, you bastard," he said.

Pike's eyes were terrified, and his last thoughts were that he wished he'd never heard of Smoke Jensen, Mountain Man.

When Smoke got back to the cabin, he found Cal inside on their bed and another man lying on their couch.

He looked at Sally. "How is Cal?"

She nodded, smiling. "He's going to be fine. The bullet tore a chunk of fat off his flank, but it didn't enter the abdomen. He'll be back at work within a week."

Smoke turned his attention to the other man. As he stood looking down at him, Sally said, "Smoke, this is

Blackie Johnson. When I was being held prisoner, he treated me with respect, and tonight he helped to save our new house."

"How are his wounds?" Smoke asked, though his expression showed he didn't care so much as Sally did.

Louis looked up from bandaging Johnson's wounds. "He took one in the ribs, but it didn't hit the lung. I think he's going to be all right."

Smoke walked over to address the man on the couch. "Mr. Johnson, my wife is a pretty good judge of character. If she thinks you are worth saving, then I am not inclined to argue. You can stay here until your wounds are healed, and then you will be free to go."

Blackie's eyes shifted from Smoke to Sally and he tried to smile, though the pain caused it to be more of a grimace. "Thank you kindly, ma'am," he said.

For a sneak preview
of William W. Johnstone's next
Western Novel,
Preacher's Peace
[coming from Pinnacle Books
in January, 2003]
just turn the page . . . .

Upper Missouri River, Saturday, May 22, 1824

Under a bright blue sky, white snow was still glistening in the mountains, but new-growth green signaled the welcome arrival of spring in the lower elevations. A tall horseman rode through a narrow valley where the river meandered along a rocky bench, wooded by pines, willow, and aspen. The rider, dressed in buckskin, appeared and disappeared effortlessly as he blended in with nature.

The river splashed and babbled over rocks, worn smooth by centuries of flowing water. From its depths, trout leaped into the air to snare flying insects that hovered unsuspectingly over the sparkling surface. In the sunlit glades nearby, wildflowers bloomed in a profusion of color, scenting the air with their sweet fragrance.

The rider who came onto this scene was an impressive man, with a full mustache, square jaw, straight nose, and steel-gray eyes staring out from under a wide-brimmed hat. He sat his horse easily and was leading two mules, both smaller animals packed to their maximum carrying capacity with beaver pelts. In a country where a man's deeds and character counted for ore than his family name, this man, who would someday be known as Preacher, was still known only by a single name, Art.

Art took a long pull from his canteen, corked it, and hooked it back on the pommel of his saddle, then shifted around to look at the two mules that were plodding along behind him. For some time now, he had been aware that two Indians were dogging him, riding parallel with him and, for the most part, staying out of sight. They were good, but Art was better. He was on to them as soon as they started shadowing his trail.

Art knew that the Blackfeet were denying white trappers access to the rivers and streams in the upper Yellowstone, but he was well out of their territory now. If these were Blackfeet, what were they doing this far down the Missouri River?

As soon as the stream rounded a bend, Art slipped his Hawken rifle from its saddle sheath, dismounted from his horse, and gave it a slap on the rump to keep it moving along. He wasn't concerned about the horse and mules getting away. They had been following the stream so rigidly that he was sure they would keep going in that direction, and they were moving slowly and deliberately enough that he would be able to catch up with them again. Using the sharp bend in the stream as concealment, he quickly primed his weapons, cocked the hammers on his rifle and his pistol, and waited.

Art didn't want to kill them, whoever they were. He knew there were times when one had to kill and when those times came, there was no place for hesitancy. He had killed more times than he wanted to recall, starting with river pirates back on the Ohio River, English soldiers during the Battle of New Orleans, and Indians in various battles in between. And he knew he would kill again, but to the degree that he could, he made a compromise with grim reality. He would kill only when he had no other choice. It was the kind of man he was. So far these two Indians had not put him in such a position.

The Indians on his trail approached his position so skillfully that he could barely hear them. Not one word was being spoken, and the rocks that were being disturbed by the horses' hooves were moving as lightly as if they were being dislodged by some wild creature.

Art watched; then as they came around the bend, he stood up suddenly, his Hawken pointed menacingly toward them.

"Ayiee!" one of the Indians exclaimed in a startled shout. His horse reared, and he had to fight to bring it under control. The other Indian raised his bow. The arrow was already fitted. He aimed without hesitation.

"No, don't!" Art shouted, but his shout had no effect. The Indian released the arrow and it whizzed by Art, coming so close that he could feel the air of its passing. Art pulled the trigger on his rifle. It roared and bucked and poured forth a cloud of smoke. The Indian who had shot at him tumbled from his saddle.

The other Indian, his horse now under control, knew that Art could fire the rifle only once. Realizing that he now had an advantage, he released an arrow toward Art, but missed. Dropping his rifle, Art raised his pistol and fired. The charge in the pistol exploded, sending a shudder through the shooter's powerful arm. The Indian's face disintegrated in a bloody red pulp as the ball struck him right between the eyes.

As the powerful echo of the last shot was still reverberating through the canyon, Art went over for a closer examination of the two Indians he had shot. As he suspected, both were dead, but something he didn't expect was to see that they were Arikara.

Why were the Arikara trailing him? As far as he

knew, the Arikara were not causing any problems. Of course, it might have nothing at all to do with any problems between the Arikara and the white trappers. These two could well be a couple of renegades just after his pelts. He knew that the load on his pack animals would tempt any thief, red or white.

Art recharged and reloaded both his weapons, then mounting one of the Indian ponies, galloped down the stream until he caught up with his animals. Letting the Indian pony go, he remounted his own horse and continued his journey.